Underbelly

S.P.M Barrett

Copyright © 2016 S.P.M Barrett
All rights reserved
ISBN: 978-1530307494

DEDICATION

This book is dedicated to my fantastic grandparents who helped to raise marvelous parents for me.

ACKNOWLEDGMENTS

This is to all of my Kickstarter supporters; Gavin Behan, Eolane; Author "Whisper in the Wind", Anthony Barrett, Maurice Barrett, David Cardoso and John Nicolay

This is also a nod to all of my talented team that helped me put this book together; David Daigneault, Sheryl Washburn, Nada Orlic and Karin Wittig.

Last but certainly by no means least, are all of my friends and family that I have subjected to countless hours fretting about plots. Much love guys!

To Anne, Mick, Daniel, Billy and Naoise

Hope you enjoy the book!!

S Barrett

9/7/16

Map of Islandari

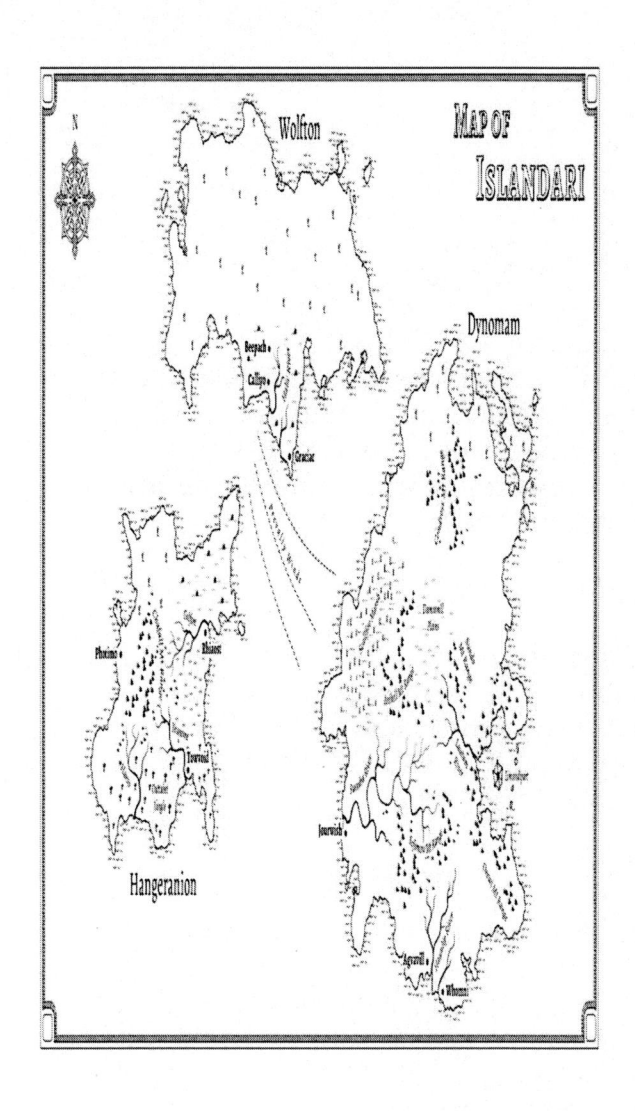

The Meeting

It was one of those nights. The kind where the sky was as black as pitch but around the brilliant moon it was rendered grey. The cold was so sharp and fierce that each breath was almost like a new ghost was escaping from my body.

I had never felt so alive.

I was walking down an almost deserted street of the city of Limondipart, the capital of the Dynomamian Empire. It was that time between people arriving home from work and night people going out for their night duties.

A quiet time.

The footpath was cracked and grey from overuse and from the constant freezing temperatures. The snow that is always threatened by the glum meteorologist would fall any time now. I plunged my hands deeply into the warmth of my coat as I walked quickly and resolutely down the silent street, cursing the fact that my gloves were back home in my apartment.

There were honking cars in the distance, but they were far away; enough that they could almost be mistaken for a dream or an errant thought.

The cold was beginning to sting my lungs and I knew I did not have that much time until my hands would be invaded by the frigid air. I was nearly there, I thought.

I stepped up to peer curiously over the railings that prevent people from falling into the Lavtum River, which divided the city in two. As I gazed into its murky depths, a memory of a pale faced girl regarded me with a placid expression. Her small pointed chin was digging into the thermal coat and her pale lips were a shy blue. It was her eyes that caught my attention; they were a caramel brown that seemed to retain the only heat in her face. The dark hair that framed her face resembled a halo protecting the face from the harsh outside world. I hardly recognised myself.

There was a splash as a flash of silver and black caught the moonlight; I saw a fish leap into the air to catch a passing moth. It smacked the water as it fell back down, but then all was still in the river. I could not help but wonder how many countless stories it had heard over the centuries from people. Here, the whispers of the running water had a recollection of all of the scandalous secrets spilt over its banks and guarded them jealously. Here, amid the rising swells and the shuddering crashes, the insidious and pure stories intermingled as though they had lives of their own.

I turned sharply to the sound of approaching footsteps. My heart was beating a little too fast. I took a deep breath in and I realised they were just a young couple walking side by side, with a large, bristly dog on a leash. I could see steam rising from the dog's spines and it panted with exertion as the young couple power walked down by the river. They did not acknowledge me as they walked past, as they were too engrossed in their conversation to take notice of anything else.

I settled in for what could be a long wait.

I stamped my feet. I was on the point of grumbling but I knew that it would not be wise to show signs of frustration. I knew that I was most likely being watched. My watchers would be uneasy if they saw any form of agitation coming from me, especially considering the recent crackdown on several of their operations.

Every other day on the news there was a new Underbelly safe house cracked and exposed like a festering wound. And every other day there was a new attack from the dark citizens of Limondipart on the law abiding citizens on the Surface.

He was an hour late, and I was beginning to think it likely that I had gotten the wrong address when I heard more footsteps approaching. My gut clenched and I instinctively knew that this was the person that I was waiting for.

I kept my expression calm, cool, and collected. Not that I was capable of much expression, the cold having immobilised most of the muscles in my face. I just hoped that I would be able to speak coherently. The man stepped forward and I saw immediately that he had a slight limp in his left leg. I noted that it might come in handy should I need to make a quick getaway.

As he came closer, the moonlight hit him at a suitable angle and revealed his features to me. He had long, dark blonde hair with a puckered face and green eyes. However, it was not his eyes or his hair that grabbed my attention; it was the livid scar that ran from the left corner of his lip to just under his eye along his cheekbone. It was a harsh reminder of the world that I was getting myself into.

He looked me up and down and said with a low gravelly voice, "Name." I knew that he was not asking for my name, but for the name the person I was meeting had supplied me with. This was of course, to ensure that I was legitimate, and not part of another sting operation. "Lad" I said in my most neutral voice. The blonde man grunted and turned on his heel. He gave no indication that I should follow, but I fell into step behind him.

He walked swiftly through the run down areas of town, and I heard the catcalls of various gangs, almost like wolves howling as they warned their rivals away from getting too close.

It was getting late and there were more people entering the streets, looking for an adrenaline high to fill in the gaps between the moment of birth and the moment that they would die.

As I was left with that musing thought, he led me through the cramped and dirty streets of the poor side of the city. The sights were not so bad but the stench was awful. No wonder these people turned to crime when the government proved so ineffective. Even in the outer suburbs of Limondipart where I live with Rena, my best friend and roommate, the homeless and less unfortunate are scorned and ignored. Many of these people don't last long on the streets. Either death or the Underbelly claims them. Death would be a kinder mercy.

We walked along the Lavtum River before we came to the old docklands. This side of the city had long since been abandoned by its law abiding citizens, but the undesirable denizens of the city had clearly moved in.

As we pushed further on, we came to row upon row of old crestfallen warehouses, seemingly fragile with old age. The blonde man began to angle deeper, his stiff legs locking with purpose as he led me further into the warehouses and I followed, wary.

He finally stopped in front of a worn out wooden warehouse and knocked twice on the weary door. A husky, "Password?" was the reply.

The blonde man snarled his response under his breath and the door swung open with a squeaky groan.

I was in.

The room was sparse, and there were papers scattered all around the floor as though a child had been running wild and had tried to make it snow with paper. The cracked wooden floors were aged and warped, like a wizened old grandmother on her deathbed. There were windows, but the permanent grime that covered them allowed none of the brilliant moonshine to shine through, and lent the room a dull, dead, atmosphere.

In front of me, there was an aged wooden desk with more papers scattered haphazardly on it. There was a small man idling behind it as he leered at me. The vibe I got off of him was distinctly unsettling and I resisted the urge to shudder.

I tried to focus and keep myself calm, aware that my blonde companion was ever at my side, constantly watching and evaluating. Every so often I heard a slight wheezing sound as he exhaled a little too loudly and it set my teeth on edge.

I paused.

There was a different kind of smell emanating from this place, a sweaty smell, and judging from the groans of pleasure that were coming from the various closed off rooms, it was pretty obvious what was the source of that smell.

I winced when a particularly loud scream nearly punctured my eardrum. I could see the small weasel man grinning at me lavishly as he said with his husky voice, "Would you like to join them love? I would dare say that there are a lot of men who would love to play with that pretty dark hair of yours, among other things." I resisted the urge to pull my gun on him and instead fixed him with an icy glare. The small grubby man backed off with his hands in the air and the blonde man laughed in a strange way, as though his vocal cords did not work properly and his wheezing became more pronounced. I looked at him but he noticed, and scowled ferociously when he caught my gaze. I quickly diverted my attention and he grunted and we continued to a lift that I had only just noticed at the other side of the reception.

It was a double door lift, each panel was rusted and flaked. It opened with a quite ping and my blonde companion stepped in and turned around to face me, daring me to enter.

I hesitated for the briefest moment, as the realisation that the culmination of all my hard work in the last three years had led to this point. My sacrifices in the Hornet's squad brought me to this moment. The blonde man smirked slightly. I felt my back stiffen in response and resolutely strode toward the lift.

I stepped in and the doors closed with a tired sigh. There was a cacophony of mechanical noise as the rusty gears began to grind together as it began the endless job of lifting people from the Surface to the Underbelly. The lift shuddered and then lowered me into the depths of the Underbelly, closer to him.

The Lift

I felt a cold apprehension settle over me, now that I was getting closer to my goal. After all of these years, I could not help but feel like all of the insignificant moments of my life had led me to this point. Another startling thought washed through me; If this is what I had been waiting for all of this time, what will happen after? Will I die then, after I kill him?

To distract myself from these crippling thoughts, I turned my attention to the lift I was in. It was not very pretty; I could see a dark crimson stain, that I was fairly certain wasn't paint, splattered against the wall to my left. The panel of buttons that indicated the levels of this building were worn, and flickered feebly in the bleaching glow of the overhead light. The metal that made up the lift was warped and rusted, and I began to seriously doubt the capabilities of the lift to remain in one piece.

I saw my glowering guardian look at the puckered and peeling steel door with a mask of indifference, which swiftly shifted to an expression of snarling defiance as he caught my eyes and growled, "What are you looking at?"

I felt terror skitter across my heart, but I refused to let it show in my face and returned his hostile gaze with a cool one of my own. I continued to study the lift. I almost lost my footing as the lift suddenly jarred to a stop.

We had arrived.

The worn and tired doors pulled themselves apart, like they have done a thousand times. We stepped out and the doors closed again with a relieved sigh, thankful it can return to its slumber. My first impression of the Underbelly was a strong scent of strawberries on the air. The next was that it was a very cold place, almost like an immense fridge. The blonde man stalked forward, like a ghost eager to leave this world behind. I could hear the quick pitter-patter of my feet as I hurried to keep up with him.

We walked in silence for some time as he led me down tunnel after tunnel and I found reassurance in the gun strapped to my leg, as well as the pair of knives lashed to the inside of my wrists. They were not my real weapons of course but it was good to know that I had hard, cold metal alongside my warm flesh, and that it could be used to defend myself if needed.

Though the twisting and convoluted tunnels were cold and dark, they were at least dry, which was something to be thankful for. Although I did see flashes of red light from the eyes of the rats that lived down there, exposed by the hanging lights that dotted the tunnels. I tried not to think about them.

I got a whiff of a distinctly musty smell that filled my stomach with dread. Whatever it was, it made me uneasy. Above the chatter of the rats I heard high chirps that silenced the rats for a time before a squeal and the sound of crunching bones. My blonde companion did not seem worried, so I attempted to convince myself not to worry.

Every so often a breath of air would hurdle down the tunnel, brushing aside that musty smell. Instead of stale air flooding my nostrils, it was the scent of strawberries. The blonde man must have noticed my confusion because he said in his gruff voice, "The boss does not like the stench of rotten rubbish, and demands that fresh strawberries be brought down every day so that it smells nice down here." I nodded and we quickly fell back into our customary silence.

It was not long before I saw a light at the end of the tunnel, and knew from the glow that it was not another old-fashioned lantern hanging from the ceiling. The blonde man quickened his pace even more, and I practically had to trot to keep up with him.

We reached a door that looked out of place among the ancient flagstone walls of the tunnel. It was a sleek and polished dark metal that gleamed malevolently. It could only be Bloodsteel. A rare ore of metal that was found in the jungles of southern Hangeanrion, the continent to the west of Dynomam. It had an unusual property, if it was treated with human blood in the foundries where it was smelted, it would expand and contract only on contact with the same blood. It was the ultimate security door, because it was not only selective in who could open and close it at will, it was extremely durable and had a high melting point. It was prohibitively expensive and I had never actually seen one in person.

It looked far more secure than the rust-bucket that we came down a while ago and I knew that we had arrived at our destination. Sure enough, a slot on the door pulled back seamlessly and revealed a pair of dark eyes.

"Who's there and what do you want?" The question fast and sharp.

The blonde man stepped forward and spoke in a low voice, "Jeffery. And I'm bringing this girl here to meet the Bossman."

The man's eyes seemed to darken but it was difficult to tell in the gloom. "Very well Jeffery, bring her in but no trouble, you hear?"

Jeffery laughed his strange laugh and grabbed me by the shoulder and pushed me through the door. I yelped without meaning to and the two men began to chortle in a raucous manner. I heard the quiet chuckling of another, younger man, behind the door. I felt my calm façade slip slightly and my cheeks burned, but I stiffened my spine and walked ahead.

They wouldn't have the last laugh.

The door opened to a seemingly small antechamber, but I walked further in and in front of me was singularly the largest door I had ever seen. It was massive. It must have been easily three stories tall and a hundred metres wide. With a shock, I realised that it was all Bloodsteel. I felt goose bumps raise across my arms as I began to understand the extent of the power of the Underbelly. I had always wondered why the Surface had not yet cracked the Underbelly, but looking at the darkly glowing metal in the gloomy light, it was clear.

The Underbelly was an impregnable fortress.

Jeffery and the other two men were watching my awed face with haughty expressions. Jeffery was laughing his gravelly laugh and the taller and darker of the men said, "It's an impressive sight isn't it? That Bloodsteel barricade covers the entire Underbelly city and is over thirty metres thick. There's not a hope in hell that those Surface bastards are getting in without our permission."

The small, pale man cleared his throat, "You know what to do Jeff, make sure she doesn't squirm." Before my alarm could be fully registered by my limbs, the small man moved so startling fast that he was an indistinct blur.

There was a pair of cool hands cradling my head, despite the gentleness of the movement there was no doubting the strength and firmness of his grip. A huge pressure built up in my head but it wasn't coming from his hands but more like…his mind? I could feel him probing in my mind and I instinctively knew that he was looking for something in particular. He was looking to see if I was gifted.

I panicked.

I felt something stir within me and it reared its groggy head, but it suddenly snapped to attention as it sensed the threat that Marcus could pose, and simply vanished. It had spread itself so thin throughout my mind that it would be impossible to sense. Not even by Marcus.

I was safe.

The pressure suddenly lifted and I saw the small pale man frown, "She's armed." Two sharp jabs came from the small pale man and I was sent sprawling onto the ground. The pale blond man stooped down towards me and efficiently removed the two knives strapped to my forearms, as well as my gun down the back of my jeans.

Jeffery was laughing his strange laugh, "Well then Marcus, what is going to happen?" There was no mistaking his menace. I tried to remember my combat training but the speed of Marcus unnerved me and my thoughts were still muddled from his invasion.

Marcus shrugged. "Mr. Forts will see her regardless, and he's been expecting her."

Jeffery scowled and I had to admit that I liked to see him taken down a peg or two.

Marcus returned his attention to me, "Apologies for that but we couldn't let you into the Underbelly with weapons." He sniffed delicately, "Besides, you're better off without those archaic firearms anyway; bullets have been out-dated for decades now. You need a good plasma-ray."

My unease grew as this soldier discussed weapon strategizing with me. Was he that confident I wasn't a threat?

Well that's not good, I thought.

Marcus nodded to the tall dark man, and my escorts led me to the imposing door, where one of them knocked on the outline of a smaller, man-sized door within the larger one. A light flashed and I could hear whirring and the sound of many bolts and locks twisting as they were undone. There was no chance of sneaking out of this place either. Jeffery motioned for me to lead the way, and I stepped through the now open door.

Jeffery overtook me soon enough, and began to navigate through the vast crowds in the Underbelly. I was expecting there to be a lot of people here, but the throngs of bodies were far greater than I had imagined; it was a whole new city beneath the other.

Over several decades, the various Underbellies had attained a fearsome and legendary status; the worst people and the most talented criminals were all living in the sprawling metropolises, and to enter uninvited was to invite certain death. I had never really believed the extraordinary tales about those places; I had known it was dangerous, but to think that it was death incarnate seemed a bit over the top to me.

Looking at the sheer number of people here though, it was now clear that I'd been wrong at least in one respect; I had never imagined this many people. There must be thousands, if not hundreds of thousands. The crowd was the most diverse I had ever seen. There were people of all shapes and sizes mingling amongst each other. I saw the small squat people of the Hangeranion jungles, their northern cousins with their pale yellow skin and dark hair. I even saw night people from Wolfton, the continent north of Dynomam, walking in plain sight. I was taken aback. I felt something shift a little guiltily in me. Before I had time to understand the sense of unease though, Jeffery whisked me away through the crowd. I just hoped I was not also wrong about it not being death incarnate.

Jeffery led me up through the Underbelly and I began to feel claustrophobic as the crooked houses started to cram in together. With no sky, it was easy to imagine them toppling over on me, crushing me beneath a flood of stone.

Thankfully, it was not long before we left the residential area and entered the market. There were more people here, but there were also more open spaces. My feeling of claustrophobia diminished to a more manageable level. What stood out were the mounds of strawberries, glistening as though they had just woken up from the long night, coated in dew.

People of varying composition bustled back and forth, peering at the plundered treasures from the Surface and evaluating their worth. It was surreal to see the severe contrast between goods on the same stall. There was one hawker who had a marble bust of Fero Jecha, the first Emperor of the Dynomam Empire, who had started expanding our borders four hundred years ago. Arranged in neat piles beside it were stacks of magazines, and hovering above those were exotic birds. They fluttered excitedly as a young night boy fed them colourful fruits, his snowy skin seemingly drawing in the light around from him.

A Dynomam woman came over and scolded him, a scene that was all too common on the Surface. But then she did something extraordinary; she pointed to her cheek, and though I could not hear what was being said, her body language had changed and the boy grinned cheekily.

He stood on the tips of his toes and pecked her on the cheek. The woman then knelt down and swept him into an embrace.

She was a human, hugging a night person. The thought was startling to me; night people just didn't mix with humans. They were dangerous.

A laugh from the boy drew my attention back to the embracing figures. I saw the flash of lavender-purple eyes that were typical of night people, and the young boy's eyes sparked with amusement.

It sent shivers down my spine. The night people were tall, pale skinned but dark featured. They had dark hair, usually black or dark brown, but it was their eyes that were the most captivating. It was always a strange, lavender-purple that seemed to glow in the darkness.

However, it was not the peculiar physical appearances of these ethereal creatures that unsettled me and the rest of the citizens on the Surface, it was their need for human blood.

Though there had been blood clinics set up throughout Limondipart, there were still sporadic reports of attacks at night on unwary humans. I'd had to clean out more than one nest of these creatures while serving under the Citizen Protection Force, or the CPF, as they are more commonly known as.

Watching the night child and human interact was difficult for my mind to process, but it was clear that others here had no problem with it. They looked at their goods with a sharp eye and bartered with experienced buyers' tongues, oblivious to the paradigm shift in my world and the racial differences among themselves.

Jeffery kept moving through the Underbelly and it was soon apparent that the Underbelly was like a mountain; the residential areas at the bottom rising toward the market places ringing the middle. As I followed him, I realised that the surrounding houses were increasing in size and grandeur. Soon, we stood outside a magnificent house that made the others around it look like pig-sties. It was resplendent in its majesty. It seemed to have walls made of white marble and a roof of emerald copper.

It was intimidating.

Jeffery was obviously not intimidated, and he walked up without missing a step and knocked on the onyx black doors. It opened automatically, seemingly without anyone behind it. I stepped into the cool embrace of the stone house and the doors closed behind me. I was now in the lion's den.

I was brought straight up the stairs that, as with everything else, was far too large. Jeffery stopped in front of a plain wooden door. He took a deep but hesitant breath, the first sign of any uneasiness in him that I had seen during our entire journey. It that did not do much to help my own nerves.

Jeffrey stepped up to the door and an indent the size of an eyeball materialised on the door. It was a glassy eyeball with a bright green iris that studiously drank in the features of Jeffery's face and then whizzed and disappeared. There was a gruff summoning from the other side of the door and Jeffery entered at the summons. I took one more steadying breath, and I followed him in.

A man was sitting in a swivel chair in front of a mahogany desk with his back to us gazing into a fire

that purred as it devoured the logs contently. Jeffery snapped to attention and said with his voice full of respect, "Sir, this is Georgina, the woman who said she wished to speak with you."

The man chuckled, "Jeffery, this is not a woman called Georgina, her name is Merissa."

Jeffery looked both terrified and confused and his voice broke slightly, "Sir?"

The man chuckled again, "I know her true name because I was the one who gave it to her."

The man finally rotated the chair around, and I was met with a face I had not seen in fifteen years. I felt my spine stiffen and my voice constrict with anxiety as I said, "Hello Father."

The Tour

My memories of my father had not distorted him beyond recognition, though there were some startling differences. He did not seem as tall as I remembered, nor as immensely powerful as I recalled. His formerly raven black hair was peppered with grey but his blue eyes were still as sharp as viroblades. Though he towered above me when I was a little girl, it was quickly apparent that we were more similar in height now, at six foot. I suddenly understood what people mean when they say the world seems different when you are younger.

Over the years and with the death of my mother, I became a totally different person than the little girl I once was, and I knew that he was not as authoritative as I had long ago believed. Nevertheless, he terrified me.

He smiled. It looked as unnatural as a snake smiling and I felt my mental defences solidify and my body tighten in anticipation. His voice slithered across the room like the serpent that I always saw him as. "So my prodigal daughter finally returns to me. To what do I owe this pleasure?"

My mouth felt as dry as the Mugaco Desert during high summer, but I made my sandpaper tongue do its job laboriously. "Mom is dead."

I saw a shadow of some emotion flicker across his face, but wasn't sure what it could be. Fear? Shame? Anger or triumph? It was too fleeting for me be sure. Before I could press him he spoke, with his slinking voice faltering ever so slightly. "How did it happen?"

I felt a flash of rage and my voice came out snapping. "You know exactly how she died. The same way all of your mistresses die. Because of you."

Jeffery raised his hands to strike me for insulting his master, but I was faster than he expected. With lightning speed, my fingers found all of the focal points on his raised arm. It swung loosely to his side, where it hung limp. He gaped at me and croaked. "You're the same as him!"

I backhanded him hard and he flew across the room, crumpling against the wall with a heavy thud.

My father showed no sign of alarm. In fact, he seemed unperturbed, even pleased, his face alight with excitement. He motioned for me to come closer, but I was wary. His voice no longer seemed cold, rather, it was warm with anticipation. "Marcus had no idea! Come, sit. We have much to talk about! Oh the possibilities are endless!"

It looked like I was going to get the conversation that I wanted after all.

My father was silent for a few moments as he tried to still his racing thoughts. This was a characteristic of him that I was very familiar with, and I knew that if interrupted, he could become violent. When I was small, I once happened upon my parents talking in the living room. They were speaking in that intense way that children never understand but instinctively react to. My mother was standing with her back tall and straight, her long golden blond hair like a burning halo in the sunlight as she defied my father. My father paced back and forth across the living room as he grew more and more agitated. I had run to my mother and hugged her legs tightly.

After what had seemed like an age I had asked, "Mommy, what's going on?"

My father flew into a rage. "You stupid little girl, if you don't learn to keep silent it will get you killed!"

He had become more aggressive but my mother simply grabbed him by his ear, and hissed delicately into it, "If you ever threaten our daughter again I will kill you, you understand me?"

"She's my daughter as well and you are well aware that she needs to learn to watch her tongue, otherwise she'll get herself killed!" my father spat.

My mother had crossed her arms and glared back at him, her anger far surpassing his. "She might be your daughter but she will never be your little girl. You long ago lost that right."

I learned a few things that evening. My mother was strong enough to stand up to the impressive force that was my father, and to speak my thoughts even in the face of oppression. I also learned that even though my father was the most terrifying figure in my life, there was someone or something out there that was more of a threat to me than he was.

As he stood pondering, I tried to calm my heartbeat as it began to beat to beat like a galloping horse. It was pounding harder than the hooves of the race-horses that ran every year in the summer near the outskirts of Limodium. Past and current anxieties pressed tightly up against my heart, making it hard to breathe.

A happier memory presented itself to me at the thought; my mother used to take me to the races, and we would get ice cream. I always chose a scrumptious caramel brownie ice cream that just dazzled and danced across my tongue or sometimes the mint ice cream that was as cool as marble and as refreshing as a blast of the ocean air after being housebound all day. My mother never changed her ice cream. It was strawberry; always strawberry. I choked back the memory and returned my thoughts to my current circumstances.

My father continued pacing back and forth, his footsteps wearing away at the luscious red velvet carpet. The matted fibers gave testament to the fact that this pacing was a common occurrence, and had been for some years. He seemed oblivious to my observation of him as his mind raced with the new information about me. I was not fooled by his seemingly warm reception; I had seen him at his worst.

I still had nightmares about he and my mother throwing screams at each other like they were sharp knives, and me running to my room and hiding under the covers with flashlights. I wanted them to stop but at the same time, dreaded the finality of their terrifying conclusion.

My father peered at me occasionally and I could practically see his brain sparking as his mind threw together ideas and broke them apart just as swiftly. I knew then that I was being involved in a game, but it was a game that I did not know all of the rules to. I would have to play nice to see what the endgame was.

Soon, he was ready to begin. So was I. He began with a simple question, asked as though he were inquiring how I liked my coffee. "How long have you been aware of your physical state?"

I shrugged. "About six years or so. It came from nowhere, I woke up one morning and suddenly it was a struggle to close the door without smashing it to pieces."

He laughed at that, and I felt myself relax ever so slightly, which I wasn't prepared for. I steeled my resolve before I continued on with my answer. "The strength came first, then the agility, and finally the mental focus."

My father was watching me with fascinated eyes and was almost whispering with excitement. "You are by far the most advanced of all of my children."

That caught me off guard and the question popped out of my mouth before I could stop it. "I have brothers and sisters?"

My father's eyes gleamed when he saw that he caught my interest, "Oh yes, you have dozens. Would you like to meet them?"

We were interrupted before I could answer, as Jeffery began to stir from his place at the bottom of the wall, moaning softly. He looked around, and remembered where he was, coming to suddenly and bolting to his feet. He drew his shock-ray in a flurry of awkward flailing, aimed it at me haphazardly, and began to fire rapidly. Deadly darts of blue electricity seared the air with a menacing hiss. I reacted instinctively and threw myself backwards, rolling behind my chair. My father was roaring at Jeffery to stop, but the young man did not hear the shouting over his fury at me, and the high hissing of the shock-ray.

I tensed my stomach and sprang towards Jeffery, twisting in the air to avoid the lethal bolts of electricity. The heels of my palms connected sharply with his forehead and for the second time in five minutes, Jeffery fell unconscious to the floor.

Father was glaring at him furiously and stalked over to him in a few angry steps. I could see the murderous intent in his eyes, and decided I would not let him kill Jeffery, though admittedly, he was not on my current short-list of friends. I drew myself to my full six-foot height and squared my shoulders, and stepped swiftly between them. My father drew himself up short at that, surprised. I thought for a second that he considered pushing me aside, but he looked at Jeffery, then back to me, and seemed to realize the he was no longer the undisputed strongest person in the room.

He chuckled briefly, backed off and said, "Ok then, darling. How about we give you the grand tour of the kingdom that your Dad has made?"

I arched my eyebrows. "Why on earth would I want to see that?"

My father looked genuinely surprised. "Because some day you and your siblings are going to rule this world, and you need to learn the skills to lead. It's harder than it looks you know."

Before I had a chance to process this, my father pressed a button on his watch. There was a loud mechanical humming sound. I felt a sudden lurch, and I almost lost my balance as the floor began to sink. I blinked, slightly panicked, and I wondered what was going on?

My father noted my confusion with a grin. "This, my dear, is where I do all of my interesting business conducts." The endearment made my skin crawl, and as he talked, the polished wooden walls began to disappear from view as we were slowly lowered down into my father's abode.

As we descended further into the massive house, the lights from the ceiling above grew dimmer. Though my advanced eyesight could more than compensate for the lack of light, it was still unnerving. Some things will always be easier to do in the dark, like murdering your daughter, I thought.

Without warning, bright lights flared on, sourced from the walls at the side and I grimaced and blinked as the light shocked my eyes. After a few seconds, my sight adjusted and I looked around to find that we had been lowered into some kind of cellar.

It was large, clean, and bright. The walls were still stone but there were no signs of dampness. The room was filled with large pens and there was that strange musty smell emitted by the pens, more concentrated now than it had been in the tunnels.

I raised an eyebrow at my father and he strode proudly over to one of the pens, stopping at the thigh high fence. He beckoned me over and I followed cautiously, making sure that there was ample space between he and I.

I looked in apprehensively, then took a few seconds to register what I was seeing. I frowned when I realized that my first impression was that they looked like dragons from a children's story-book. What on earth were they?

My father was beaming. "These are the result of a collaboration between my top two scientists, Dr Terry and Dr Oslo."

I looked at him, aghast. "You mean these are genetically modified organisms?!"

GMOs have been banned for decades on the Surface, ever since a lab tried to combine sheep and cows together to maximise wool, milk and beef production. It resulted in the mutation of a rare virus that was able to infect not only the GMO animals, but also the purebred sheep and cows. It decimated all three populations and resulted in millions starving.

My father waved his hands at my horror in contempt. "Don't be naïve Merissa, those GMOs were inbred and immunocompromised. They were a ticking time bomb from the moment they were created. These GMOs are from genetically diverse populations; they are as healthy as oxen!"

He paused for a second and frowned. "Well, as healthy as wild oxen, not their inbred domesticated brethren."

I was still unsure about that but since countless millions of people aren't relying on these animals for food, I figured that there's not much harm in making them. I felt my curiosity become more aroused as my analytical brain kicked in. I looked at them curiously despite my earlier trepidation, and I could not help asking, "So what are they a mix of?"

My father's answering smile was satisfied and smug. Damn. I guess that meant he knew that I was interested. "Well, there are actually three animals used to create these little guys."

Just then, one of the animals went still and looked up and it seemed to recognise my father and it began chirping. Not like a bird; it was deeper than that, but it was the closest description that I had for the sound. The others heard the chirping and looked up and began to chirp alongside their pack member. They all rushed to the side of the pen and stood up on their scaly hind legs, their whip-like tails thrashing back and forth with enthusiasm.

One of the larger ones arched its back. Dark purple, feathery wings stretched out and pushed some of its pack mates to the side. I gasped. I had never seen such a beautiful creature, with its elegant dark blue pointed face, piercing green eyes, and deep golden body with delicate purple wings, it was sight to behold.

It had small horns extending from the back of its jawbones and other small spines that ran around the skull. Its golden front feet were splayed up against the fence and its ivory white claws were extended.

It was simply stunning.

My father watched my reactions and I got the distinct impression that he was pleased with them. My father continued on in a lowered voice. "They're not really dragons, but we call them dragons anyway. They're a careful blending of a snake, a lizard and a bird."

I raised an eyebrow. "But which ones, and why did you use them?"

My father shrugged. "I don't know the ins and outs of it exactly but from what I have gathered, the Yewsome snake was used because it's quite a tame breed of snake. The Prince Wagtails has a huge wingspan naturally. I think they were going to use the Condress falcon, but they are only a little larger than Prince Wagtails and not nearly as pretty or mild mannered."

I was distracted by the odd chirping noises and I looked down to see the larger one gazing up at me imploringly and my father laughed. "Be careful or she may imprint with you!"

I looked back at him in alarm, "What do you mean?!"

My father shook his head. "Don't worry, it's nothing to be afraid of. It's odd, they seem to have this bizarre tendency to pick one person as their own and they are fiercely loyal to that one person. Observe."

He whistled and I heard a loud thump and the snick of talons clicking against the stone floor and the dragons grew quiet and I smelt that strange odour again of mustard but this time there was a tang of strawberries in the air.

My father called out. "Come here, Frans!" And this huge creature came out of the shadows. It was as large as a horse and as well built as a bear. It was jet black apart from its eyes, which were a startling ice blue in colour. It snarled at me.

For a split second I felt blind terror.

My father began to sing to it, and for a second I was dumbfounded. I had never heard such a clear beautiful voice, and to hear it from him was particularly startling to me. After a moment, the black dragon began to hum alongside my father. It was a strange, hauntingly beautiful duet, the high clear notes of my father were complemented by the deep bass of the dragon.

After a few moments the dragon came forward and still singing my father gestured me forward. I hesitated but stepped towards the huge black dragon. It had stopped humming and was watching me intently, I could not help but feel like it was able to read my mind.

I stopped in front of it and gingerly placed my hand on its snout, it did not move and I noticed that it was surprisingly warm. Suddenly it reared back on its hind legs and its huge four-metre-wide glossy black wings spread out from its back and it hummed even louder.

I heard a small sigh of relief from behind and I noticed that my father had stopped singing. I turned around and Frans bumped me with her nose, soliciting more attention. I quickly placed my hands back on its snout.

My father chuckled. "I guess she likes you now, don't you Francesca, old girl?" I placed my hands underneath her chin and tickled her, and was rewarded with a deep hum.

Frans suddenly jumped towards my father, and he laughed even louder. "No, I can't go for a fly with you now." Frans whined and stretched her wings even further. "Frans! Behave yourself!" My father admonished the huge dragon, "I haven't seen my daughter in a very long time and there are plenty of things that we need to discuss." He rubbed her snout lovingly though. "I promise that we'll go for a fly tonight ok?"

Frans seemed satisfied with that and she turned to prowl around the pen of younger dragons, flicking her tongue out occasionally to scent the air. The younger dragons mimicked her every move with youthful enthusiasm and chirped in greeting.

Satisfied with their apparent submission, she ambled over to the far side of the room where I saw that there was a large alcove fitted with plush bedding that she settled into contentedly. As she closed her eyes, she vanished from sight, surprising me once again.

My father looked at me critically, mulling something over, before apparently making a decision and pressing a few more buttons on his watch. I was unexpectedly surrounded by people dressed in smart uniforms, and was whisked out of the room with my father leading the way, strutting like a king. As I was leaving I heard the low keening of one of the young dragons. When I looked back at the sound, I saw it was the beautiful blue faced one peering out of the grille in the fence watching us walk away.

My father began speaking informatively as we walked. "The Underbelly is divided into three basic areas, the lower, middle, and upper rings. The lower being the residential area, the middle being the markets and the upper being the administration area." He paused for a moment. "Obviously there are far more layers than that but you'll get used to it after a few months."

I stopped abruptly at that, startled. A few months? Just what was my father playing at? The smartly dressed staff grabbed my sleeve and pulled me along impatiently.

I could have easily resisted but I'd rather not put more people in hospital if I can help it. I resumed walking while I mulled over the brief events of the day so far. Alright. I'll play his game for a little while longer. I could feel my apprehensive nerves falling way to my inner tiger, confident in my newfound resolve.

I was led out of the cavernous cellar and into a breezy tunnel. I shivered in the cutting air, drawing into myself to conserve warmth in this dismal place. Father noticed my shivering and snorted derisively. "You've been made soft by the Surface. A few more weeks here and we'll have toughened you right up." There it was again, this notion that I was going to be here longer than I intended.

His casual assertions made me uneasy.

We exited the breezy tunnel into a green park. I halted in my tracks, startled by the sudden intense colour. I could hear the river running over the riverbed and there was a cloud of flies darting back and forth above the clear water. I could see frogs and fish feasting on the banquet on the wing.

So much life in such a dark place. It was hard to take it all in.

Resting on the riverbanks were otters, stretched out basking in the heat of a huge orb of black light. My father was watching my reaction, I pointed at the massive orb. "What is that exactly?"

My father puffed out his chest in pride. "T[hat] dear, is why all of the Underbellies are able to function independently of the Surface." He loo[ked] slightly sheepish as he admitted, "I must confess that I don't understand the intrinsic details. All I know that it's a form of energy that is more efficient than electricity. Some would argue that they are also more efficient than the sun, but I really don't know. They don't produce the same amount of energy, obviously, but they are more concentrated. Of course, I think it's just the physics' department positing that to get more funding."

I blinked. I felt a dawning comprehension draw over me. This technology would make the Underbellies far more dangerous than the Surface had previously feared. We assumed that they have been living like rats in tunnels, hiding and stealing to survive. If they already had this degree of independence and infrastructure, it would not be long before they were confident enough to challenge the Surface.

Perhaps they already were.

We still had time to diffuse the situation though, I reassured myself. The Surface might not be able to choke out the Underbellies' resources but we would still manage to drown them in bodies alone.

My father was watching me intently, studying my reactions. I thought saw a flicker of unease flash across his face, but I wasn't sure if I had imagined it or not. He shrugged and began walking down the gravel path. "When the Underbellies began to emerge three hundred or so years ago, there was an obvious problem of getting the energy needed to run each of them. Initially they had siphoned it from the main grid but as the Surface grew more and more unstable and more people sought the protection and shelter of the Underbellies, we began to grow exponentially. Our physicists came up with the ingenious solution of the black suns."

He paused as a flash of red darted across the path and a small dragon slid into the water, disturbing the ducks that were wading amongst the reeds. My father fell silent as he watched the young dragon slice through the water like a sleek new boat, making the otters scatter and plunge into the water to flee.

When the dragon had disappeared amongst the reeds, my father continued on. "So as our Underbellies grew we needed to find alternative sources of energy. In the early days we had used nuclear power, but that greatly increased tensions between the Surfaces and the Underbellies, and we knew we were not prepared for direct confrontation."

He paused for a moment as I took time to digest this. We were of course taught in school about the formation of the Underbellies but I had never heard this level of detail being told before and I had to admit that I was fascinated.

We left the park and arrived amongst several large houses. I looked down the end of the street and I saw my father's house standing alone as it gazed down, like a ruler amongst its subjects, at the rest of the houses.

My father led me away from the Upper Ring and we descended to the lower levels. As we passed through throngs of people I became aware that I was drawing attention to myself. With the Underbelly leader and his cohort for company, it was no real surprise to attract a little attention. It was however, unnerving to realise that I could not remain incognito, as people would easily recognize me.

I was running out of time.

As we passed through the market square, I noticed something strange. I struggled for a moment, attempting to pinpoint my sense of unease I studied a pair of men conversing colourfully as they haggled over the prices of exotic fruits. The large swarthy trader was scowling as the beady eyed buyer attempted to lower the prices.

After a few moments, he threw his hands up in agreement and the beady eyes man grinned widely, but then all animation on either of the men's faces went still. After a few seconds the beady eyed man smiled again and the large swarthy man nodded his head and the purchaser walked away with his goods.

"I guess that even other criminals are not immune to be extorted against." My comment had come out harsher than I had wished, and I internally winced when I saw a few of the servants exchange looks but my father was looking at me in amusement. "Oh that wasn't an extortion, it was a sale. Look around."

I did and I saw that there were people engaging in the same behaviour, their faces going slack before life flooding back into them. I frowned and my father saw my frown. "Can you figure it out?"

I felt my brain struggling to put the pieces of the puzzle together. People spoke normally before coming to coming to an agreement on a price. But then they would lose all facial expression for a few moments, before coming back to life, and some sort of agreement that was not visible and the buyer would take the goods.

A ludicrous thought entered my head, what if they could read their thoughts? I felt a cloying presence envelope myself and it felt both protective and invasive at the same time and I turned my attention outwards to see my father gazing at me intently but upon seeing my questioning gaze he smiled and raised his eyebrows. "So did you figure it out?"

I shrugged. "The only thing I could come up was that they're reading minds."

Something flashed across my father's face and I got a distinct vibe of unease. But then it was gone. It was strange because it did not come from me, almost as if it had come from outside of me. It was surreal.

My father shook his head. "Not too far off of it I suppose. As you can imagine we are a little unorthodox here in the Underbelly and for the last few years I had been trying to come up with a viable trading currency, that did not involve physical money. If there was one thing that living on the Surface had taught me, it was that money itself was not a bad thing, it was just a tool just like any other but it was the love of money that had corrupted many people. I wanted to develop a vaccine for that I suppose."

My father was talking as he guided me through the market place, nodding and smiling at the various traders that saluted him. "We had tried bartering at first but it was too subjective. How does someone put a value on the countless different goods in the market place against other goods? Not to mention that many people of the Underbelly do not actually visit the Surface to source goods to trade so that system quickly fell apart."

Father was silent for a moment as he collected his thoughts. "It was one of our brightest minds that had solved it. Dr Yuyo, a night walker." I had inadvertently frozen and my father sighed deeply, rolling his eyes as he looked back at me. "Really, Merissa. You Surface people need to let go of your prejudices. Yes, there are bad night walkers out there, just as there as there are bad humans out there, but the vast majority of them are decent hard working people."

I glared. "You've never had to break into a feeding frenzy of those monsters then, have you? Casually carving up humans for sport? Do you know how many families have been torn apart by those monsters?"

My father looked unmoved. "Like I said, there are good night people and bad night people. You would be wise not to paint everyone with the same brush Merissa. I thought that your mother had taught you better than that."

I saw red as he referenced my mother, and I felt my heart rate increase and blood began pounding in my ears. I felt something stir sleepily inside of me but it settled down after a moment as I fought to control my rage. After I had gotten all of the information that I thought would be useful, I would kill him.

My father looked at me with his unreadable dark eyes and he continued slowly. "Dr Yuyo is an absolute genius and is a very compassionate man. He then decided to mix the two together and developed a brain implant."

I started at that. I did not like where this was going.

My father continued on. "He designed this implant to connect to our black sun cloud."

Seeing my confused expression, my father hurriedly explained. "Dr Yuyo will explain better to you later, but basically the black sun cloud is just a vast reservoir of information that is wireless. Not too dissimilar to the clouds of information used by the Surface, but ours is unique in that its powered by our black suns. This makes them both impossible to hack as there's no point of control, and it makes it possible to erase sensitive data should we need to, by destroying a particular black sun. So our banking is in the black sun cloud but instead of using money as our currency, Dr Yuyo had the ingenious idea of using reciprocal altruism."

I had heard of reciprocal altruism, of course. It was a system of scratch my back and I'll scratch yours. However, I struggled to see how this could be used as a form of currency and then father leaned in like he was going to let me in a secret. "If you're nice to someone it's registered in their implant, and the degree of the appreciation will determine how many points you get. It pays to be nice you see."

Oh wow. That was well and good but I couldn't help thinking that a society that relied on being nice as a form of currency was not going to be a threat to the Surface.

Father rattled on and on about the different places as we passed by, but I was not really paying attention. I was focused on taking note of how to get out of here in a hurry when I needed to. Other than the way I came in, there seemed to be no way obvious way out. If I knew my father the way I thought I did, there were almost certainly a few secret passages out of here.

The tour got even more interesting when Father stopped in front of a large Bloodsteel door that was three times as thick as the entrance gate. Though I had been paying attention to the direction and location, I had not noticed the change in the appearance and feel of the surroundings. I knew that I was in the Lower Ring. Most of the people in the crowd were wearing practical hardy clothes and moved with the grace and ease of constant movement since birth.

I noticed again the various night people but, as they mixed with the other people with practiced ease, I felt myself starting to understand that they weren't considered a threat here.

At an unseen signal, the smartly dressed staff diffused into the crowd that was thronging around us and I suddenly felt very alone, despite the crowd. My father was looking at me intently and I felt a probing sensation that was similar to when Marcus had placed his hands on me but this time instead of feeing like it was inside my mind, it was a feeling of being completely enveloped. "This is the Academy, where people like you and I learn to master all that we can, a place for you to reach your full potential."

I shook my head in exasperation. "I don't need to do that, I trained for years with coaches and martial arts experts, not to mention the various professors in their areas of interests. I am the best I can be at this moment in time. I just want to focus on me."

I was coming up to the point and I think he could sense it too because he dropped his voice. "I know you want closure but if you let me show you this place, I will let you choose your own path. Only a fool would rush into a situation without looking at all options, and you, my daughter, are no fool."

With that he walked up the stone steps towards the gargantuan gates and to whatever was waiting inside. I looked after him and bit my lips, what did I want to do?

A flash of my mother appeared in my mind, her worn tired but happy face that was filled with strength gazed steadily at me. She did not say anything but I could almost hear her saying, Go on honey. You know what to do.

After a few moments of hesitation, I followed suit.

My first impression of the Academy was that it was warm, and it was only then I realised how cold it was out in the Underbelly. Despite the heat of the various black suns that I had seen scattered across the Underbelly, there was a lingering bite in the air that stung my skin.

The second was comfort; whoever designed this place had a lot of comfort in mind. It contrasted with the hard practicality of the Lower Ring outside. Aside from the flashy goods in the market that I saw when I first arrived, the Lower Ring was the baseline of the Underbelly and did not need to be extravagant to display its power. In the Academy however, it was obvious that whoever lived here was used to living in style.

Lining the pale cream walls were plush couches, a deep scarlet red. The cushions scattered amongst them were the colours of every gemstone imaginable, creating an illusion of being inside a vast treasure trove. The floor was covered in a deep purple carpet and I could feel the feathery softness through my worn boots.

Hanging on the walls were large luxurious holograms that showed footage of nature, cascading waterfalls, gently blowing green trees, and huge herds of wild hera, a large bovine creature with small miniature horns on either side of its head, roaming the Damoomill plains. Until today I had assumed that they had long since disappeared from the planet.

I could see my father watching me through in my peripheral vison, and I knew that he was evaluating my every move. It gave me confidence to think that someone who once terrified me would give me this much wary respect.

Though, admittedly, it unnerved me and reminded me that I had to think everything, lest a rash move invoked his rage and retribution. It did not do much to soothe my nerves that every time I noticed my father paying particular attention to me, I felt that cloying presence enveloping me.

I still wasn't sure what it was.

He led me down a straight corridor. There were no doors leading off the corridor, however, there was an archway at the end the hallway that gaped open wide like an ominous mouth. The walls were not bare. There were about a dozen small alcoves carved into the walls and opulent holograms dressed the spaces, and I could see that these were not holograms of landscapes, but of people.

What amazed me about the holograms were that that they were in colour, and not the static blue of standard holograms. They looked so breathtakingly alive that I jumped when they began to move, pose and laugh in their alcoves. I peered closely at one that drew my attention.

With a flash of anger, I recognised the young woman who was smiling in the painting. Her face was much younger than in any pictures I had ever seen, but there was no mistaking her look of strength and confidence. It was my mother. Her long blonde hair was flowing like wheat blowing in the wind, her tanned skin rippled with the muscles that she had from her days in the army, though their hardness did not make her any less striking. In fact, her strength had always added to her beauty. When I was in school, I had always boasted that my mom was the prettiest, strongest and smartest mom ever.

Even now as I gazed upon her likeness, she was still my hero.

Her sky blue eyes sparkled with mischievous laughter and I felt a lurch in my heart and my breathing became harder to control. Before the tears could start to fall I saw that there was a little inscription below the alcove; Jessica Forts was first wife to esteemed leader of the Academy Underbelly Alastair Forts. Her role in the setting up the Academy and acting as First Mistress during its birth was pivotal, and she will always be remembered as our Mother.

My father walked slowly towards me and I turned to him incredulous. "My mother set this place up!?"

My father answered with a slow nod, and I detected a distinct tinge of sadness in his voice. "She did, indeed. We had decided a long time ago that we would keep this from you."

I stared at him. "What does that even mean?"

My father shook his head and the sorrow lifted from his eyes, "That is a long story, but this is not the place for it. I will tell you, but not here. Even here the walls have ears."

I suddenly felt more exposed and my father nodded in almost agreement and I felt a spark ignite in my own my mind. I wasn't sure what it was, but something important had just dawned on me. I just needed time to sort it out, and articulate it to myself.

My father turned and began to walk towards the impending archway, and I followed him, resigned. I felt more helpless than I had ever been. With every passing minute that I spent in the Underbelly, I found myself more tangled in its webs.

We reached the gaping maw and I peered down and I saw that there were a set of glass tubes leading down. It was dark, but not completely. There were glowing points in the walls and I could feel my keen eyesight adjust until I could see as well as if it were a sunny afternoon.

My father grinned and I could see the gleam in his eyes that was reflected in my own and I repressed a shiver. I hated to be reminded that I was not entirely normal.

My father turned and plummeted down the tube. With only a brief hesitation, I dove in after him. Though I could see through the gloom, I could not help but feel I was descending into a different kind of darkness. I was falling deeper into the convoluted webs of the Underbelly.

This is going to be one hell of a ride.

Family Reunion

The plunge was not that long, and a landed with a soft thud on a remarkably soft surface. When I stepped off of the padded cushion I had landed on, I felt my foot connect with a hard stone floor. So much for the illusion of comfort upstairs, I thought. This was not too dissimilar from the flagstone of the dragon breeding pens. I followed the swiftly moving figure of my father down the dark corridor. It felt more like a tunnel though, with the curved low ceiling overhead, and I felt a somewhat claustrophobic in the cramped, dark corridor.

He stopped in front of another Bloodsteel door. My father placed a hand on the centre of the door, and I realised that there was no handle. I heard my father hiss slightly, and watched as a thin trickle of blood flowed from his palm, down his wrist.

He withdrew his hand and I saw a small puncture wound on it. I looked at the door and found only the smallest hint of blood smeared on the surface. My father looked at me and said. "The door will only open if there is a blood offering, and only if it's a special kind of blood. Our kind of blood, to be precise."

Morbid, I thought. I pinched my lips in distaste. "How does that even work?"

My father shrugged. "Apparently, there's something that's special in our blood that they can detect and even if someone had a packet of our blood it wouldn't work. This door and those like it are able to detect how fresh blood is by the amount of live cells in your offering."

With a soft drone the door opened. My father finished his explanation, as I was greeted by an assault of noises. We were at the top of a set of steps that led down to some sort of training grounds.

It was set up like an amphitheatre, but it had no ceiling. I could see the rough underside of the roof of the Underbelly, and flying in and out of the amphitheatre were numerous jewel coloured dragons. There were dozens of children running around on what appeared to be the most insane obstacle course known to man. There were some parts of it that would be impossible for normal humans to even hope to overcome, including a large, sheer, wooden wall that was twenty metres in height, and a firing range that shot at the darting figures.

Amongst the darting people, I saw that there were dragons working in tandem with them. A petite young woman, with a riding helmet and leather outfit, was riding an emerald dragon, the size of a large wolf. They were streaking down a runway and at seemingly random intervals, humanoid robots sprung up from the runway and shells of electric pulses erupted from their open hands.

The dragon and young woman were not perturbed, however, and dodged them with practiced grace. I gasped when three figures in red sprang in front of them and they trained Tracker weapons on them. I had never used Tracker weapons before but I had heard of people in my unit curse these weapons before, with horrifying tales of these weapons used by the Underbelly and other factions. They were non-lethal, but had a nasty charge that often knocked out the target, and rarely missed. They were wired into the nervous system of the user, and so tracked the movements of the user's target until the hit was landed.

	Sure enough, when they all fired initially, the girl and dragon easily evaded. But instead of firing off in a straight trajectory, they all curved around and began to harry the young woman and dragon.

	The young woman began to look pressured and the emerald dragon was losing steam and flying erratically. Suddenly, the young woman pressed a button on the back of her helmet and a visor dropped down to cover her youthful face. She crouched deeper into the dragon and with a roar the dragon spread its wings wide and bounded forward. With one huge push with powerful legs, its wings strained and lifted them into the air.

The Tracker weapons did not relent, however, and they continued to harass the pair and dog at their heels. Although the dragon was as graceful as a ferret on the ground, it was abundantly clear that it was more suited to the air. Using its long pale green tail as a rudder, it glided through the air with enviable ease.

Within moments the dragon had outmanoeuvred two of the three Tracker weapons as it spiralled tight circles through the air. The two Tracker weapons collided with a mighty explosion and erupted into a firework of sparks. The third one was not so easily dispatched.

No matter what the dragon did, it could not seem to shake the last Tracker weapon. Eventually it turned laboriously in the air, looked at the rushing oncoming mass of electricity, and hovered in the air with its forked scarlet tongue scenting the air. With a flash of her hands, the rider unhooked herself from the green dragon and drew out a blunt weapon.

With a screeching yell, she jumped from the dragon's back towards the approaching crackling ball of energy. She thrust the blunt weapon into the ball, and amazingly, it went out with an audible snuff. As she was tumbling through the air her dragon swooped below her. With a crow of victory, she grasped one of the long spines that ran along the dragon's back and hauled herself onto the saddle.

With a roar, the dragon dive-bombed the racing track and blew past the finish line below. The young woman jumped off of her dragon's back and patted it on the snout fondly and it nuzzled her in return, both of them heaving from the exertion. She removed her helmet, shook out her hair, and grinned at the crowd forming around her in congratulation. With a shock, I realised that she was not a young woman at all, but actually a girl, maybe twelve or thirteen at most.

My father beamed proudly at the spectacle. "That is Yelena, your youngest sister. It looks like she just graduated!"

I unexpectedly felt a swell of mixed feelings; excitement at the thought of having a younger sister, but also uneasiness at the thought of seeing physical proof of my father's infidelity, and lastly, a little bit of awe. Seeing her in flight with that perfect partnership with the dragon was a sight to behold.

Yelena was not the only one performing amazing feats. Elsewhere, I saw two young men darting back and forth as other men and women in red shot at them with red lights. The flickering red lights were moving blindingly fast. Yet, even as the lights flashed through the air, not one of the blurry figures faltered. They were dodging them! That was incredible!

Even as watched this demonstration, my attention was pulled to another young girl out of the corner of my eye. She ran up to one of the sheer walls, and jumped cleanly up half of it, then scrambled her way up the rest of it. I looked on in amazement. As I processed this, my eyes were drawn to another end of the running track, where a portion was aflame with in a solid expanse of fire. I saw flickering shapes appear, and retreat into it, as both people and dragons ran through. I felt my jaw drop open when three young kids leisurely trotted out of it. A place to train people like us indeed.

A small group of young boys, about thirteen years of age, saw us and zipped up the stone steps towards us. It would have taken the average person about a minute to sprint up the steps, but they managed it in less than five seconds. It was more than a little unnerving, and reminded me of the deadly speed of the guard, Marcus, at the gate.

They stopped sharply in front of us and grinned cheekily. Father, pretended to be mad but it was clear from his manner that he was only teasing them as he scowled. "Shouldn't you boys be running more laps or something? I think I could still run laps around you!"

I stared at my father, quite dumbfounded, as the boys retorted with easy sarcasm. This was a totally different facet of the man that I had known growing up. Lost in my attempt at reconciling what I thought I knew about him with what I was witnessing, I missed what the boys actually said.

It was quickly apparent that I was the focus of most of their attention. Father grinned and gestured towards me. "Lads, what do you think of your oldest cousin?"

I took a step back, and stared at them with new awareness. When my mother decided that she had enough of my father's schemes and left him, she and I had always been alone. There was never really anyone in our lives apart from sporadic visits from my father, and suddenly I was faced with having three young cousins in front of me. I hadn't really believed my father when he said I had dozens of cousins and siblings, but here was the evidence, grinning before me.

This knowledge changed everything. I no longer had to be alone. I felt the weight around my heart that I had felt since my mother's death shift ever so slightly. The isolating fist that was clenched around my heart loosened and I could breathe a little easier.

I looked at them intently, studying their faces in an attempt to discern any common features between us. I noted the odd features, such as an arch in an eyebrow or a quirk in the corner of a lip. One of them had a shade of brown hair that was identical to mine. There were some alien features on them however, showing that we did not share the same parents but enough similarities that it was possible to see them as family.

My father cleared his throat. "Merissa these are your cousins, Isaac, Tommy and George. Boys this is your big cousin Merissa." Isaac was a slight willowy boy with deep amber eyes and chocolate coloured hair. Tommy was much taller, but just as slim and looked stretched thin and with similar colouring to Isaac. George had a more athletic build and he was paler than the others and had green eyes.

Father looked proudly at his nephews. "Isaac and Tommy are twins, but George has different mother but they were all born roughly at the same time so are more or less triplets." I felt slightly uneasy at how he was talking about them, it almost seemed like a proud farmer discussing the merits of his livestock.

The three young boys looked at my father expectantly. They must have seen something in his face because they all narrowed their eyes and adopted defensive positions and glared at me. They suddenly looked much older than they should and I felt the hairs on the back of my neck rise and I felt my heart rate increase. I was suddenly convinced that these young boys were far more dangerous than trained soldiers.

Father looked at me and smiled. "Good. At least living with and being trained by the Surface has not totally destroyed your senses. Come, there is someone I want you to meet."

I left my cousins, who calmed down once father spoke. They were grinning like children again and began to scamper around like a pack of puppies. I ignored them and followed my father down towards the centre of the amphitheatre.

As I had noticed before, it was more or less a giant obstacle course but the difference this time was that all the figures that were in constant motion previously were now stationary, me being the focal point of their attention. Both humans and dragons were as still and observant as statues, with the exception of the dragons' tongues flicking as they took in my scent as I passed them. I felt my back stiffen in response to their scrutiny. Despite the sea of faces looking at me it was apparent that I was the oldest by several years.

That gave me some comfort.

Then as I followed father I saw that I was mistaken. There were people dotted amongst the young faces that were around my age if not older. Since I knew that I was the oldest child in my father's family, I wondered who they were. They were all dressed in red uniforms, so maybe they were some part of group that helped train the students here?

It was obvious that I was going to get my answer soon, as my father was angling for one of these people, a tall dark haired man, who towered over even me.

With an uneasy lurch of my stomach I saw that he was a night person and I recognised him as the sole trainer who had managed to use his Tracker weapon to pin down the girl Yelena and her green dragon up until the last moment.

My father gestured back to me. "Chaz I'd like you to meet my eldest daughter Merissa." Chaz's dark lavender eyes brightened and I could see the interest in his eyes light up his entire face. Then without warning, he jabbed out with his hands at my right shoulder but I twisted my body so that I avoided it. He nodded to himself. "Your reflexes are on point, let's see what else you've got!"

With a roar he lashed out with kicks and punches, I had to really stretch myself to avoid them. He was fast, but I was faster. Then, three other night people joined in. It was clear from the matching red uniforms that all of them including Chaz, were wearing, that they were part of some sort of team and that I was being tested for something. The four of them pressed in for the attack and I was hard pressed to defend myself.

Eventually I felt myself growing weary and what had started out as me dodging the attacks, became me blocking them which in turn became landing solid strikes on my body. One of them, a small lithe blonde woman, slithered through my defences and used her nails to rake my face.

I tasted blood.

I felt an unfamiliar sense of power course through me but it was not totally alien. I had felt it once before; the night my mother was murdered. I grabbed the woman by the wrist, my first offensive move of the fight, and I could see alarm in her eyes in the shift of my tactics. I focused the power in my core and channelled it down my arms into my palms. I felt it slam into her and cause havoc with her nervous system and she began to scream shrilly at the pain.

The other three froze before exploding into action, whenever one touched me they crumpled beneath my gift. Chaz was the last one standing, of course. He was in a kneeling position as my hands rested on his shoulder, pain rippling through his body. I looked deep into his dark lavender eyes. "If you or any of your friends ever lay a hand on me again, I will kill you. Do you understand?" Chaz bared his fangs and spat at me so I increased the pain intensity and my voice was remorseless. "I asked you a question and I expect an answer."

Chaz's eyes began to roll in his head and he moaned a quiet agreement. I let him fall unconscious, my breath hard and fast as I recovered from my explosive use of my gift. I looked around at all of the shocked faces. "I'm leaving now, I thought that I could get what I wanted by coming here but I don't think that's the case anymore."

I turned to leave, but my father spoke calmly. "If you leave Merissa, you'll die."

I whirled around, still gripped in the rage of my gift. "Are you threatening me old man?"

My father looked unruffled. "Hardly, especially after seeing what you did to them. The people who want you dead are the same people who killed your mother and did this to me."

I stopped and with a sudden rush the rage left me. I asked with a calmness I did not feel, "Who murdered my mother?"

My father stretched out his hands. "Come with me and I'll explain to you what happened. I'll tell the story of how I was abducted and experimented on as a child. I'll tell you how I escaped and how your mother got wrapped up in all of this, and how it led to her death. Come with me and I'll explain everything."

He wagged his fingers though and said, "You have to promise that you won't have any more temper tantrums however." With that he turned heel and headed towards the opposite side of the stadium expecting me to follow, after a few moments of deliberation, I did.

Sad Story

We entered a bar just off of the running track. It was obviously my father's favourite viewing point considering, how many whiskey bottles there were stacked on top of the glass shelves behind the bar. My father clapped his hands as he walked in and several small black light lamps sprang to life, casting a sharp angle on everything in the room. He strode right over to the bottles and poured himself a generous glass of the golden liquid. He raised his eyebrows questioningly but I shook my head in polite refusal.

I was never much of a fan of whiskey.

I strode over to the enormous window that spanned the wall and looked out onto the athletic field. It was still crazy to see people achieve such amazing feats. They were working in teams now and many people were riding dragons of different sizes, though none were as large as Francesca, some came close. Chaz and his team of trainers had already recovered and I had to begrudgingly admit to myself that they must be phenomenally fit to recover so quickly.

A cough brought me out of my wonder and I turned to see my father sitting on a reclining chair. Its gleaming leather caught the light blazing from the three black suns radiating onto the fields. He gestured to the couch in front of him and I walked over to it slowly, still wary, and I sat myself down.

He swirled his whiskey around in his glass for a moment as he collected his thoughts. He was frowning. I frowned in return, confused. My father, unsure of himself? It was then that I realised it was very possible that my father has never spoken of this before. It was a new side of him and I wasn't sure how I felt about my father showing me his vulnerability.

He cleared his throat with a large harrumph and sat up straighter. "I never knew my parents Merissa, which is the reason I was a bad father to you." I arched an eyebrow in disbelief at that and my father threw up his hands in hasty admission, "Ok, ok. It's one of the reasons I am a bad father to you. Now that that's out of the way, I'll continue my story."

He got into a comfortable position and continued. "As I was saying, I never knew my parents and I don't mean in the way bratty kids today say it about their daddy or mommy not having enough time for them, I mean I grew up in the Empire's care." I was sitting very still, I never had any proper conversations with my father, and any attempts were certainly not alone. My mother was always in the background hovering, radiating cold fury in his presence.

It was surreal to listen to the big scary man in my life to talk like this, "So I grew up in an orphanage not far from here actually. I stayed there until I was about fourteen. One day I was walked into the head matron's office and was told that I was being adopted. There were three women in suits with her and they told me to pack my bags because and that I was leaving right there and then with them. I was, as you can imagine, shocked and more than a little upset since I had made friends in that place that were like family to me."

He smiled to himself and I got the feeling that he was not really talking to me but rather to himself and I listened closely, he could very easily let slip information. "I was even sweet on a girl there and I was bawling my eyes out when I told her goodbye and she gave me a kiss on the cheek as a goodbye present. I still have the little plastic flower she gave me on our first date..."

I cleared my throat in impatience, he looked up almost like he was surprised that I was there and then his expression cleared,

"Apologies for that Merissa. I was reminiscing. As I was saying, I was taken by those women and I soon found out that I was one among dozens of young boys taken by these women."

I felt like I was bringing up old and awful memories but I had to know the truth. "We were told that we were being recruited into the army to be part of a new program. They called us the Spliced Soldiers. At the time I did not know what that meant, but as time went on they trained us more ruthlessly. Every so often, a boy would go missing overnight and we would not know what happened." He paused to take a swig of the golden whisky as though to ward off a particularly nasty memory.

"One night though, I was with one of the other boys, Thomas. We had grown close, and we were exploring after curfew. We heard screams and naturally we followed them down the dark corridors. They were horrible screams, almost like the very reason for a person's existence was being torn apart over and over again."

My father took a sudden gulp of his drink again and waited a moment before continuing, clearly perturbed by what he remembered. "What I saw I'll never forget. I know the Surface people don't think much of us Underbellies but what they do to each other is far worse than anything I have ever seen. I saw four boys roughly my age but I couldn't tell who they were since they were torn apart like an overexcited dog with a rabbit."

I could vividly see what my father was describing, four young boys slashed open on pristine steel operating tables as figures cloaked in white pulled and twisted to see what they could do.

A younger version of my father and his friend walking in on that and their childish innocence disappearing forever as they whiteness the nightmarish scene.

My father then gulped a little more whiskey and continued on. "Thomas and I must have screamed ourselves because suddenly there were masked figures pulling at us, we tried to fight back but they must have injected us with something because we were suddenly unconscious. I won't tell you what they did to me but you can rest assured that what Chaz and the other trainers felt when you touched them was like a walk in the park in comparison."

I blanched at that.

My father was quiet for a moment. "I'm going to fast forward about five years when the last of my training was complete. Of the dozens of boys only eight survived to that stage, the rest died while they were playing God with their genetics." I swallowed. I felt like he was reaching the climax of his story and that one way or another I would have to make my decision. For the first time since I came here, I questioned my intentions.

My father was looking pensively into the golden brown liquid as he unwillingly unpacked his memories and looked at them. "I was brought into the army at nineteen, and there were just eight of us. We were a special ops force and were to undertake unofficial missions.

"Basically we were a hitman squad. As I'm sure you're aware, along with our extra physical and mental capabilities other so called "gifts" were unlocked in us. Each of us was different. One guy could tell you something and make you want to do it, a charismatic. Another could predict every possible outcome and tell you what was going to happen, a seer."

I cocked my head, interested in spite of myself. "So what can you do? What's your superpower?"

My father laughed loudly and it was a laugh of self-loathing. "Oh that's good! Superpower!"

I felt myself blush and spoke through gritted teeth. "Just answer the question, father."

My father wagged his finger at me, having regained his humour. "Remember Merissa, no temper tantrums now, ask nicely."

I rolled my eyes at his antics. "Can you please tell me what your gift is?"

My father sniggered. "I think I preferred it when you called it a superpower, seemed cooler but to answer your question I am an empath."

I looked at him blankly. "How on earth are you an empath? You're as compassionate as a slug!"

My father smirked "See that's a common misconception. An empath is just someone who can feel other's emotions and manipulate them. Many empaths like to feel loved to so they are generally people pleasers so that they can feel better about themselves."

I rolled my eyes again, if I kept rolling my eyes they were going to fall out of my head if I wasn't careful. "Not you of course, you're too clever to be a people pleaser aren't you?" Then a sudden thought blazed into my mind, was it possible that my father was manipulating me as we spoke? Was there any way for me to know that the emotions I felt were my own?

My father shook his head, seemingly unaware of my internal panic. "On the contrary; I am a people pleaser, but one that is a people pleaser in the long run as opposed to the short term. That is where your dear mother came into this."

I perked up at this and decided that I would have to sort out my messy emotions later. My father continued with his story. "You see, by being surrounded by men for the last four years I had obviously been deprived by a woman's loving touch so I went wild."

I held up my hand and abruptly snapped. "I did not come here, Father, to hear you regale me of your past conquests."

My father's eyebrows drew together. "You need to loosen up Merissa, call me Dad. I insist."

I felt instantly repulsed by the idea and I opened my mouth to object but he glared at me and I felt the two of us lock eyes.

Then I felt it, the cloying feeling as though I was being wrapped in clouds and I hissed. "You're doing it again!"

My father looked at me in surprise. "You can sense that? That is most curious, you're an empath also?" My father looked distracted and I knew that unless I had felt that suffocating feeling, my emotions were my own. I also knew that I was actually feeling myself at a crossroads, not one that was being induced by my father. Or rather, my Dad.

"So Dad, you were enjoying your time in the army." I prompted.

He grinned like a little boy. "Yes, my dear, I was. It was then I met your mother. Oh, she was beautiful! She had no time for me of course, she just saw me as a reckless jarhead that was after every skirt that would let him near. Truth be told, she was right. Something changed though when I met her. Her resplendent golden hair when the sun was shining was simply divine."

He eyes glazed over and I swear that I saw a tear. When he spoke, he had to clear his throat a few times. "When you told me that your mother had died, I admit that I was in shock. Still am if I'm honest. Not only was my oldest daughter suddenly on my doorstep. but she tells me that the love of my life is dead."

He looked at me suddenly. "You have her hair you know." I touched my dark black hair absently, my mother used to tease me saying that my hair was darker than some of the darkest suns. At the time I never understood what she meant, but now I did. She was talking about the black suns of the Underbelly.

I shook my head in disagreement, flashes of nightmares where mom would be brushing my hair and I would be dozing in her lap only to feel her slipping away. I would always wake up crying.

Dad shook his head in turn. "No. you do, it's not the same colour but the same texture and everything else." He trailed off and we were both silent for a moment remembering her.

Dad continued on. "So, I corrected my ways and eventually your mother thought that I was acceptable enough to be with and we were happy for a time."

I frowned in confusion. "If mom was the love of your life, why were you never there and why did you have all of those mistresses and those children?" I pointed to some of my half siblings running on the fields, "Some of them are only a few years younger than me. That hardly seems like the way you'd treat the woman you claim to love."

He looked at me sadly. "I did that so that she would hate me."

Now I was really confused. I felt my voice go up an octave as my surprise coloured my voice. "Why would you do that? That's the craziest thing I have ever heard!"

My Dad looked at me with sorrow in his eyes. "To protect you… and her, of course."

Dad took a deep breath. "Your mother and I had decided to leave the army together and for a time it seemed like we were going to have our happy ever after. But remember Tommy?" I nodded. "Well he was one of the people who survived the experiments and one night he paid me a visit." He gazed blankly into his glass that was already running low again, and he continued. "He came to me one stormy night and told me of the Spliced Soldiers. and how they were disappearing one by one. He was convinced that the Surface was the culprit for their disappearing."

I listened with rapt attention, my mother had never told me of this. and it was a deep relief to finally get answers to this part the past. My Dad continued. "One day, your mother and I were browsing in our local market for food when I felt the distinct aura of soldiers closing in around us." I felt my heartbeat begin to race as I listened to the story. "I didn't think. Tommy's warning was still fresh in my mind. I grabbed your mother and I fled the little town that we had made our home in."

He was silent for a moment as he thought about his past life and with a slow mournful tone my Dad continued. "Your mother and I were running for years, and after too many close shaves we began looking for a sanctuary." Dad abruptly stood up and poured more whiskey for himself and he began to speak over the cascading golden liquid. "We had heard of the Underbellies, of course. We never paid them too much mind. They did seem to be everywhere though, whenever your mother and I tried to lay down roots before the Surface found us, the Underbellies' influence was always felt. No matter where we were."

Dad threw back his head as he downed another gulp of whiskey. "So we decided that if they were that spread around the globe, they must be able to resist the Surface on some level and they might be able to offer some protection to us."

A dragon screeched as it flew past the window as an indistinct blur and Dad and I both jumped, my own heart beating a little too fast. We both looked at each other and laughed. I felt a little bit of that that tight feeling around my chest loosen even more.

My Dad chuckled and continued. "This next part wasn't so bad. Your mother and I were quickly accepted into the Underbelly, since it was Tommy running the show."

I raised my eyebrow and Dad laughed again. "The sly old fox infiltrated the Underbellies years ago and worked his way up. When he realised that the Surface was eradicating the Spliced Soldiers he had come to find me personally and warn me."

My Dad sighed. "It was only for another year or so that we were happy. Your mother and I had gotten married and had just found out that we were pregnant with you. But, as I'm sure that you're aware, good things must always come to an end."

My Dad's face darkened as he thought about past wrongs. "Tommy was one of the Underworld bosses. He was in charge of an Underbelly several cities away from here, and that Underbelly was in charge of food production and distribution. About twenty odd years ago he was assassinated and his entire family was butchered. There was absolute uproar and the Underbellies were thrown into disarray as food became scarce."

My father glanced out of the window. "Your mother and I knew that if the Underbelly fell that we and you wouldn't be safe and so we did our best to save it. I used my own gift to quickly get people to trust me and to provide some support and stabilised the Underbellies. Your mother was absolutely incredible. Though she was ungifted, she had this drive that made people believe in her. While I was placating the masses, she had decided that the gifted people of the Underbellies were our greatest assets, but also our most vulnerable. So we went about setting up the Academy."

Dad clicked his fingers again, and several small black suns sprang to life throughout the room, offering more light and warmth. He continued on. "You were very young when it happened, maybe six months or so, but someone had decided that I had grown too powerful in the Underbelly and wanted me gone. Since they knew that I would detect a threat head on, they had decided to go for you and your mother."

Dad was rigid with rage. "Your mother was well trained and her days in the army gave her the strength to hold them off. When I arrived I lost all sense of civility and lacerated the skin off of their bones. And it was right there and then I knew that the two most important people in my life could not be exposed to that again."

He looked away and I got the distinct impression of shame. "I told your mother to take you and hide on the Surface. It was no place to raise a child, I said." He snorted. "Naturally, she called me out on my bullshit, and I was starting to panic that she would get us all killed. So I did the only thing that seemed sane at the time. I made her walk in on me sleeping with another woman." We were silent for a long time. He gathered himself up. "Even after all I did, she still died." I shook my head, feeling a righteous rage uncoil within me. "No. She didn't die. She was murdered. And I want you to help me get revenge on her murderers."

It seems I finally made up my mind what I was going to do, I was going to avenge my mother after all by continuing the fight she started twenty years ago.

Soul of the Butler

There was a knock on the door and a young guy was standing there. He had dark, unkempt hair and wore ripped and tattered clothes. I studied him, and couldn't help but feel like that there was something slightly off about him.

My father stood and looked at him with a warm smile on his face. "Max! Excellent timing. I was just thinking that Merissa could do with meeting Doctor Oslo and Doctor Terry, don't you think?"

Max looked towards me with interest. "So, you're her?" I raised my eyebrows in surprise at his abruptness.

"What do you mean?"

Max grinned widely but before he could reply I saw a flash of movement behind his head. I watched as a small dragon circled once, then landed on his shoulder. I was mesmerised by its scales, which were a translucent colour and caught the light of the black suns at odd angles, casting minute rainbows off of its scales. His coal black eyes looked at me piercingly, and I could almost feel the sharp intelligence in its gaze.

Max looked at the dragon that was perched on his shoulder. "Oh. This is Tyson. He's my eyesight." I frowned, unsure of what he meant. I stared a bit longer than was polite, and finally looked past the grime and dirt on his face. I was startled to realize that his eyes were clouded over.

He was blind.

Max grinned again. "I'm gifted too, but my gift just makes life easier for me, unlike the superpowers everyone else seems to have."

My Dad broke into the conversation and said, "Yes, Max here has a useful gift here that lets him perceive life from other life form's perspectives. This manifested just after Max began to lose his eyesight, a few years back. As such Dr Oslo and his wife Terry have been studying him to see if there is any relationship between our genetics and how we develop our gifts."

Max was silent during our exchange but as he swung his head left to right as he observed us, the dragon Tyson mimicked his movements. Interesting, but eerie.

Dad cleared his throat. "Since you are the oldest of my children, Merissa, and also of your cousins, Dr Oslo and Terry would very much like to meet you. They have a few hypotheses they would like to confirm."

I suddenly had a flash of being prodded and poked at by people in masks and lab coats, and felt as though I were being slowly entangled in an invisible web. When I thought I had it figured out, a jarring motion would stop me in my tracks, entangling me further.

Dad must have sensed my sudden anxiety because he raised his hands and splayed them open in a placating manner. "Relax Merissa, there's nothing to be worried about. They won't be using any invasive techniques. They're actually quite nice, for scientists."

Max was grinning again. "Don't worry Merissa! Dr Oslo and Terry are really nice! They even sometimes give you chocolate if you're good!" Max's eyes started to glisten and I thought I saw a tear forming, but then saw his salivating mouth. I realised, with a small sense of relief, that he was just really looking forward to the chocolate and not tearing up at the thought of pain.

Tyson began flapping his wings in agitation and Dad laughed, "Ok Max, go and get your chocolate!" Max snapped back to reality and grinned at my Dad again before turning his attention to me. "Now, don't you be upsetting my scientist friends; chocolate is very hard to come by down here!"

My voice was dry when I replied. "Oh, I wouldn't dream of it." I could feel my eyes itching to roll again but I restrained myself.

Max continued to lithely bounce down the corridor as he led me even further from the athletic field, and deeper into the Academy. We passed by corridor after corridor and it was with a small surprise that I realised that this was like an Underbelly within the Underbelly. I wondered what secrets I'd find down here.

We walked in silence and despite the constant chatter radiating off of the young boy, I could not help but find him endearing. He had no nastiness about him at all, and he was a breath of genuine fresh air of enthusiasm in this dark place.

We entered a massive courtyard that was filled with a small forest, and the smell of pines and deciduous trees wafted up my nostrils. With an appreciative deep breath, I tasted the fresh air and I heard a rustle of wings and with a piercing chirp. Tyson spiralled up amongst the trees and as my eyes followed the clear coloured dragon through the deep green foliage, I noticed that Max was standing stock still.

I nudged him gently, and I heard a shriek of alarm. Tyson came hurtling out of the small forest baring his teeth. It was the first time that I realised dragon's teeth were serrated like sharks, and also as numerous.

I held up my hands in a placating manner, though the dragon was only as big as a large cat. With the speed it had returned to Max, it was clear that it was a force not to be crossed.

The dragon stood protectively in front of Max and hissed voraciously, but Max laid a placating hand on the enraged dragon. "Tyson, it's ok. She just scared me a little by accident. I'm sure she wasn't trying to hurt me." Tyson stopped hissing but watched me with his night black eyes, unblinking. After a few seconds he relented and retreated back up to Max's shoulder where he could keep a closer eye on me.

Max grinned ruefully. "Sorry about that. He's really protective of me. One time one of the older guys tried to trip me up, but Tyson saw him and went ballistic. He was only a young dragon at the time, a fledgling about the size of a kitten, but he went mental and went right after his face. Ever since then, we've been bonded." He looked up at the quietly chirping dragon and smiled widely and the dragon nudged him in response.

Max bounced to a stop in front of a huge oak tree, placing his small hand on the centre of the tree. With a whistle of wonder, I saw that the wood was actually breathing. There was a delicate fluttering of several of the branches near the top of the tree, and a couple of faded leaves drifted through the air and settled by our feet.

The tree seemed to pull itself apart, revealing a passage. Within its murky depths, I could see a faint light running along the inner wall in a dotted line formation. Max stepped forward without hesitation into the massive hollow tree. After a brief pause of unease, I followed suit.

In the centre of the mossy ground within the tree was a stump. Max ran over to it and pressed at a little nodule that made it sink into the ground silently. With a low hum, the surrounding ground sank and retreated to reveal a set of stairs. The lights that ran around the inside of the tree were also visible here, lending a nurturing glow.

It was a marvellous piece of work.

I followed Max and Tyson down the stairs and we found ourselves in an earthy chamber. The roots from the trees above protruded from the walls, and the air was damp and warm, like a greenhouse for exotic tropical plants.

Max strode forward with practiced ease and I tentatively followed. He stopped in front of a large slab of rock that had intrinsic runes inscribed along the edges. The language looked old, and I had no idea what it said.

"Fire, Earth, Water, Air and Spirit. The elements of the universe, protect and worship them against yourself or you will become your own worst enemy."

I looked at Max in surprise. "Is that what it says?"

Max shrugged nonchalantly, "I'm not sure but that is what I see every time I look at it. No one else even knows what language that is."

I peered a little closer at the inscriptions and could almost see what Max meant, the individual symbols made no sense, but when looked at together its meaning revealed itself. It felt like a warning.

Max placed his hand on the centre of the slab of rock and bright blue light radiated out from it in a star-like pattern. When it reached the end of the slab of rock, there was a high melodious ring that reverberated through the air and seemed to make the tree roots dance. It was such a beautiful sound.

The rock door opened down the middle and pulled itself apart to show its contents. Inside was a small antechamber that Max dragged me into. I was still dazed by the beautiful musical ring from the rock. Suddenly, a blast of foam erupted from the wall and thoroughly drenched me. With a yelp, I almost sprang out of the antechamber but Max had a firm grip on my arm. He tried not to laugh at me, but failed miserably as he snorted through his fits. Even Tyson was regarding me smugly and I glowered back but before I could say anything the doors behind us snapped shut and a wave of oppressive heat blasted through the small room, drying us instantly.

Max had calmed down somewhat and said with a grin. "Since outside is so dirty, Dr Oslo and Dr Terry want to make sure that everything is nice and clean before coming into the lab."

He frowned as though remembering a bad memory. "One time we didn't wait to get clean and they got mad and wouldn't give me chocolate for a week."

It was my turn to laugh, the look of petulance on the young boy's face was endearing to see. Max grinned and exclaimed, "Let's get going so! There's chocolate to be had!" With that Max sprinted through the open door at the other end of the room. Tyson was watching again, and I felt myself shuffle somewhat uncomfortably under his scrutiny. I mentally shrugged and followed the bouncy boy into the lab.

I had done science for a couple of years in school but I might as well have been playing with a kid's chemistry set for all the good my knowledge would do me here.

We walked onto a raised dais and there was a glass workbench in front of us. Max and Tyson fluttered over to it and peered curiously into it. I joined them and I was about to ask what it was but the question died on my lips when I looked down from the dais into the cavernous room.

There were rows and rows of glass workshop tables, and on each one were the various stages of experiments. I felt a chill as I walked past them, feeling warily like each one had enormous implications.

I stopped by one glass worktable and saw a couple of white mice darting back and forth in the cage. One of them caught sight of me and squeaked in terror, then promptly vanished from sight.

I blinked, sure that I was seeing things, or rather not seeing things. An electronic voice interrupted me. "Excuse me, ma'am, but you are interfering with the experiment and I would ask you to please step away." I turned to see a six-foot-tall robotic humanoid figure looking at me with electric blue eyes.

I gasped and stepped away as it requested, stumbling into Max. He laughed and began clapping his hands in glee. "Oh, you got her butler!" He began to chortle. "You should see the look on your face Merissa!" I felt myself go red and the continued snickering of Max was not helping me regain my composure.

I took a closer look at this butler. There was no doubt, it was a robot. At six-foot tall, it could eyeball me. It was pure silver but there were no facial features other than those startling blue eyes. Everything else looked remarkably human, though. There were wires and nuts and bolts that added definition to the robot's body.

"Ah I see that you've meet one of our butlers." I turned to see that another person had entered into the room, a pleasant looking man that looked like he was used to spending time in the sun, a rare attribute in the Underbelly.

He smiled warmly. "You must be Merissa." I nodded in reply and he continued. "Well my name is Oslo." I smiled myself in answer and the doctor looked at the butler before continuing. "I suppose that you want to know what he is don't you? Most people are alarmed when they first meet my butler." I pursed my lips in response, not really sure how to respond.

It's been illegal for decades for members of the public to own any robots that could function independently. It was considered a security risk and only the military was allowed to continue to develop them. As the Artificial Intelligence became more and more advanced, the military became increasingly paranoid that the robots would eventually turn on them and had discontinued them.

Every so often on the news, an undercover factory would be found producing these machines and agents would be sent in to demolish the operation. I've even been on a couple of these raids, it can be terrifying to go up against an entity that is immune to most of your electric charges and doesn't feel pain. This meant that we had to rely on archaic weapons that punched holes in them.

I understood why they were considered a security hazard. In the wrong hands, intelligent robots are lethal weapons of destruction and the fact that the Underbelly had these robots was very worrying.

It would mean that if they had enough resources, which thanks to the black suns they might, they could wreak absolute terror on the Surface.

I didn't want everyone to die.

As these thoughts were racing through my mind I could see Dr Oslo gauging my reaction. He must have seen some form of unease because he began to talk in a soothing voice, guiding me back to the dais as he explained. "I understand what it must look like Merissa but these butlers are only research robots. They simply help my wife and I conduct experiments more efficiently."

I bit my lip. "That may be so, but how do you know they won't malfunction and rebel against you? I've seen what these machines are capable of." Dr Oslo looked pensive for a moment then gestured for me to follow him to one of the workbenches.

He stopped at the workbench on the raised dais and the workbench appeared empty but Dr Oslo touched something on the underside of the table and I could hear something coming to life beneath the workbench. There was whirring noise, and in one fluid motion another butler extracted itself from underneath the bench and waited for instructions in front of Dr Oslo.

I rounded on Dr Oslo, alarmed. "Just how many of these machines do you have?"

Dr Oslo shrugged casually. "Underneath each experiment is a butler." I looked around the room in horror. The laboratory was a vast room, and there were hundreds of workbenches. Dr Oslo flicked a switch on his watch and hundreds of butlers soundlessly slid out from underneath the workbenches. The mass of silver then began tending to the hundreds of experiments, as tenderly as a gardener nurturing a delicate sapling. There was no menace in their graceful movements, but I could see their strength. One of the butlers pressed a button on its workbench and an opaque force field bubbled around it. The butler jammed its fingers into a rock and with a grinding sound, as it slowly ripped apart the rock and revealed a slumbering creature. With a jolt I realised that it was not a rock but rather an egg!

Dr Oslo beamed and hurried us over to the edge of the shield and gestured towards the newly birthed creature. "This is amazing! We have just created a totally new animal!"

I frowned at him. "What is it a mix of?"

Dr Oslo shook his head, "No! You don't understand," He exclaimed. This is a totally new creature." Seeing our confused expressions, he sighed, and then said, "This isn't my experiment. I'll leave it to Dr Terry to explain it to you."

I turned aside as another butler passed me carrying a heavy crate. Dr Oslo nodded and we left the experimental floor, and headed for the raised dais. From the higher vantage point, I looked back down to the experimental floor and I saw a flood of silver. That was a lot of weapons. In the wrong hands, they could cause mayhem.

Dr Oslo smiled gently again. "You know, I had much of the same worries as you when I started this project. I wanted to make sure that there was no chance these machines would ever cause deliberate harm to people, and so for a long time I looked for a solution."

He turned and looked fondly at the butler that was standing there silently and patiently. "This is the original butler that I made about fifteen years ago. He's not as good as the newest models, but in some ways that makes him superior. You see Merissa, I knew that there was a chance that if someone wanted to, they could kill me and my wife and seize control of these butlers so I worked to solve the problem."

Max was clearly enthralled with the story that Dr Oslo was weaving, but I was still sceptical. Yet the Doctor continued. "Merissa, how much do you know about the human brain?"

I was startled by the sudden question and I fumbled for an answer. "It controls the body?" My response was questioning as I doubted my own knowledge.

Dr Oslo swung his head side to side like a pendulum as he pondered my answer. "Not quite, but that's how most people understand the brain so I'll forgive you. The brain is actually a reservoir of information. I won't get into the nitty gritty details, but basically, I converted the information in my head into data that a robot would understand. Now, the butler understands everything that I do, including what I consider important in the world. In return, they give me the information they have assimilated from their experiments."

My own brain was starting to hurt. "So what does that even mean?" I asked awkwardly.

Dr Oslo grinned like a little boy and spread his arms to encompass the entire room. "It means that I put my soul into each and every of these butlers."

The Doctor and the Missus

An opaque glass door on the far wall slid open and a woman stepped through. She was engrossed in a hologram that floated in front of her. She was constantly poking her long fingers into the hologram and revolving an image of a person. It was moving too quickly for me to see any details in other than it was male.

However, when the woman switched off the hologram and saw us she smiled brightly. Her skin was very dark, not the kind of darkness that was a result of being out in the sun frequently but a darkness that one was born with.

A tall slender man then followed her, a dreamer's face lost in another world, but it was the colouring of his face that caught my attention. He was snowy skinned with jet black hair and lavender coloured eyes.

Another night person.

He ambled over to us with the unnatural grace that was characteristic of his species and smiled politely at us. I felt my hackles rise when I saw his fangs. Perfect for puncturing human necks and draining life giving blood from us.

Dr Oslo cleared his throat and said in a brusque voice, "We might as well get this out of the way; Merissa, this is Dr Yuyo, our most brilliant mind in the Underbelly. And this amazing woman is our most accomplished geneticist-who happens to also be my wife-Dr Terry."

Once I got over my initial shock of seeing a night person, I saw that Dr Oslo's wife was a spectacularly beautiful woman. Her deep black skin seemed to glow as it radiated light like a black sun, and her facial bones were exquisite. Her unusually frizzy hair stood out in a condensed sphere and added character to her face. Her lips were scarlet red but it was her eyes that were the most captivating feature, they were a dark chocolate colour and they were filled with such a thirst for knowledge and passion for life that it was impossible not to instantly like her.

Dr Yuyo was …strange. He felt off, like he was almost on a different radio frequency as the rest of us. The thousands of micro expressions that take place on the human face were totally absent on the night walker's face, making him unsettlingly hard to read. He nodded his greeting to me as Dr Oslo introduced us. "A pleasure to finally meet you Merissa. Your father, the Underworlder, has told us much about you over the years."

Dr Yuyo must have seen the confusion in my face as he explained. "The Underworlder is just the title that your father is given as the ruler of this Underbelly."

Dr Oslo smiled. "It really is becoming an Underworld with the introduction of night people into the Underbelly."

Dr Yuyo grinned more widely, fully exposing his fangs. "Please, Dr Oslo, you know we prefer our original name. Call us vampires, please. We must always respect our roots that have allowed us to grow such beautiful leaves and flowers."

Dr Yuyo then raised a dark eyebrow at Dr Oslo. "Your heartbeat is racing. You should relax."

Dr Oslo scowled. "I hate it when you ruin surprises."

The human angel then spoke with an exasperated voice. "Are you being theatrical again dear?"

Dr Oslo grinned unashamedly. "I was just telling Merissa about how we put our souls into our work." He chuckled at his joke and the beautiful woman sighed and raised a delicate hand to her forehead. "I would have thought, dear, that after a couple of decades that you would have calmed down, but you're still as immature as the day that I met you."

Dr Oslo beamed at her and turned back to me and Max. "This perfect creature you see before you is my darling wife, Terry." Dr Terry smiled gently and flowed forward. She clasped my hand in a firm and warm handshake. "It is truly an honour to meet you at last Merissa, your father has told us much about you. I cannot wait to begin our work together."

Dr Yuyo nodded his agreement.

I felt slightly overwhelmed, and the three scientists seemed to pick up on this. They smiled again to reassure me, and Dr Terry said, "We just want to monitor your progress and help you become the best you can be."

Later on, after Dr Oslo and Dr Terry had shown me around their labs, and Dr Yuyo asked me my opinions on a few engineering problems that were way above my ability to solve, they then told Max to take me back to the dorms of the Academy. He had pouted initially, but they had given him a bar of chocolate and he and Tyson were practically chirping with joy.

I was now laying in my bed, trying to think about the day. So much happened in such a short space of time that it was hard to process everything. I got up and took a shower to wipe away the dirt and grime of the day.

As the water ran over my body, I felt myself begin to relax, and my thoughts ran freely. I was suddenly hit with a burst of clarity. In the last several hours, I had learned that everything is not what it seems in the Underbelly. They have dragons, vampires and even their own suns down here. The economy is based on being a decent person, and somehow it is impossible to cheat the system. Though I felt a little uneasy at the fact that they put brain implants into people's brains, I hoped they didn't do this to children. I also wondered at the ethics of using kindness as a currency. How does one know when someone is genuinely being kind or just doing it to pay their bills? Since its based on the intensity of the recipient, would this system eventually fail once people grew used to a certain standard of kindness?

I stepped out of the shower, dried my hair to the best of my ability and wrapped it up in a towel. Feeling refreshed, I slid into my bed and it felt like I was being cradled in silk. My eyes grew heavy and my mind began to drift. Strange visions began to form in my mind's eye. My mother and father stood in front me with clasped arms, and a colourful dragon grinned at me as though it had just found me after searching for a long time. A pair of dark lavender eyes, searching my own dark brown eyes, picking at who I was as a person, testing me, for what I was not sure. The dark lavender eyes vanished and were replaced with a warm wooden room filled with smiling people. My family. As I drifted off to sleep, for the first time in a long time, I felt a little warmer and safer.

Limitations Are Only Illusions

I woke up with a headache and could feel someone hovering over me. I yelled and lashed out. I felt my towel roll off me and flop onto the floor. I heard an unfamiliar grunt and a rueful voice broke through my groggy mind. "I guess I had that coming to me, come on! You're going to be late!" I opened my eyes to see a young girl, who was about thirteen, looking at me with earnest big blue eyes. With a jolt of realisation, I saw that she was the girl who was riding the green dragon yesterday. It was surreal to think that this young girl was soaring through the air yesterday on a flying dragon.

She grew uncomfortable with my gaze and she began to tug at her light blonde hair shyly. "I'm Yelena."

I cleared my throat. "I know; I saw you yesterday on your dragon. I'm Merissa."

Yelena grinned in response. "Everyone here knows who you are after we saw you kick some butt yesterday!" Her face screwed up in worry and her pale skin crinkled. "Seriously though, we're going to be late, get up!"

I threw off my duvet and stood up, with Yelena moving back hastily. Then I heard a chirping sound and saw that there was a dragon sitting on a pillow that was strewn on the ground. It was wagging its tail furiously, and with a gasp of shock I recognised that it was the same colourful dragon that I had seen in my dream. Yelena grinned. "She was begging to get in here this morning when I came to get you." It was the rainbow coloured dragon that was crying when I left the dragon pens yesterday. I stood stock still, remembering what Dad had said; "They have a tendency to imprint with a human." Does this mean that this dragon was trying to imprint with me?

The dragon could not contain herself any longer and she chirped shrilly, bounding over to me and rearing up on her hind legs. The light casted off a myriad of colours, and I saw that in the day since I'd seen her, a new colour was added to her body. It was a scarlet coloured moon on her chest. I marvelled at her beautiful markings and bent down to touch her and she went still with suppressed tension. I heard a sharp intake of breath behind me and I turned my head to see that Yelena was practically radiating excitement. I frowned, I wasn't sure but it seemed different somehow, like I could really feel what Yelena was feeling, it was coming from her instead of me just processing it.

While my thoughts distracted me, the little dragon lost patience and bumped her dark blue snout against my palm. With a sensation of cold shock, I felt an enormous pressure enter my mind Merissa.

With a yelp I stumbled back and Yelena clapped her hands in delight, "That's amazing! You're not even here a day and already a dragon's bonded with you! And not just any dragon, number 73!"

I swallowed. "Number 73?"

Yelena nodded eagerly. "Oh yes she's a special dragon, she's one of the oldest here, older than Frans even. But she's never picked her bond-mate until you came along, so she's never told us her name. She's also the only multi-coloured dragon here and Dr Oslo and Dr Terry think that's important."

Wow.

I don't know what to even to think, I was bonded to a dragon? Other thoughts came crashing in. Could I bring her to the Surface or was this some sort of contract? Did my father do this to further entangle me in the webs of the Underbelly? What did I have to do with her? Did she need to be treated like a dog, fed, walked and washed?

The thoughts were becoming panic-tinged but I felt the strange pressure again. Even though the little dragon was no longer touching me, I saw the total devotion and commitment already forming in her mind. With a start, I realised in the back of my mind that I had been searching for her for a long time too, even if I had not known it.

The dragon looked supremely pleased with herself and touched my hand again. I felt the pressure build again, but it wasn't as intense. Merissa. I have waited a long time for you. I blinked, how would I talk to her? Do I talk normally or can I talk to her with her in my mind?

Merissa. I heard her laughing lightly in my mind and I was surprised at the maturity of her vocal tones. She sounded like a woman in her mid-forties, as opposed to a child. *When we are bonded I can hear what you think and you can hear me. With a little time, we will not need to be touching to hear each other. In time, we will also learn to discipline our own thoughts and not intrude on each other's privacy.*

I felt a flash of annoyance. I never said I wanted someone privy to my innermost thoughts, and I felt a little sadness come from the little dragon. *Neither did I Merissa, but when we are born dragons are bound to humans and it is a match best suited to both dragon and human. This is not a conscious decision on either of our parts, we must simply make the most of it.*

I mulled it over for a moment but the flash of anger had disappeared and I accepted it, it wouldn't hurt to have a dragon on my side. I felt approval radiate off of the little dragon and she laughed her light little laugh. *Merissa, my name is Ellesera but you can call me Elle for short.*

I grinned. Right Elle, let's do this!

I strode over to the bathroom, with Elle on my shoulder and looked at the arsenal I had at my disposal. Since I was on a time limit I would have to make do with minimal cover. I grabbed my basic survival kit and began to lather my face to make me semi human looking. In the last few years I had noticed wrinkles forming. After a small bout of self-pity, I had gotten over it and just learned to cover them up. I could see Yelena looking at me wistfully, I smiled and gestured to the lotion in my hand. "Would you like a bit of moisturiser?"

She nodded eagerly and was soon giggling as I rubbed some onto her cherubic face. She hardly needed it but I guessed that she didn't have many interactions with other girls. This was confirmed when she said, "I've always wanted a big sister." I was brushing her hair when she said that and I paused for a moment as I realised the implications of what she just said, but she did not seem to notice. "I mean, I love my big brothers, but being the only girl and the youngest is not easy. I'm still way stronger than the other girls in school though! So it's not too bad." I could feel my eyes widen in horror, was this girl being trained to fight in my father's war?

She turned to look at me so I had hastily schooled my expression. "Are we ready? The coaches are going to be mad if we're late!"

I patted her thick hair. "Don't worry I won't let them get mad at you." I shook my head. "I need to get something to eat, is there anything quick to eat?"

Yelena pursed her lips thoughtfully and skipped from the bathroom. I heard a crow of victory and I laughed and followed her, with Elle sniffing curiously from my shoulder.

Yelena was pouring grey coloured beans into a bowl, then poured water on them from a standing jug. With a hiss, the beans broke down and became a mass of grey porridge. There was steam rising from the bowl of food, but it did not look appetising. I grimaced, and Yelena laughed, rummaging in one of the cupboards, and then picked out a jar of strawberry jam. I squinted my nose at the strawberry jam, but Yelena smiled and delicately plopped a spoonful of the scarlet fruit onto the grey mush. Then something magical happened; the scarlet jam spread seamlessly throughout the unappealing grey grain and every colour of the rainbow emerged, chocolate brown, jade green, baby blue and royal purple. I tentatively took a bite, and a riot of flavours danced and ran over my tongue.

It was scrumptious.

Elle saw my reaction, and I felt her desire to try it too, and so I brought my spoon up to her for her to taste a scoop of heaven. She darted out her snake like tongue, and a small lining of the rainbow porridge coated her tongue. I may have only known Yelena about twenty minutes, but I already could feel a bond being forged between us that was going to be very strong and when Elle and I had finished she raised her eyebrows in a questioning manner and I nodded, "Yes, let's go."

I threw on my hoodie and followed Yelena out to the fields. I heard a deep chirp and I looked up to see a green dragon swan dive towards us. Yelena shouted with glee as the dragon pulled to a graceful stop in front of us. Yelena hurried over and hugged the green dragon and grinned back at me. "Merissa meet Jandre. Jandre meet Merissa."

I felt a light pressure on the fringes of my mind and Elle placed a paw by my cheek. *He is asking permission to talk to you, that is what that pressure is.*

I nodded and I heard a low musical male voice echo through my mine. *Well met Merissa. I am honoured to meet Yelena's eldest nest-mate at last.*

I bowed my head in response. "And I am honoured to meet you also Jandre, you flew well yesterday."

Distinct pleasure and pride radiated from Jandre, and then I felt him divert attention to Elle who was watching the proceedings in my mind. Their communications were not word based; they used images, feelings, and some odd sounds, almost like metal flowing. I got the impression that even though Jandre was twenty times the size of Elle, he was giving her the respect one would give to a superior. I wondered why?

The two dragons then sprang into the air and intertwined each other and danced through the sky, joining the rest of the dragons in their exercises. After a few moments, Yelena led me over to a small group of red uniformed coaches, my stomach was a little uneasy when I saw Chaz among them.

Yelena was all smiles when she reached them and a strict middle aged night woman with greying hair and horn rimmed glasses glared at her sternly. "Yelena you were sent to get Merissa not to have your hair brushed and makeup done."

Yelena blushed furiously and I interjected. "I'm sorry, it was my fault. I was doing some basic foundation, and I wanted Yelena to try."

The stern woman turned her glare on me. "This is not a beauty salon Merissa. This is the Academy, where exceptional individuals learn to become freedom fighters."

I returned her gaze coolly. "You're asking children to fight and die for you. If you are going to be that cruel you might as well let them indulge in normal pastimes every so often."

The stern woman began to bluster but Chaz cut across her. "Relax Ésme." He turned to me, his gaze attempting to cut through me. "You need to learn some respect. Now go warm up and come back to us when you're ready to listen." He turned away in clear dismissal.

Yelena started to drag at my arm and I complied. She sprinted towards a large group of guys, ranging in age from just older than Yelena to only a year or so younger than me. One of the older guys looked at me with hostile eyes before he seethed. "What is she doing here? She's a Surface bitch."

I chose to ignore his antagonism, but one of the more athletic guys punched the surly dark haired surly guy on the shoulder. "Chill out, Zack! Dad says that she's cool and since when has Dad ever been wrong?" He turned to me with his smile bright. "Ignore my twin, Zack. He gets hormonal despite the fact that he's twenty-one years old. I'm Ray, and I guess Zack and I are your brothers!" The rest of the guys cheered and I could not help a little smile in return.

Ray turned to the rest of the guys. "Now let's get this party started! Last one to the wall is a rotten egg!" He turned and began to holler at the top of his lungs. The other of the young men followed with enthusiastic screeches.

Yelena grabbed my hand and pointed to a climbing wall about five hundred metres away. She grinned and began to flit towards it and I quickly followed her.

We arrived last and Yelena was gasping with giggles. I could feel another little shift somewhere inside of me and I laughed too. One of the younger boys, with red hair and freckles dusted across his face, crowed with delight. "She's the rotten egg!"

I smiled at that but then Zack cut across. "Of course she is, she's as soft as a Surface mundane."

I ignored him but Ray frowned. "That's hardly true. She took on Chaz and the others, and won pretty handily if I do say so."

I winced internally. While I was thankful that Ray was standing up for me, I could not help but feel like I was causing a rift in this community, and that Ray was only making things worse for me.

Zack stomped away furiously and began to scale the wall. The others shrugged and followed his lead. I eyed the five story wall uneasily. There were no handholds to grab, and it was sheer. Yelena was half way up when she saw that I was not following. She dropped and landed lithely beside me. She smiled encouragingly. "It's not as hard as it looks, you just need to let go of your inhibitions and go for it."

I eyed her doubtfully and she nodded at me earnestly. "I was the same way, I swear! But then they showed how strong I can be when I believe in myself, and that the limits we put on ourselves were illusions." She didn't sound like a thirteen-year-old girl, but a much wiser woman. I nodded resolutely and placed myself at the base of the wall.

As I started to climb, I refused to think about how. I just did it. Then I made the mistake of letting my concentration slip and my fingers lost their grip. I fell on my back and cursed loudly. Yelena looked at me with a small smile. "That's ok. It took me a while to get all the way to the top too." She pulled me up and brought me around the wall to where all the others were stretching. By now, the group had grown to several dozen. The rest of my family had arrived.

I ignored the curious stares and followed Ray's stretching instructions. Pretty soon, we were all sweaty and quite warmed up. A mischievous grin spread across Ray's face, and I had a feeling I knew what was coming.

Sure enough, he bellowed: "Last one to the coaches is an old fart!" Everyone groaned good naturedly at this. Well, almost everyone. I was still sore from climbing a five storey wall.

We all sprinted towards the coaches, a tidal wave of flesh. We stopped in front them and they looked at us with raised eyebrows and I heard amusement in Chaz's voice. "Well I gather that you all have energy to spare. Go with your tutors and meet back here in three hours for lunch." He looked at me with a slightly annoyed expression, "Merissa, follow me."

Everyone else was drifting away towards their tutors, and I saw Yelena go off towards Ésme, the stern lady with the horn rimmed glasses. Several of the other younger kids went with them. I obediently followed Chaz, and found myself mildly irritated to see Zack accompany me. I perked up a bit when I saw that the grinning Ray had also tagged along.

This should be interesting.

Chaz took us into one of the small rooms that branched off of the main athletic field. It was simple enough, with grey walls and wooden floors. There were several bean bags scattered about the room, adding a bit of much needed colour. Chaz collapsed onto a blue one that looked bright behind his pale skin. He gestured for me to sit on the yellow one across from him. I complied as Zack and Ray each found one and dragged them over, their eyes alert with anticipation.

Chaz looked at us thoughtfully and began to speak. "We're going to experiment with your gifts today." The other two boys looked puzzled at that, and I felt nervous. I couldn't help but feel like this was a test to see just what I was capable of. Chaz continued on. "Merissa has had no formal training, and so she will need to have this all explained to her." He then addressed me directly. "Zack is an illusionist and Ray is a charismatic. Today, we are going to classify your gift. Most gifts fall under Endo or Ecto influences. This means that you can either change how your view changes, or how someone else's perception changes."

He paused for a moment, frowning. "Judging from our first fight together, I would say that you are an Ecto; someone who influences perception outside of yourself. Pain, in your case." He pointed at both Zack and Ray. "As an illusionist and a charismatic, they are both Ectos as well. We'll give you a little flavor of how their gifts work to see how it feels, then we'll look at yours."

He nodded to Zack and before I realised what was happening, I found myself in a jungle. The smell of rotting vegetation wafted through my nostrils, the cacophony of the birds sang through my ears, and the warm breeze slithered along my skin like a sinuous snake. I heard a disturbance in the melodious concert around me, like a spider web that had just been disturbed, and I turned to follow the sound. I saw a black panther growling, its velvet hide glistening in the noon sun.

I could hear Chaz's voice in the background, explaining. "What Zack is doing is reaching into your brain to where all of the sensory data is processed by your brain. As long as Zack concentrates, he should be able to make you see, hear, smell, touch and taste anything he wants."

The black panther began to stalk towards me, growling menacingly. I felt undiluted terror sweep through me. Then a part of my brain began to twist and turn. It felt strange, almost like it had a life of its own. It wrenched itself from its prison and coursed through my veins.

My eyes snapped open, back to the grey reality. I looked around, slightly dazed and I felt a flash of shock when I saw that Zack had a nosebleed and was looking at me with wide eyes. Chaz was looking at me, his expression unreadable but I could feel suspicion radiating off of him, like a cloying flavor covering my tongue. He turned his attention to Zack. "What happened?"

Zack shrugged as he dabbed his nose with a tissue from the tissue box at his feet. "It was going fine. She resisted a little at the start, but then everything was going ok. Then, out of nowhere, she pummeled right into my mind and I lost control."

Chaz was silent for a moment. "Alright then, Ray, you're up. In order to understand how Ray's gift works you'll have to see its effect on someone else as it's too subtle to detect when its used on you."

He motioned towards Zack, who had just dabbed at his nose to stem the blood flow from his nose. "Go on Ray, a small demonstration if you will." Zack's face went sour as Ray's face lit up with mischief. As the guys got into position Chaz continued with his lecture. "Ray's gift is almost like the power of suggestion."

At that Ray began to speak, his voice deep, soothing and hypnotising. "Relax Zack, go to your happy place." Zack's previously sour expression evened out and a look of serenity washed over his face. "Zack, I want you to do a handstand for me."

Ray made Zack do many things after that, each with increasing difficulty. Zack did each without any hesitation whatsoever. Eventually Ray said, "Zack I want you to stand upside down on the ceiling." For the first time there was a moment of hesitation from Zack, but then he began to run towards the wall at full pelt and when he reached the wall he pounced and began running along it. I stood there, with my jaw agape. It was impressive to say the least.

Zack reached the ceiling and began to run along it, but when he reached the centre, he hung there for a moment like a humanoid bat. The spectacle ended with him crashing to the floor in an undignified heap.

He got up immediately, and began to run at the wall again but Chaz cleared his throat and Ray nodded. The vacant look left Zack's eyes and he stumbled to a stop, turning to glare at both Chaz and Ray.

I couldn't help a little smile, but then Chaz looked at me with a glint in his eyes and said. "Ray why don't you try it on Merissa?"

I opened my mouth to protest, but Ray locked eyes with me and I felt my mind drip into a liquid state, being bathed in endorphins. The sheer joy was rapture, I felt subtle strings being pushed and pulled within me. The euphoria was distracting, but I could feel a tightness curl heavily in my stomach.

I felt my own gift respond sluggishly, as though waking up from a restful nap. It ambled towards the source of discontentment in my stomach. In my mind's eye I could see a dark ball of writhing shadows, flickering and darting into the surrounding tissue of my body.

The dark shadows seemed to clasp onto the electric currents of my spine and shimmy up like monkeys clambering up a tree. The shadows cajoled the blue electrical impulses and directed them away from where they were originally destined to go. Making them move the muscles the shadows wanted to move.

That is a scary gift and it was time to stop it.

I felt my gift become more alert as it sensed the invasion, and in my mind's eye I could see it glow a golden colour and stab at the shadowy mass in the centre of my stomach. The shadows rapidly dissipated and my eyes flew open.

It took me a moment to understand where I was, then I saw Ray breathing deeply as he tried to recover. His skin was sweaty and clammy and Zack was patting his back, comforting him.

Chaz was looking at me in exasperation and suspicion. "What are you? You can do far more than anyone else here and now you can resist others? It's almost as if you're both an ecto and an endo!"

I shrugged. "Maybe that's your problem. After all limitations are the illusions that one places on oneself, no?"

Ray was rapidly recovering and he was leaning forward excitedly. "What can you do Merissa?"

I looked at him carefully, weighing if I can tell them my theories. I caught Chaz's sharp lavender eyes looking at me with a pinched expression and a dark gaze. I need to get him to trust me or he might tell everyone here I'm not to be trusted, especially now that I can do so much more than the others, it seems.

I sighed. "I think the best way to explain it is that I have complete control over my nervous system. It's a really basic and crude way of explaining it but I think it's the best way to."

Chaz was listening intently and so I continued, "I'm not sure exactly what I can and can't do. I discover new things all of the time. Take today for example, I never knew I could redirect other people's gifts until I was exposed to them." Chaz's face was becoming more and more dark as I spoke.

However, Ray and Zack were both looking at me with rapt attention. I had said as much as I wanted to. Chaz then found his voice and spoke with a heavy voice, "Ok then, Merissa. Show me what you got."

I hesitated. There was always a chance that the vampire would see something that he shouldn't, but I decided it was a risk that I would have to take if I was going to complete my mission. I stepped forward, accepting his challenge.

I felt a slow and uncertain grin spread across my face, and my voice was nervous and excited at the same time, when I said, "My pleasure." My hand outstretched to show him my world.

Ghosts of the Past

I felt my mind settle into a calm trance. Chaz's cool, pale hands enveloped mine and I could feel spikes of energy scatter between our palms. I ignored them and focused on the pressure building up in my head, just above my nose on my forehead. People in the psychic communities call it the third eye and since discovering my gift, I have often wondered if they were on to something.

I could feel my mind fold in on itself, almost like a collapsing water column. With a resounding roar it crashed and rushed from my mind, I felt it race along my arm, reaching hungrily for its escape.

My fingertips began to buzz, not too dissimilar from when Chaz first took my hand. I felt my gift swell and rush into Chaz. This part of my gift was very familiar to me, however, this was the first time I had paid it this much attention. It was the next stage that I was far more unsure of.

It was almost as though my gift could sense my hesitation and was also unsure of itself. It cruised from my fingertips and flowed into Chaz's hands. With no directions from me the gift continued to mill and swell about in his fingers.

Suddenly, I felt my eyes squeeze shut. My neck snapped back and in my mind's eye I could feel the flux and flow of my gift coming from me and sweeping into Chaz. It was as though I had become my gift!

Incredible!

I felt like I was suspended in liquid, and was disoriented at first. With movements in my mind that felt like aqueous acrobatics a swimmer would do in a swimming pool, I oriented myself, and I could see the pathways of the nerves in Chaz's hands spread out before me, almost like roads on a map. Each nerve was a silvery blue hue and made it easy to distinguish from the mass of red flesh around it. With wondrous enthusiasm, I began exploring.

It was more than a little strange. Since I was in both of his hands, I was split down the middle, and felt as though I was in both of his hands at the same time. It was like holding a wet slippery ball in one hand and a dry rough ball in the other at the same time, being aware of the differences but also thinking of them as the same. I played with the different textures of his nervous system, but focused as I rejoined up with myself, in his torso.

I spilled out into his torso and I could see his heart and his other vital organs. The heart was a phenomenal sight, there were smattering of pulses of electricity as it continued on its ever demanding job of contracting and relaxing to pump the blood in the body.

The silvery blue lights were strong here, almost hypnotic.

With a start, I realised that the nerves were not actually the silvery blue colour, but that it was the pulses of electricity that I was seeing. Similar to the pulses of colour that I saw Ray manipulating when he used his gift on me.

His lungs pushed and pulled at the air currents and the silver and blue lights were dancing within his lungs, as though they had just been set free, dancing with wild abandon. Each breath was like a fireworks display, so dazzling.

I managed to drag away my gaze and I located his spine, a tall mass of silver and blue. I decided I was going up. I wanted to see what I was going to find in his brain.

I felt like I was Dorothy following the yellow brick road, except I was following the nerves of Chaz up to his very essence. I felt more and more apprehensive as I approached my destination, I had no idea what was going to happen, as I'd never done this before.

I just hoped I didn't kill him.

I finally reached the brain and my, oh my! What a sight it was. The combined lights of the vital organs and the spine had absolutely nothing on the brain. It was a blinding mass of silver and blue, a shining brilliance that glittered and dazzled as the neurons sent messages throughout it.

Curiously though it was shaped as an orb as opposed to an actual brain shape. I tentatively reached out with my gift, and when it touched the membrane of the light, a ripple streamed across the orb.

"Merissa?" I went cold all over. That couldn't be right. Was I hearing voices or did I actually just hear Chaz's voice just there? Am I reading his mind? I heard him again. "Merissa, what's going on? You've been stone still for nearly an hour now. Is everything ok? Do I need to do something?" I withdrew my tendril and the voice went silent. Interesting.

I splayed out my gift, preparing to touch the orb in various spots. I gently prodded the orb and I felt a chorus of voices wash over me before finally settling on one. "Dear Creator Merissa! What did you just do?" I took a deep breath and spoke back with my own mind. "I think I managed to make contact with your mind, I've never done this before. But then again, I don't normally force this, so maybe this is actually what happens when I use my gift without thinking."

My own mind was reeling and I almost lost my concentration. I felt my gift falter and I had to quickly re-establish my focus, and my gift continued flowing nice and thick. I wonder...

I sent a wave of power through my connection and felt it reverberate through my mind link with Chaz. His mind retreated, and I pursued and established another connection. "Merissa, would you please stop doing that! I would very much like to not get a headache today please."

I felt a little guilty and Chaz must have picked up on it because he grumbled. "It's ok. How about we leave this part of the experiment alone for now? I would rather talk to your father and the rest of the scientists before continuing. To see if they've had any experience with this."

A curious thing happened then. I could see a dark entity flit about in the silver blue mass of colours and I instinctively chased it. I could feel Chaz's growing alarm. "Merissa, what are you doing? I want you to stop! You could break something!" It was too late I had surrounded the black entity and it darted back and forth in my cage, morphed from my gift, in terror. I sent a tendril towards it, curious.

The shadow attempted to evade me but I simply sent more tendrils after it, determined to see what it was. As soon as I made contact my mind was catapulted to a sitting room. The setting was still ordering itself, couches and bookshelves jumped into existence. The fireplace sprang to being and the fire was burning merrily. Along with the fireplace was a rug and a young night boy was sprawled across it, listening avidly to a young human woman, reading to him from the couch while she occasionally glanced out the dark window.

I couldn't hear what was being said. There was no sound but it was clear from the adoring expression on the boy's face that he was cherishing the time spent with the woman. With a jolt of understanding, I realised that this must be the boy's mother.

Suddenly, the woman looked up and the boy's face became even paler with fear. The woman abruptly stood and whispered to the young boy before rushing from the room. He boy stood frozen for a moment before running over to one of the bookshelves that lined the wall and pulling a book.

The bookshelf swung out from the wall, revealing a chamber, and the boy stepped in. A tidal wave of sound crashed in on me and I could hear harsh grunts and scuffling from beyond the room. Then, a single scream. I could hear the quiet sobbing of the young boy as he waited in his hiding place. Suddenly, there was a bang and the horrendous stench of burnt flesh, followed by a terrible silence.

The door the young boy's mother had run through swung open and two men walked in. I recognised them, not because they were extraordinary looking. In fact, they looked very unremarkable. Of course, they had to be in their line of work. Agents Higgins and Slattery looked around. Agent Higgins was sporting a bruising face. Clearly the woman had put up a fight.

The two men looked around the room, with sharp, cruel eyes, before Agent Slattery spoke. "He had a son. We do not leave until he's found. All of the night children must be purged." Agent Higgins nodded and began to search the room. They searched fruitlessly for several moments before Agent Slattery spotted something. "Come here Higgins." The young ginger man ambled over and agent Slattery pointed at the bookcase. "There are groove marks on the floor. This is a moving bookcase."

In one sinuous movement the two men holstered their Shockrays and began pulling at the books. I could sense the palpable fear from the young boy, it was almost like I was really there experiencing the moment. The two men could sense it also, and were pulling at the books with predatory fervor.

Eventually, Agent Slattery located the correct at a book, and the bookcase pulled away from the wall. The men trained their Shockray on the young figure hiding within, no mercy in their soulless eyes. Before they could pull their triggers, they both collapsed and began screaming in pain.

They continued to scream, blood frothing at their mouths, the boy looking at them with wide and lavender eyes filled with horror. The movements lessened, and then they stopped and went still. The boy stepped gingerly over them and left the room.

"Enough."

I was wrenched out of his head and suddenly I was aware of my brothers Zack and Ray looking at me intently. My chest was heaving and I could feel the sweat clinging to the hollow of my throat. I gulped and looked at Chaz, who was glaring at me with a dark and pained gaze.

"Wh-what was that?" My voice felt loud after the quietness of his mind.

Chaz looked at me. "A very bad memory." I balked at the sudden realisation. "That young boy was you? How did you do what you did? I didn't think that vampires were gifted?" My brothers looked perplexed.

Chaz had a faraway look in his eyes. "That's why I know it's the right thing to go to war with the Surface. They are ruled by animals and they will hunt us until we're all dead. Ironic considering that they consider my people to be the animalistic hunters."

The penny dropped and Ray began to gesture excitedly. "Does this mean that you're gifted, too?" Zack looked at Chaz in shock before Chaz said. "It does indeed."

I frowned, my thoughts racing. "Then why don't you train with us? It may be unorthodox for a vampire to train with us, but would it not make sense?"

The haunted look returned to his eyes. "Because every time I use my gift, I can hear my mother's screaming. Since I can't use my gift like that, I train all of you so that you can survive better. It's my penance for killing my mother."

I jerked back in shock before saying. "You didn't kill her. Those men did!"

He set those cold eyes on me. "By being born the way I was, I threatened the existence of the Surface, and so I was to be killed, along with my family."

I felt rage stir within me and my gift began to swell again. "How dare you? It was those bastards that killed your mother, just like they killed all of our parents. It's those bastards fault not ours! I will not be told that you were the fault of your mother's death! IT IS NOT OUR FAULT!"

Silence followed for a moment before Zack broke it dryly. "Well hear, hear, I agree. It's those bastards fault. And we are due our revenge, so what do you say Chaz, shall we make them pay?"

The glazed expression fell away from Chaz's eyes replaced with an unholy fire. "Yes, let them burn. If they want to rule, let them rule hell."

I felt a sense of foreboding rush over me, but it was gone before I could comprehend it. This was going to be the turning point. I could feel it.

With a small dawning realisation, I recognised that I no longer saw Chaz as a night person, but as any other person who had suffered under the rule of the Dynomamian Empire. And just like any victim, he deserved justice. We were going to get it, not just for him but for all of us.

The Barracks

I heard a loud gong ring through the Academy and Chaz smiled wanly, "I guess it's time for lunch." Zack and Ray got up sharply but Chaz gestured for me to wait a moment. "Your father wishes to see you, Merissa, he is waiting for you in the bar. Do you know where it is?"

I nodded, "I do."

Chaz returned the nod, "Well, then you should probably get going. He is not a very patient man, your father."

He got up to leave and was almost out the door when he turned and said, "I'll pick you up afterwards." He was gone before I could reply. While the words themselves were innocent enough, the meaning underneath was complex. What the exact meaning was a little unclear, it felt both like a threat and a gesture of politeness.

Men are far worse than women for sending mixed messages, in my experience.

I gladly left the training room and crossed the deserted training grounds a to the bar my Dad had brought me to the night before. Was that really just last night?

He was waiting for me behind the bar, serving himself some fresh strawberry juice. He had some mint flavoured water waiting for me, and I drank it rapidly, thirsty from the last three hours of workouts.

We sat in silence for a few moments, enjoying our drinks. After a few minutes, Dad spoke, "I wanted to check up on you, make sure that everything is going ok."

I shrugged, "It's all strange, of course. Everything that's happening. But nothing seems to be actually harming me."

Just then, there was a loud chirp and I saw Frans slink out of the shadows, we bowed our heads to each other at the same time. I felt a questioning nudge from her and I nodded my assent. *Thank you for talking to me Merissa, I must apologise for my…erratic behaviour yesterday. I had thought you had meant harm for my bond-mate and indeed at the time you did. But I saw something else in you. You're not a bad person Merissa, you have a good heart. Angry? Yes. Misguided? Perhaps. I am glad Ellesera has chosen you to be her bond-mate, my sister deserves to be happy.*

My Dad yelped with surprise and I heard Frans chuckle quietly and she spoke to us both. *I have never told anyone of my elder sister as she wished no one to know until she had bonded with someone.*

I glanced at Dad. "How did you not know that they are sisters? Surely they would have been young once and you would have reared them?"

Dad shook his head but it was Frans who answered me. *We do not have brothers and sisters the way you understand them Merissa. We have all been born in a lab. It's only been the last year or so that some of us older dragons have begun to feel like adults. Maybe we will have hatchlings naturally, or we may not, only time will tell. Until then when a dragon calls a fellow dragon sister or brother then that is the ultimate friendship bond that a dragon can form and is only second to bond-mates.*

Elle joined us soon after, and the two sister dragons looked happy to see each other and began talking to each other in that peculiar dragon-speech of images, feelings and liquid metal singing through the air. My Dad and I began to talk, about everything really. I had never seen him so relaxed and a thought blurted out of my mind. "Why do you trust me, Dad?"

Silence greeted me and I noticed Elle creeping closer to me, anxiety pumping off of her. If I could feel it, then Dad definitely could. But he gave no indication that he did.

His calloused hands rimmed the edge of the glass he was drinking from, lost in thought. I watched him wary for any signs of anger but he just seemed thoughtful and he eventually broke his silence. "At first it was interest, you were so bright and brilliant. When you stopped me from punishing Jeffery, you were so angry. It wasn't a vicious anger though; it was a righteous anger."

"Once I had seen that I knew that I had to get you to see reason, and what we stood for in the Underbelly. I knew that I was doing the right thing when Frans looked into your mind and she saw your potential also."

I didn't know what to think at that. But then, I hadn't known what sort of answer I would get, and I was surprised to get an answer at all. A loud knock yanked me from my thoughts and I saw Chaz standing at the entrance. I felt bone white terror run through me. How much had he heard?

Dad grunted as Chaz moved into the bar with the slow sure movements of a predator. I was still not sure how he had processed my seeing his most private memory. I did not want a vampire as an enemy.

The slow, graceful and purposeful walk was for him to remind me to watch my back. I took his warning seriously. He turned his attention to my father. "The Surface forces are patrolling again. Two of my boys have found traces of them not too far from the front gate." Dad pursed his lips. "I see, well I want them found and if you do find them, I want them dealt with."

Chaz nodded in agreement and my father turned his gaze onto me and I saw a glimpse of the man that he had to become to save me and my mother resurface. "You don't know anything about this, Merissa, do you?"

I shook my head resolutely. "Of course not. I have nothing to do with the Surface security, I was working in an office for the last three years after school." This was a lie, of course.

Dad believed me, but Frans' tail twitched, and I worried about that. "Good. It would be nasty if you were caught up in that lot. Not only are they the most corrupt people I had ever had the misfortune of knowing, but the people here do not take kindly to traitors, and would have torn you apart." I could feel the inside of my palm sweating and I was desperately hoping that Dad was not reading my emotions at that moment in time. He did not seem particularly enraged, however, and he gestured to Chaz. "Take Merissa to the barracks and get her kitted up. Tell her about our grading system. I want her graduated in three months. She can start her official training, immediately."

A vein in Chaz's neck visibly throbbed at that, and his nostrils flared. But he remained composed and replied in a level voice. "I'd recommend against this Sir. She is an unknown and that will make people nervous, especially with the increased activity on the Surface. Not to mention she displays gifts that we have never seen before."

Dad looked at him coldly. "I turned my back on my daughter once, I will not do it again, do you hear me? Now do as I say or I'll make you live out your worst nightmares for the rest of your life. "

My father snapped his fingers. "To ensure that Merissa gets the best training she can get, I'll assign you to be her tutor permanently. Expect her to be among the best of them, you understand?" Chaz nodded stiffly and turned heel. Dad chuckled. "You'd best follow him, Merissa. He's a little miffed at the moment and is none too pleased to be taken down a notch or two because of you."

Lovely.

I hurried after the stalking dark man, with Elle perched on my shoulders. He was halfway across the athletics field by the time I caught up with him, and I was breathing a little more heavily than I would have liked. He looked at me from the corner of his eyes appraising me. "You're out of breath." He didn't have to say anymore. I could hear the disdain in his voice.

I felt my hackles rise. "Well I was just in a mental fight with a group of lunatics not an hour ago, and used my gift to do things that are apparently impossible! So I'm sorry if I'm a little out of breath!" Elle mirrored my irritation, baring her fangs at Chaz.

He looked at me again, a little taken back by my outburst and Elle's hissing, and said a little stiffly, "I apologise. I didn't mean to be so harsh, but maybe, if your gift takes that much out of you then you should be more sparing with it. Zack and Ray are the next oldest after you and have only started to show the first signs of their own gift in the last couple of years."

"We have only had your father for guidance for how to use the gift, and he wasn't sure how his developed and it was decades ago. It's been a lot of hit and miss. But it does seem to rely on mental strength, and that is a finite resource so guard it well. But we have no idea how it works really."

He whirled around suddenly to face me fiercely and I was caught up in his emotional storm. "Most of these kids have no one to turn to outside of here and I would do anything to protect them. If you compromise their safety I will end you. The boss' daughter or not. Do you hear me?"

I was actually afraid and I had to swallow past a lump before I could say, "I've been alone with my mother for a long time and I have no intention of endangering the rest of my family." I felt my own temper rising in response to his. "But if you make a habit of threatening me, I will end you myself." I pushed past him and walked quickly ahead, fuming. Elle had her tail sticking straight up to show her own contempt for Chaz.

After a few moments, I heard soft footsteps following me and I could see him walking beside me. After a brief silence, I could hear his low voice. "I am sorry for that. I am very protective of these kids. I've helped raise most of them."

I looked at him in surprise. "You hardly look older than me! Are you thirty or something?"

Chaz chuckled, "No, I'm twenty-six. But I've been here since I was fifteen helping out and most of these kids only got here about six years ago."

I raised my eyebrows. "You're only two years older than me so." Elle was laughing to herself and when I tried to get her to explain she just said, *it's just funny to see you try to flirt with someone you were just spitting venom with a minute ago.*

I was aghast, I was not flirting with him! I was just commenting on his age difference! Not to mention he was a vampire! He was probably waiting for a chance to drain me dry. *Say what you will but you and I both know that you have a weakness for dark eyed men and even I can see his attractiveness, though his face is a little too flat for my tastes.*

Chaz looked at both me and Elle, "Just so you know that is considered rude, to mentally talk to your bond-mate privately while talking to others. I'll forgive you this time though, as you're both getting used to the bond." We arrived at another set of doors leading off of the training grounds and Chaz gestured for me to walk ahead with a sardonic grin. "Ladies first."

To which I replied with my sweetest smile, "Age before beauty."

He glowered and waited for me to walk ahead but I stayed where I was. He rolled his eyes and walked in ahead of me. Ha!

You're flirting again. Shut up. *It's really obvious.* I strove to ignore Elle as she continued to laugh lightly in my mind.

We walked into a smartly dressed room. It was all monochrome, silver and glass, a very distinct masculine feel. I looked around, trying to take in as much detail as possible. With the walls being pale silver, I almost missed the robotic remote controlled spider-cams mounted on the walls but once I saw the first one, I saw half a dozen more. I felt that the scrutiny was a little excessive...

Chaz led me down another corridor, and as we passed through the white hallways, automatic doors slid silently apart as we walked through. He stopped in front of a Bloodsteel door and I almost rolled my eyes. Of course there was another Bloodsteel door. Maybe Bloodsteel is so bloody rare because the Underbellies are hoarding them!

Chaz raised an eyebrow quizzically and I stared back at him blankly. He sighed impatiently. "Come on, Merissa. These doors can only be opened by those of your particular genetic makeup."

I felt my face go red with embarrassment. "Oh. Right. I'll do that then." I pressed my palm against the cool steel and I felt my palm begin to warm the steel and I felt a sharp sting and almost hissed in surprise.

I withdrew my hand sharply and massaged my bleeding hand and looked at Chaz reproachfully but he maintained an innocent expression. The door hissed open and I straightened my spine and stepped through.

And stopped right in my tracks. This room was packed to the hilt with weapons. I could guess some of them, like the ion grenades and some of the plasma-rays and even heavy assault laser-fire weapons that I had seen on TV, and even a few of the small hand-chargers. But most of them I had never even dreamed of, much less seen. I felt my jaw fall open.

Chaz walked past me and lounged easily against a small armoury of deadly looking blades. "Ok pick something to practice with so we can get this started."

I gaped at him. "Why on earth would I even think about touching one of these?"

Chaz's eyes hardened. "For the war against the Surface of course."

Wait, what?

Eskrima

I took a moment to compose myself and felt my voice come out far calmer than it should have been. "What do you mean the war with the Surface? Are you suicidal?!" I could feel the hysteria beginning to bubble to the surface. "You will all be annihilated! They would cover you in bodies! The only reason you've even been left alone is because they only consider you a nuisance, not a threat!" Chaz was regarding me far too calmly and that made my temper overflow. "What about all of those children? The ones you said that you cared for? Are they going to be in this?"

Chaz nodded solemnly. "They are going to be on the frontline."

I deflated. "This is insanity."

My whispers were low and broken. I could feel tears brimming behind my eyelids. I looked at Chaz. "Why would you do this? Why, what do you have to gain?"

I could see the fury reignite in Chaz's eyes and he practically roared at me. "We have everything to gain! Don't insult my intelligence by telling me that the Surface is a fair and equal place. The lucky ones managed to escape to the Underbelly but most of the people are slaves up above, regardless of race. They have to live the lives laid out for them and if they deviate from it, even slightly, they are exterminated or exiled."

I swallowed past my beating heart. I had heard the stories of course, a teacher teaching what he shouldn't, a writer writing what she shouldn't and then disappearing overnight. I had always disregarded them, thinking that they were just urban legends to scare people but looking at Chaz now and the passion in his eyes, it was not possible to deny it any longer.

Another jolt went through me as I considered what he said, he said regardless of race. Does that mean that it wasn't just vampires but also humans? Has the Empire conditioned the Surface society to pit itself against each other so that we could not stand against it? Why would it do that?

Immediately, the answer sprang to my mind and I felt Elle agree with me, Power. It was always power. But why subjugate an entire species for power? Why allow contempt and disgust to flourish?

This time the answer came to me much more gingerly, it was waiting all along for me to ask these questions and now that the moment had come, it was apprehensive, aware of the future consequences.

Because the Empire is only as strong as the people allow it to be. If all of the people believed that the Emperor is unfit for duty, then we could all easily topple him. That is why he wants to keep us distrustful of each other so that we would never rebel.

It had almost worked on me.

I thought about my reaction to Dr Yuyo, an intelligent man who had done nothing wrong to me in the slightest, though he was a little strange. Then of course there was Chaz. Although he and I had our differences and he infuriated me, I could not help admire his strength after seeing that memory of his mother's murder.

And yet my reaction to him had been was an instinctive repulsion. Why was that? I had always thought that I was above social pressure and that I had made my own opinions, but this new perspective humbled me a bit. Maybe I wasn't as unbiased as I'd though, but this realisation was the first step in the right direction.

I suddenly felt tired and Elle glided from my shoulder, settling in a corner. I said to Chaz, "So what will a war accomplish? Even if you're right, and the Surface is repressing its own people and vampires, they out-number you a thousand to one. And that's not even taking into account that all the Surface cities help each other and will come to each others aid one if they're attacked."

Chaz grinned, exposing his fangs. "Trust me little Rissa, we have thought of that. But, since you're still in training I'll not fill you in the finer details."

I was not sure what was more unsettling; the fact that he called me Rissa, or that he honestly believes that he can take over a city of millions with a couple of thousand criminals. Then, with a cold shock of realisation, I thought of what the Underbelly had at its disposal; dragons, black suns, robots and vampires.

They actually might have a chance.

The thought ran through me like a bolt of lightning, both freezing and scorching at the same time. It raised goose bumps all along my arms. The pieces of this puzzle were coming together with alarming speed, and if I had known this information a couple of days ago, I would have fled to the CPF and reported it.

But now I just wanted it to stop escalating. Some things are worth living for and worth keeping the peace for.

He was still watching me, waiting for me to pick up a weapon. I gravitated towards the viro-blades, made up of a combination of steel and a recently discovered metal called Netac, incredibly light but really resilient. It was still too rare to make entire structures from it until more sources are found. Most ores are located in the north of Wolfton, and the tensions between the Dynomamian Empire and the natives are still high keeping supply low. The metal also had the curious ability to sustain colonies of a particular bacterium, commonly called Death's Metal. Microbiologists are wary of this microbe as it is highly toxic to humans.

Makes for a really good weapon though.

I swung the blade and marvelled at how easily it turned in my hand, and I heard Chaz murmur. "Maybe not something that would kill me if I get a slice."

Sighing, I laid down the beautiful weapon and cast a critical eye over the remaining weapons. They were all fantastically crafted and though many of my squad had always ridiculed me for my preference of hand combat, I had always had a soft spot for blade dancing. Heart pumping ferociously, the rush of air scraping down my throat, and my muscles singing in tandem with the dance of my blade; it was exhilarating.

I rarely felt as alive.

I saw two longish daggers on the other side of the room. They were gently curved and perfect for catching longer blades, locking against them and then sliding past the defence of my opponent. I had trained in Eskrima, an ancient Hangeranion martial art that helped me master blade work. When I graduated, my instructor gave me two blades himself, saying that he made them for me. At thirty centimetres long each, they were long blades but were also retractable and made it easy to hide them up my sleeves. I still hadn't got them back yet from Marcus the guard at the entrance of the Underbelly, and I was going to have to do something about that. I had those blades for too long to lose them now.

I went over to the weapon's shelves and ignored the more modern laser-blades, long shafts of metal that ignited lasers from their tips and melted most metal. I picked up two long curved daggers that were similar in size and weight to my own blades. Chaz widened his eyes in surprise. "Ok then, can you use those?"

I grinned. "Of course."

He grunted and strode over to a wall of equally lethal looking blades, choosing a pair of katanas, long thin blades that were prefect for slashing.

I threw up my hands. "That's hardly fair! They must be both be twice as long as mine!"

I could see a wicked sparkle enter his eye. "Hasn't anyone ever told you that all's fair in love and war? Now back outside we have got to make you a soldier of you in a couple of months."

Oh right. The war. His response seemed almost playful, and it infuriated me.

See, he's flirting back. Look what you've gotten yourself into Merissa. I don't know how you've survived this long without someone pointing stuff out to you. I ignored Elle's observations and her grumbling eventually stopped.

We soon found ourselves in a small enclosed mesh arena, and Elle was standing guard outside of it. The overhead lights were as strong as the sun and I was beginning to sweat. Chaz was standing in front of me with wooden versions of the katanas in his hands, and I had the wooden versions of my daggers in mine. I was wearing just a worn black vest and tracksuit bottoms. His snowy skin contrasted starkly with his own clothes, while his lavender eyes sparkled with supressed mischievousness.

Apparently they don't like to cut their students on the first day. But every other day was fair game. According to the vampire anyway.

I flexed my muscles and sighed with contentment as my strength began to return to me. I bit my lip, unsure. "Not that I'm complaining but why are we practising martial arts? If I'm to be fighting Surface soldiers, would it not make more sense to train me with shockers?"

Chaz shook his head. "Nope, this isn't really a training exercise for armed combat; martial arts have always allowed one to hone their connection with their own bodies. This is especially useful to gifted humans as you all need to understand what's happening in your bodies to use your gift most effectively."

I smiled and said "What about gifted vampires?" Chaz growled and said nothing.

Be careful Merissa, Chaz has still not fully recovered from the death of his mother. I know that you mean well but you of all people should know that a person does not easily get over the death of a parent. Elle was right. I was mortified at how callous I sounded.

Chaz shifted his stance. "I know you're able to take me on if you don't hold back, but you can't rely on your gifts alone. We also need to push you to your limits physically to see what you got."

Without further ado, he began slashing at me. It was the same as before, but this time I decided to experiment a little, instead of reacting to his attacks I decided to act a little. I danced to the side and noticed that he was ever so slightly off balance. I used my momentum to slip in behind him. He saw his mistake and quickly snapped his blades behind him to protect his back. My wooden daggers raked across his katanas, jarring my arm. He pressed his advantage used his superior weight and height to force me into the corner.

I was trapped.

His blades were too slow to hit me, but too fast for me to get through his defences. I knew I would lose the stamina race and had to do something, quick. So I threw my dagger at him and he yelped in surprise and stepped back. I reached for his exposed wrists and felt my gift reach into him, immobilising him. I held him for a few seconds before releasing him.

He sucked in a huge breath. "I thought I told you not to use your gift?"

I shook my head. "No. You said not to rely totally on my gifts and I didn't. I only used it as a last resort."

Chaz looked at me in surprise. "You thought that the situation was that bad already?"

I frowned. "Yes. It was obvious that we were at a stalemate and that it would come down to who could keep going the longest. Since I thought that you would probably beat me, I decided to use my gift."

Chaz shook his head. "It was by no means that bad, if you had been creative enough you would have seen half a dozen opportunities. Why didn't you just jump over me? Why not go between my legs? Even when you had me temporarily stunned you could have just finished me with your daggers."

I opened my mouth to object but he interjected. "If you want to get revenge for your mother you need to fight smarter. Your enemies are strong and there are a lot of them."

I blinked. How had he known about my mother?

He faced me again and before I could ask him about my mother, he continued. "I want you to fight me again but this time no gift. You're powerful but even you can't use your gift to take down the world."

I nodded warily and approached him again. Our blades clashed as we fought to dominate the other. We fought for a few hours and by the time we were nearing the end, I could feel my muscles screaming at me to stop.

When we did finally stop, Chaz stood there sweating as he looked me over. "You've improved a good bit, after a couple of weeks you'll be at the top if you improve as much as you did today, every day. Now come on, I need to bring you to your room where you can clean up and recover."

He straightened up and groaned as his back cracked, I followed suit and felt a little relief as my spine straightened itself out. Elle waited for us outside of the arena and I saw that she was excited to go home. We walked out of the small arena that we'd practised in, and Elle flew alongside us lazily.

We strolled back to my rooms and I could already feel my limbs protesting from the rigorous workout. I had always been fit, but I have never fought someone as skilled with a weapon as Chaz, and his reflexes were really good. I've also never fought a trained vampire but the sheer lethality of his blows during training confirmed my suspicions that the children of the night were a fearsome people.

I noticed that, too, agreed Elle, *he may not have developed his gift but his physical prowess more than makes up for it…as I'm sure you've noticed.* I swear I could've hit her and her laughter did not do much to temper my mood.

Chaz was grinning, bearing his fangs fully and the light of the black sun burning high in the sky of the Underbelly sparkled darkly across his fangs.

I narrowed my eyes at him. "What are you smirking at?"

Chaz just laughed. "It's just funny to see so many emotions fly across your face. Elle's said something to annoy you, hasn't she?"

I shrugged and Chaz grinned again but this time it was subtler, and his fangs were not exposed. This did something funny to my stomach and it squeezed a little too tightly.

Before he could say anything else, we were standing outside of my room. I saw that it was number seventy-three, and Chaz motioned for me to go on through. "The servants do all of our laundry while we are training so everything should be fresh. Grab a quick shower if you want. I'm going to run to my room and get cleaned up myself, I'll be back in twenty minutes or so to get you."

I frowned. "Servants? Why don't you all clean up after yourselves? Are you too good for that?"

Chaz raised one dark eyebrow. "Hardly. We all have different roles in our campaign of the annexing of the Surface. For some it's training night and day to act as soldiers, and for others it's to run domestic chores so that order is maintained."

I was still not satisfied. "I don't buy that, it just seems like to me that this has the potential to lead to classes and corruption in Underbelly society. Why would the Underbelly be any better than the Surface?"

Uncertainty then clouded across Chaz's face, but it was Elle who answered me. *Remember Merissa, remember what your father said? The currency is based on reciprocal altruism. So long as that you don't take what others do for you for granted, harmony will be maintained and respect given. Is it perfect? No. Will it last? Only time will tell.*

Chaz must have realised that Elle and I were talking because he remained silent during our exchange, dark lavender eyes taking in every detail of my micro expressions. He must have seen my understanding because his normally inexpressive face relaxed and the minute lines that were lining his forehead smoothened out.

Chaz sighed in relief and said "Ok, I'll collect you in about twenty minutes."

I frowned again. "Why are you collecting me?"

Chaz looked at me as if I had two heads. "Do you want food or not? Everyone eats in the communal area in the market downtown."

I felt rising panic at the thought of meeting more people of the Underbelly. Chaz's eyes hardened ever so slightly. "Will that be a problem?"

I shook my head and he relaxed and then grinned like a sweaty child. "Ok! I'll see you in a few minutes!"

Oh would you just kiss him already. It's getting nauseating listening to this all of the time.

There and then I knew that if Elle ever had an interest in someone, I knew that I would mortify her to the extreme. Elle's dry voice commented, I'll hold you to that.

The Marketplace

I closed the door and slid down against the solid support of it, my aching legs thanking me for the respite. I knew that I did not have much time. Chaz's reaction to my initial hesitation reminded me that I was still not totally trusted and had to be on guard.

Elle padded over to the giant cushion one of the servants must have laid out for her, and she stretched contently and clawed at the edges of the cushion, ripping up the soft fabric. I rolled my eyes at her antics.

I stifled a moan as I rose back up to wander further into my room. I saw the bathroom immediately off to my right and so I hastily stumbled in. I was in a rush in the morning with Yelena and Elle so I hadn't really paid any attention to the details of the bathroom. It turned out to be nothing more than a plain bathroom, just the bare essentials. I was almost disappointed that there weren't any plundered treasures crowding the sinks or extravagant paintings hanging artfully from the wall. Though, I supposed it would be a bad idea to have paintings around where there would be a lot of condensation.

I saw the small shower tucked into the corner and hobbled over on my aching feet. I peered in and saw that the essentials were already laid out for me, and I turned on the water. There was even a towel ready, and I couldn't help but feel slightly touched. After three years of being totally reliant on myself, it was a strange but welcome experience to be cared for. I hadn't experienced that since my mother's death.

I stepped into the now steaming shower and moaned in pleasure as the warm water cascaded over my bruised body and acted as a balm to my aching muscles.

I could get used to this.

We don't have that much time Merissa, and frankly, I am starving. I could eat a whole cow. Elle's voice cut across my daydreaming and I gasped with shock at the intrusion.

I mentally expressed my outrage, Elle! I'm in the shower! Can you please give me some privacy!?

Elle's reply was both confused and chagrined. *Sorry Merissa. I hadn't realised that this would be a private moment… I walk around naked all of the time and I forgot how humans are about such things. Again, I'm sorry.*

I grumbled but accepted her apology. I quickly grabbed one of the nondescript shampoos that lined the rim of the shower. It was surprisingly silky and when I washed it from my hair I could already feel that it had given my hair much needed revitalisation. My thick dark hair was getting long, reaching down half way my back when it was completely straight, I couldn't even remember the last time I had got it cut. I might be due…

I was startled by an abrupt banging on the door and I nearly fell over.

As my heart calmed down a bit, I switched off the shower and stepped out of the warm cubicle. I quickly towelled myself dry, looked at my hair, and resigned myself to the fact that I would have to go down to dinner with wet hair.

"Just give me a minute!" I hollered in the direction of the door. I could feel Chaz's impatience leaking through. There were some tracksuits that were laid down on the bed that I quickly grabbed and threw on. Elle was pacing by the door, impatience rolling off of her, as well.

Breathless, I opened the door and I saw Chaz there dressed in a dark pair of jeans and a shirt, looking every bit the dark and brooding vampire. He raised an eyebrow at my ensemble, but said nothing.

I almost blushed. Probably not a good idea with a hungry vampire greeting me for dinner. *For the love and honour of all that is holy Merissa, can we please GO! I am starving!*

He tapped his foot and pressed his tongue against his inner cheek, clearly thinking along the same lines as Elle. I grabbed my fleece that I had left hanging on the door and stepped out to join him.

He sighed impatiently. "I am starving and you're about as quick as a starfish running after its prey."

I looked at him baffled and he elaborated. "There is a species of starfish in the great barrier reef that actually eats other starfishes. If you just look at it for a minute, it looks like it doesn't move. But if you leave a holo-recorder there for a couple of hours, you can actually see them moving if you speed up the camera."

I see. Looks like he's more than just a moody vampire, he is what I believe you would call a nerd, Merissa.

He shrugged self-consciously. "I used to watch a lot of nature documentaries when I was younger and a lot of it stuck with me." He cleared his throat and began walking on. With his long legs, even I had trouble keeping up with him and I had to push my protesting legs to stay level with him. Elle was being lazy, perched on my shoulder. *Since you insist on all of these ridiculous rituals before eating I am forced to take drastic measures to conserve my strength.* Drama Queen, I thought. *Whatever.*

By the time we reached the stone steps of the Academy leading down to the Underbelly, I felt like spiky spiders were dancing up and down my legs and I came to a stop at the bottom step. Elle saw what I was about to do and hopped off of my shoulders, grumbling about me taking too long to get to dinner. I sat down and began kneading my legs to rub some of the pins and needles away.

Chaz was looking at me with a torn expression. I laughed. "Go and get some food, I know where the market is from here!"

He almost looked guilty but he turned heel and began power walking towards the enticing aroma of the various curries that laced the air.

Even I understand the sacred relationship between man and food. Well vampire and food, I was a little confused about what nouns to use. *It means that you're starting to see Chaz as a person as opposed to what you were raised to believe on the Surface. But seriously, can you hurry up? I really need to eat.*

I sat there for a few more minutes and when the drive for food began to overcome the uncomfortable sensation of the pins and needles, I flexed my legs one last time and swung upright in one motion to avoid the chance of falling. I began to walk towards the succulent scents teasing me in the air and Elle padded alongside me.

It was strange to see the Underbelly so quiet at this time. Every other time I had walked through here there had been hundreds of people, but now, there was hardly a soul to be seen. Apart from a young couple that were embracing outside of an open door.

I meant to walk past without paying attention, not wanting to violate what was clearly a tender moment, but the young man had turned around and he was still smiling with post kiss bliss when he saw me.

Zack's face dropped instantly and went deathly pale. I felt confusion well around inside of me, and knew something was amiss. He looked like he had just seen his worst nightmare come to life in front of him, and that it was promising to be there for the rest of his life.

Then I saw who he'd been embracing. A young man stepped back from me but into a pool of light that was spilling from a beaming black sun above him.

Oh.

Zack looked back at his lover with a crazed expression and his lover nodded and sprinted back into the house. Zack looked at me with both terror and fury in his face. "You will never speak of what you saw again, do you hear me?"

Elle hissed at him but then a large golden dragon came out of the side alley by the house and rumbled threateningly. Elle fell silent, but I could hear the two of them communicating with whistles and images in their minds. My focus was on Zack.

Zack's rage and fear was beginning to wear on me and I held my hands up. "Chill Zack. It's not a big deal. To be honest, I was just surprised."

Zack looked at me in surprise. "You're not disgusted?"

I laughed and I saw Zack's eyes harden, I raised my palms up again, placating. "Sorry, it's just that this sort of thing was never an issue back on the Surface. Even my roommate Rena is a lesbian. So it really is not a big deal."

I walked over to Zack and he stiffened. "I mean it Zack, you're my brother, I'm not going to let something as silly as the gender of your lover be a source of contention between us."

Zack looked at me oddly, and then to my horror and embarrassment, I could see tears falling from his eyes. He grabbed me in a fierce hug and I could feel his wracking sobs rubble through me. The golden dragon has stopped growling and was bowing respectfully to Elle. I heard his voice as he turned his attention to me. *Well met Merissa. My name is Feron. I am Zack's bond-mate.* I nodded in reply and Zack stepped back, smiling embarrassedly. "Sorry about that."

Before I could reply I heard a door opening and a soft lilting voice asked, "Is everything ok?"

I looked over Zack's shoulder and saw that it was his boyfriend. I smiled. "Everything is just fine."

The Feast

My stomach was grumbling and Zack stepped back even further, a little embarrassed and I grinned ruefully. "I haven't eaten all day so I'm starved."

Zack nodded and looked for a moment at his boyfriend. Feron rumbled and Zack swallowed. "Erm… Merissa… I'd like for you to meet Christopher," he said, his voice halting with uncustomary hitches.

Christopher stepped forward with a beaming white smile. "It's lovely to meet you Merissa." I was immediately taken in by his warm personality. His chocolate coloured eyes with long eyelashes went a long way to make him very approachable. Christopher continued to talk. "Zack had of course told me of you." I felt a slight hesitation and I couldn't help but laugh.

"Oh. It's ok. I know that Zack is not my biggest fan." Christopher blushed and I could see his bashfulness wash across his caramel coloured face.

Zack coughed. "I'm not going to lie Merissa, I did consider you a major pain in my ass, but I gotta admit you're actually pretty cool for a stuck up Surface girl."

I guess some things just don't change.

Zack looked at Christopher and I could see them communicating silently. I wonder…Was there something more going on than just lovers talking in their own special way? Elle shared my curiosity but it was tempered with wariness.

I felt my mind draw myself towards Christopher, and Elle did something interesting, her mind almost melding with mine, and I felt her adding strength to my mental ability. I could sense that she was wary and she didn't know why but her astuteness was becoming more apparent by the hour, and lending me to feel a little wary myself.

Christopher was just about to say something to me but faltered when he saw the look on my face. Before he had a chance to react I placed my hands on his exposed arm and I felt him try to jerk it back, but I kept my grip firm. I felt my grip well up and project itself into Christopher, I ran along the nerve highways and quickly found myself in his mind.

It was strange. When I had mind-linked with Chaz, I had to forge the connection myself to his mind to talk to him but I could not do that in Christopher's mind and it set me on edge.

Hello? I was echoing my message into the expanses of his mind. For a moment there was no reply. Then, in my mind's eye, I could see Christopher forming.

He seemed curious, but also wary, this was obviously a new experience, but not outside of his comfort zone. Clearly he knew what Zack could do.

Yes? The answer that echoed across the fields of his mind to me was laced with hostility. I felt myself grow even more wary in response and Elle was coiled tightly in my mind, ready to unleash her wrath should Christopher try to harm me.

Merissa? A new voice joined us in Christopher's mind. What was going on? Then I could see Zack materialise in front of us. Zack is an illusionist. He shouldn't be able to bridge minds like this, should he? I felt Elle's own confusion, too. As far as I am aware they can't. If Zack's not doing it, then…it must be the human Christopher.

I turned to Christopher with my fists clenched. "Care to explain this?" I send a probing thought to him and I rifled through his memories, while his mental defences were strong enough to stop me from seeing specific memories. I could get a general impression and I saw something horrible.

It was Christopher, but also not Christopher, he was standing in front of a masked man, with an electronic voice. The Christopher that I could see was a much harder version of the Christopher that I had just met. His brown eyes were hard like stone, and his warm smile was nowhere to be seen. The masked man spoke, "You will join the team of agents in the Underbelly. When the time comes, you'll know what to do."

I whipped back to Zack. "I can't believe that Dad doesn't know about Christopher and his gifts!" Our voices had a strange echo quality to them.

Zack held up his hands. "Hey calm down here-"

I felt my rage boil over. "You do not tell me to calm down! We have moles in the Underbelly, and don't you think that Christopher might be a tad bit suspicious? A gifted man that was not trained by the Academy?"

Zack frowned. "What? Don't be stupid!"

I could see he was getting upset. The air about him was beginning to flicker with shadows, his gift warping reality about him. I forced myself to take a deep, calming breath, readying myself to be completely frank with him. "I know that it's hard to hear this Zack, but you've got to look at the facts. You're high up in the gifted hierarchy and would know things that the Surface could use to usurp our efforts." Then I needed to drop the bombshell. "Zack, I can see his emotions and from here I can tell that he's been lying to you the whole time."

Christopher was silent, awaiting our verdict as Zack and I spat at each other like opposing suns. Zack's eyes hardened. "Are you calling me a fool Merissa?"

I felt myself soften in response. "No, Zack. I'm saying that your love for Christopher has made you blind."

I then heard Feron's voice emanating from Zack; *You know that this is a possibility Zack. I have wanted you to be happy but now that you finally are confronted by the truth, dispel this illusion you have placed on yourself. Seek the truth amongst the lies.*

Zack's eyes were vast pools of hurt and I could almost see his torn soul as he turned to Christopher. "Is this true?" Christopher said nothing for a moment but that hesitation said everything that Zack needed to know.

Black shadows with burning embers flickering inside of them sprung out from Zack and swarmed around Christopher, I could hear Christopher screaming as the shadows slashed and burned him and wrapped him up like a bloated cocoon.

I looked at Zack, both feeling a need to intervene, and to let events happen. "You need to keep him alive. Father will want to interrogate him."

When Zack turned to me I could see that his eyes were totally black and that shadows were continuously leaking from his eyes. His voice was deep, and sounded demonic. "I will make him hurt for eternity, Dad will not be able to punish him more than me." I stepped towards Zack, but he sent a wave of shadows at me unexpectedly and bowled me over.

Well then.

Elle merged her mind with mine and I felt her bolstering my strength. Feron began humming and the dragonsong and seemed to calm Zack for a moment. He seemed to sway for a second, but then the shadows swelled and flooded from his eyes and he screamed as the shadows were shorn from his body, imprisoning Feron in a black, inky cloud.

I scrambled to my feet and tensed my legs in preparation to sprint to Zack. As I was just about to propel myself towards him, he sent another wave at me but this time I was ready. I felt my own gift roar in response, and shadows laced with gold sprung from me and swatted aside Zack's shadows. Elle was darting back and forth as she dodged the residual splashes from Zack as he launched shadow after shadow.

He grunted and turned his full attention to me, and I could see in my periphery that Christopher was released from his cocoon. He was oozing blood from the multiple shallow lacerations all across his body.

Zack screamed, and an enormous wave of shadows curled up around him, raising him up on a shadowy pillar. He looked down at me with a deranged expression.

He was quite possibly insane.

With another demented scream, he began hurling bolts of shadows at me like he was some demonic God. I responded by forming a shadowed dome around myself, and tried to withstand the barrage.

Christopher began screaming again and begged something to Zack. Slowly Zack swung around on his shadowy pedestal and glared down at Christopher, "That's because this is Merissa's dream, and only she can end it."

Christopher looked at Zack in dismay, "What do you mean? She's an illusionist like you, otherwise she wouldn't be able to manipulate the dream the way you do!"

Zack shook his head gleefully. "No Merissa is different from all of us. Even with your web of lies, you never learned about our most powerful weapon. We are going to pulverise the Surface, and it's because of Merissa."

He actually threw back his head and laughed, he might be my little brother but he was definitely weird.

It was time to end this.

I let my shadowy barrier vanish, and sat down, and trying to tune out the ex-lovers spitting across at each other. I settled inside of my own mind and I could perceive a stream of energy flowing from my mind. Elle was there also, floating in my mind, as she guided me towards the source. I curiously followed and I could see it rushing towards Zack and Christopher.

Hmm I wonder…

I imagined a pair of scissors, and used them to sever the rope of energy connecting Zack to my mind. He suddenly popped out of existence. I laughed, and swiftly did the same for Christopher, and he too, vanished from my mind.

I was alone. I could feel myself waking up, and found myself back in the streets of the Underbelly. Christopher was curled up on the cobblestones, bleeding lightly from the cuts and slashes that decorated his body.

Zack was standing above him, breathing heavily. There was a deranged look in his eyes and I braced myself for more violence but he turned to me, his derangement turning to panicked pleading. "What are we going to do Merissa?"

I was taken aback by the naked terror in his voice, and I was rendered mute. Zack was beginning to sound hysterical as word after word rolled off of his tongue. "What are we going to do? How am I going to tell Dad? What am I going do?!"

I strode over to him and slapped him across his face. The rising floods of panic receded, and fury took over. "What was that for?!" Feron growled angrily and made to step towards me but a hiss from Elle made him hesitate.

I grabbed both sides of his face and made him focus on me. "We can sort this out. Trust me. You need to go get Dad. Right now."

I saw that a question was forming on his tongue but I cut him short. "Do it. Now. I'll keep an eye on Christopher."

Zack nodded and I could sense his emotions calming down. "Ok, I'll go get Dad."

I nodded and let him go, and he began to backpedal away from us, towards the marketplace. I turned back to examine Christopher, but not before I saw Zack jump on Ferron's back and fly towards the marketplace.

I turned my attention back to the broken traitor, who was still curled up on the ground, though he was no longer spasming. I hunched down beside him and I could hear his rasping breath, I began to wonder if what Zack had done to him might kill him. Elle sniffed at Christopher, *I think he will be alright but shadow illusion is notoriously unpredictable.*

Just then, she turned her blue snout towards me and I saw that there were new marks on her face, bolts of black lightning under each eye. The overall effect was quite frightening, and Elle picked up on my unease. She dove into my mind and saw what I saw, *Oh wow. That's a new one. It's…different. I like it.* Her sense of satisfaction was growing stronger as she recovered from the shock.

"I love him you know."

I started, distracted from my internal conversations and I peered down at the prone figure. "By accident or on purpose?"

The bleeding man coughed great wracking coughs before answering meekly. "Does anyone ever really fall in love on purpose?"

I mulled that over in my mind before saying and I felt Elle pay particularly close attention to what I was going to say. "I suppose not, but you've got to admit that what you've done is more than a bit damning and it might make it difficult for certain people to believe you. Like me, for instance."

He was silent for a moment, "I know, but it doesn't change the truth. I do love him, I was never supposed to, obviously. In fact, I never felt anything like this for a man before, but somewhere along the way of pretending to be in love, it stopped being an act, and started being real."

I processed that for a moment. "I take it that you're a spy for the Surface?"

I already knew the answer but it would be easier if Christopher confirmed it. Christopher coughed again and I felt torn. Should I heal him or not? Christopher's coughing subsided and he murmured. "I was raised by the State. I am an orphan and never knew my parents. Truth be told, I never really cared. But when I was found to be gifted, I was drafted into the CPF and trained."

He uncurled himself a bit, and I could see his slashed face gazing up at me. "I was sent here to be one of the State agents in place to aid in the cracking of the Underbelly. There are dozens of us of course, so finding me will hardly do much for you."

I bit my lip and decided to do it. I placed my hands on him and felt my gift running though him and his nervous system and I could myself accelerating his healing.

He sat up and looked at me with a wary expression. "Why did you do that?"

I grinned. "You'll see." At that moment I heard footsteps pounding against the stone paths and I could see Dad rounding the corner, with Frans, Zack and Feron.

Dad rushed over and landed a solid punch on Christopher and he went out cold instantly. Dad stared down furiously at Christopher, and I could see that murder was on his mind. He spoke then, his voice dripping with anger. "I should execute him now, like the rat that he is."

Frans was equally furious but her rage was more focused and she nudged Elle, seeking to reassure herself that her sister was unharmed.

For the first time in a long time I didn't know what to say but then Zack replied. "No, Dad. He deserves a fair trial."

Dad turned on him, his eyes blazing with rage. "Zachery! This man is a spy and who knows how many of our people he had ratted out? He has their blood on his hands!"

Zack shuffled his feet, clearly uncomfortable with confronting Dad. "Maybe. But he means a lot to me, and it would be only just for us to give him a trial anyway. Otherwise, we're no better than the Surface."

Dad continued to glare but a thought must have suddenly struck him like a thundering truck on a motorway. "What do you mean he means a lot to you?" His tone was suddenly cautious and emotionless. Frans was paying attention now and I saw her send questioning probes to Feron, who refused to answer. That of course, resulted in a low growl from Frans.

Zack went deathly white, similar to when I saw him first with Christopher, he opened his mouth but no sound came out. Dad's face went stone still, I suddenly had a flash of him turning his rage on Zack.

I tuned into Zack's emotions to see what it was that Dad would see. The fear and shame pulsing from Zack was unmistakable, but the source was unclear. I instantly knew what conclusion Dad would draw from peering at Zack's emotions. He would think that Zack was also a traitor.

"Care to explain yourself Zachery?" My Dad's voice was deceptively calm. It reminded me of a snake getting ready to strike, preparing to claim the life of a rat. The stillness before the explosion of speed that would end in the ultimate climax of a life being snuffed out.

Zack looked like a deer caught in headlights. His fear was total and paralysing.

I knew I had no choice.

"It's because Zack loved Christopher."

My father took a step back, his aggression leaving him, deflating him. He turned to look at me. "What?" His face was cloudy, a mixture of sadness, uncertainty and relief.

I shrugged my shoulders. "It happens to the best of us, the heart wants what the heart wants." Then I fixed him with a glare of my own. "Although, maybe if you had a more open relationship with your kids, he wouldn't have felt the need to sneak around and this whole fiasco might have been averted."

Dad took in a huge breath and exhaled noisily. "Maybe, maybe not. No one can predict what might or might not have happened if we did something different, not even you Merissa." He turned back to Zack. "Having said that though, Merissa is right Zack. I am sorry for making you feel like you had to sneak around me." He held open his arms and Zack went to him, crying softly.

I watched the two of them embracing and I felt a bittersweet song start to sing in my own mind. I was delighted that Zack and Dad were getting closer, but I could not help but think of all the missed opportunities I had growing up.

I turned to walk away, but Dad called me back. "Where do you think you're going Merissa?"

I turned back, confused. "I'm hungry so I'm going to grab some food." Dad barked a laugh. "Oh you've already missed dinner because of this drama. Don't worry I'll send some to your room for you."

I smiled my thanks and started to head back to my room but Dad called me back again, exasperation in his voice. "Will you please take up my hint? Get over here for a family hug!"

I tried to protest but both Dad and Zack ran over laughing and grabbed me in a bear hug, for all of my protesting, I couldn't help smiling as I got the hug I'd waited years for.

Sometime later, after Christopher had been taken away by the guards to be locked away until his trial, I was finally heading back with Ella to my room. I saw a familiar character leaning up against the doorway of a sweet shop. I rolled my eyes when Chaz fell in step with me.

He was silent for a moment before casually commenting. "That was some serious guts to talk to the Underworlder of the Underbelly like that."

I stumbled slightly with surprise. "Were you spying on us?! I would say that would be gutsier than anything I could have said to my father!"

Chaz grinned that small smile again and I felt my stomach do that little flip again. "Maybe so but it's part of my job. When Zack came into dinner all flustered and whispered to your father and he immediately stood up and marched off with him, half a dozen of us tailed them to make sure that there was no trouble. It's pretty logical really."

Maybe so but it was a royal pain in my ass. *Talk about invasion of privacy*, commented Elle.

My teeth were grinding together. "That was a private family moment. Did you not think that would be a little intrusive? Besides, with both Dad and Zack together it would practically take an army to take them down."

Chaz shrugged. "You're probably right, we left once we saw that there was no threat. I figured that you'd probably come back this way, so I decided to wait for you here."

I felt strangely flattered but it was cut quickly when Elle sniped. *See! I told you so! You like him.* I swear Elle was worse than a preteen who thought they understood what love was.

I strove to ignore her and replied to Chaz. "As sweet as that is, why were you waiting for me? I know how to get back. I won't get lost."

Chaz looked lost for words for a moment. "I suppose I wanted to keep you company and make sure that you were all right, especially since you never got to experience Mama's cooking."

Elle was practically crowing with victory and her giddiness was leaking over the bond into me and I struggled to retain my composure.

I raised an eyebrow, "Who's Mama?"

Chaz's eyes glazed over, "Only the best cook in the world and she's in charge of cooking dinner for the market feast. I think I might even give my life for that woman."

I laughed, "That's the way to your heart is it? Through your stomach?"

You're not fooling me. Shut up Elle. *Never.*

Chaz and I continued our banter and I realised I was actually enjoying myself for the first time in a while. Before I knew I knew it I was standing outside of my room in the Academy.

I turned and felt his hand clasp around mine, I felt a surge of energy jolt up my arm and I looked up at him with shocked eyes. "What are you doing?"

Chaz was still grinning. "I know I was hard on you today but for what it's worth, you did well today and I think you'll make a fine Underworlder of the Underbelly." I rolled me eyes at him in reply and he continued. "We start at six in the morning so get as much sleep as you can!" He turned around and walked back towards the amphitheatre exit, towards the canteen, I presumed.

Merissa. Shut up. *You felt a zing.* Shut up. *There's no coming back from this.* I swear to god Elle. *You're going to have pretty babies.* I went to swipe at her but she saw my intention and neatly jumped off of my shoulder and grinned at me with her teeth bared.

I couldn't help but laugh at the smiling dragon, it looked as daft as a lizard beaming. Elle chirped and I heard *it's been a long day Merissa; can you open the door. I'm tired.* I nodded. I was tired and I was looking forward to resting my head.

I turned and entered my room. It was a plain room with nothing too fancy in it, it had a comfortable grey single bed nestled by the wall, a large white wardrobe in front of it and the best part was actually the floor. It was carpet, I kicked off my shoes and socks and moaned in pleasure when the soft carpet caressed my sore toes.

Humming contentedly, I continued to explore, to see if anything had changed. I found the bathroom which had a modest supply of everything that I would need, shampoo, conditioner, razor blades, tissue, toothbrush and toothpaste. I eyed the shower and shrugged. My tired muscles were still bothering me, and I would sleep better if I was warm. Besides, I did not really get a chance to enjoy my last shower. So I stripped quickly and stepped into the steaming shower. Oh, it was heavenly bliss. The heat quickly soothed my aching muscles and I felt myself relax fully for the first time all day.

Soon, I was washed and I felt a million times better. I ambled out of the bathroom, enjoying the feeling of the plush carpet snaking through my silky soft toes. Elle was tearing into a rump of steak from the butcher, and I saw a plate of steaming food set on the small dining table beside the bed. I sat and wolfed it down immediately, the sweet sauces of the curries complementing the rice and succulent chicken. It was divine.

Once I finished eating, I was unsure what to do with the plate, so I left it where it was. I didn't think there weren't any rats around here.

I scampered over to the inviting bed, but I knew I was just far too excited to be going to sleep. I slid between the crisp covers and sighed happily, I stretched out and felt my hair splay out around my head, enjoying the smell of strawberries wafting from my hair. I could feel myself getting drowsy; it had been a seriously long day. Elle scampered up on the bed and curled up beside me, settling into the duvet.

I only thought of one thing as I began to drift off; what kind of nickname was Rissa?

Like A Rat

I woke up suddenly and sat upright far too quickly, and then sank back to the pillow in pain. I groaned, kneading my temples as I tried to work out where this sudden and vicious headache had come from. I swung my feet out of bed, slowly this time. I sighed in momentary satisfaction as my feet touched the luxuriously soft carpet, but the headache drove me to the bathroom and I stumbled over to the tap and let the water flood from it and guzzled it greedily.

Once I was satisfied, I rolled my shoulders to work out the tension of my shoulders. I stretched my hands upright and groaned with pleasure when I felt the cracks reverberate through my spine. I looked into the mirror that reflected my tired face and I saw the source of my headache. There was a pulse rapidly beating on the temple of my head. With a trembling finger, I gingerly pressed against the quickly pulsing point. It sent its signal to my ear and I heard a voice say, "Meet us now."

My sleepy heart began to race in my chest like a sprinter after a race. Dammit. I quickly got dressed in clothes that were left out for me, a tracksuit set in a grey colour. I took one look in the mirror and decided that at the first chance I was going clothes shopping in the market square. This outfit was simply atrocious.

I took a deep breath; I was trying to distract myself from the terrifying task ahead. I closed my eyes and thought of my beautiful mother and felt some of my nerves fade and be replaced with steely determination. I went to stride out of the door without a backwards glance but Elle was waking up, *Merissa? What's going on?*

I cursed and I felt Elle rustle rapidly through my mind and I fruitlessly attempted to block her but it was too late, she had seen it.

Merissa! What are you doing?! If you had asked me a couple of days ago and I would have known the answer without hesitation but now things were more complicated. Elle was getting frustrated. *We're going to war Merissa! You can't afford to be indecisive. We are bound, what you do affects me and the same likewise. Please think of that.*

I was shocked by that, in the short time that I have known Ella I know that she is not prone to begging and that was what she was doing.

I don't want your pity Merissa. I want you to grow up. You're going to become a very important woman someday. You're too gifted not to be, and with all of that power comes responsibility. You need to be mindful of your actions.

Elle's words resounded in my head and I felt it beginning to spin and another headache was forming and I saw shadows beginning to flicker in the background. Elle began to hum her dragonsong and it cut through the mental anguish washing through my mind. It began to settle me down and I felt like it was something solid for me to hold on to in the hurricane in my head.

After a few moments the shadows subsided and I rubbed Elle's snout in silent appreciation. Elle hummed again and I felt the last of the confusion vanish. *Do what you must Merissa. I know that you will do the right thing.*

I bit my lip, suddenly unsure what it was that I was going to do. Then, I thought of something and Elle broke out in her dragon smile. *Yes, why not be a spy but for us? Be a double agent!*

I nodded and grabbed my hoodie, pulling it on, and slipped out of the room without any more fuss. I could hear Elle in my head, a silent observer, nestling on her cushion as she rested her body to focus her mind in my own.

The amphitheatre was deserted and would have been pitch black if not for the faint lights that ringed it. I ignored my instinct to stay near the light and headed straight across the athletic field, trusting that my night vision would kick in before long. I reached the exit of the amphitheatre with no major mishaps. A deep sigh of relief escaped my lungs. So far, so good.

I reached the giant door with that was the entrance to the academy with relative ease. I could feel my heart beat begin to calm down and my breathing got a little easier, too. I slipped out into the market district of the Underbelly and glanced around to see if anyone had noticed me. Apart from a few small groups of merry people, the streets were deserted. With my hood pulled up around my ears, I crept through the streets.

The previously bustling marketplace was eerily quiet and it was unnerving to think of the throngs of people that were here earlier had all gone. The energy of those people almost seemed to linger on, as if they had marked their territory, and I was trespassing.

I pressed up against a tall, leaning building, that judging from the smell of it was full of chocolate and my stomach rumbled enviously. I could see the thick steel door that I had come through the day before. I knew that I would have to sprint from where I was now to the door.

I eyed the open space between nervously. I swallowed and thought of my Mom to calm myself down. An image of Dad also popped into my mind unbidden and I was surprised at the soothing effect it had on me. I took a deep breath and ran.

My legs and arms were pumping furiously and I was streaming oxygen from the dry air straight to my lungs. My feet were flying and I knew that if I could see myself in a mirror that I would actually be spending more time in the air than on the ground and yes, it felt good.

I was suddenly at the door and in one fluid motion I unbolted it from the inside and slipped through. I raced through the thirty-meter door, wincing as the creaks and groans reverberated through me.

I was breathing heavily and each breath was filled with the scent of strawberries and I almost laughed with euphoria. I was out. It was almost too easy. My euphoria was suddenly shredded when I thought of the spidocams in the barracks. What were the chances that there were more dotted around the Underbelly and I did not see them? Elle's voice echoed through my mind, *Your father will understand. Trust me.*

I cursed my idiocy regardless. Well, there was nothing I could do about it now, might as well continue on. I passed through the strawberry scented tunnels and came to the old dilapidated lift. God I hated that thing. I hoped that I wouldn't have to input any codes to activate it, but once I pressed the button to call for the lift, it began to beep and whirr and I could hear its shuddering descent. All I had to do now was wait.

As soon as it opened, I stepped into the lift and pressed the button to get me up to the Surface. The stains in the lift were still there and my curiosity got the better of me and I traced my finger over it. It peeled away and with a start I realised that it was not blood, but paint. Curious.

The lift opened with its customary shudder and groans, and I stepped out. I saw that the weasel-like man who was here the first time I came through with Jeffery, had been replaced with a younger man, but this time I did not lose my step. He frowned and started to walk towards me, I knew that I had little to no time so I acted swiftly and without thinking. I had seen with Chaz and the other night people that they can move extremely fast, and I had no room for error.

I exploded towards him and made sure that my fingers connected with his forehead, I felt my gift slam into him and I knew that it had worked. I felt my voice go deep and melodious. "You did not see me here and when someone asks if you have seen me you will tell them that I was not here."

The young man nodded absently. I breathed a sigh of relief. Then I heard a ding and I felt my blood turn to ice, someone was coming out of the lift.

I whirled and jumped through a door. Then I heard the groaning and shaking and I remembered that this was a brothel, and that this was a room for business. I turned around, horrified at the possibility of seeing a couple together but then I frowned. The room was empty but there were groans coming from all over the room, then I saw the old fashioned speakers. The groans were coming from them and occasionally a squeaking noise would emanate from it also. It was bizarre. Was it all just a façade?

The person who stepped from the lift was talking to the young man outside, but I was so distracted by the speakers that I missed what was said. The young man had obviously not told the person about me because the person was exiting the room to outside, to the city. I knew that I would have to wait a while before it was safe for me to leave the room.

Several minutes later I decided that it must be safe and left, the young man did not even look up from his desk as I walked past him. I stepped out into the fresh air, although it had only been a couple of days since I went into the Underbelly, I found the warm embracing air to be seriously reinvigorating.

Not much had changed. The same pungent smells lingered in the air, the saggy ramshackle warehouses leaned to the sides, and there were still gang members howling into the night.

I breathed in a deep warm breath, comforting after the cold air of the Underbelly. I looked about me, seeking the two agents that were supposed to meet me here. I quickly walked between the warehouses and then I saw them leaning against a worn doorway, dressed in leather and spikes. The silver spikes caught the flickering light above it and was glinting like a signal for me to follow, for all I know that may actually have been their intention.

I approached the two Agents, who, despite their edgy attire, worn to blend in this environment, were among the blandest featured people I had ever met. They had to be, to remain inconspicuous in their line of work. They both looked at me warily and I lowered my hoodie in response and they both visibly relaxed, waiting for me to speak. I cleared my throat. "My father is still alive."

They both looked displeased to hear this, not that I could blame them, considering that they paid me to kill him. The taller and darker of the two, Agent Slattery, spoke. "Why is he still alive?" I looked at him calmly. "He's too well protected to kill easily and even if I did kill him, the Underbelly would be able to continue without him. He's not the source of their power. He just happens to rule it at the moment."

They were silent for a moment and I felt them weighing up what to say next, I had expected for them to ask who was the source of power but the other man, a younger red headed man, Agent Higgins spoke. "Does he have any other unnaturals with him, apart from you?"

I bristled inside at the insult and I think the agents noticed and I replied stiffly. "No, not that I'm aware of. I've been put into his private quarters and I'm surprised that I was able to slip away unnoticed. I don't think I could do it again so I won't be able to help you storm it from the inside."

Elle was faint in my mind but she was roaring to make sure I would hear her, *Merissa! Remember that they have other agents in the Underbelly, don't trip yourself with your own words.* Damn it.

The agents were still mulling it over. Agent Slattery then spoke. "Stay in this cess pit for a little while longer and if an opportunity arises, take him out. Other than that, gather as much information as is possible and find a way for it to reach us."

I nodded. "Of course. Am I to work independently or do I have support in the Underbelly?"

Without so much as a goodbye, the two agents turned heel and walked away with their leather squeaking and their spikes glistening. *They don't trust you Merissa, what do you do that makes people both simultaneously love you and hate you at the same time?*

I expelled a lungful of air in relief and laughed at Elle, now all I needed to do is find a way to...

A sudden humming noise brought me out of my musings and I froze when I heard a familiar voice say. "Nice evening Merissa, for meeting old friends, isn't it? Turn around real slow and I won't kill you, just yet."

I turned around as slow as possible, to give my brain enough time to process just exactly what happened. I could see a tall man facing me and looking at me with lethal intent in his lavender coloured eyes, fixing his shock blaster on me. I could feel my heart race and my lungs seemed to have trouble dragging in oxygen.

It was Chaz.

I looked at his face for a moment, but it was not his face that I was interested in, it was the shocker that he was pointing at me. The steel nozzle was glowing faintly as it began to heat up with the building energy of the shock blaster. He looked at me with steely resolve. "I told you that I would do anything to protect those kids."

Then he fired.

Warehouse

I reacted without thinking and threw myself to the side. A sharp pain snapped along my arm and I felt a shocking inability to raise it. I picked myself up and began scrambling through the dark, imposing warehouses. I could hear my ragged breathing as panic rose up in my throat. My thoughts raced, breeding chaos in my head. I heard a roaring sound in my head and I wasn't sure if it was my own screaming, or Elle's.

I leaned against the rusted iron door of a dilapidated warehouse, the smell of rot emanating from the sagging wooden beams inside. A sudden thought formed in my mind; I needed to confront Chaz. I had to explain. He would understand me.

Wouldn't he?

I slumped down against the door, pressing my cold fingers onto the bleeding, burning wound. The pain was rapidly fading. I wasn't sure if it was because I was growing used to it, or if I was going into shock. My thoughts were muddled again. What was I supposed to do?

I stared at a rusted flake of iron hanging on a spider's web for the longest time, unable to order my mind. I watched the dew forming on the silky strands, oddly fascinated. With a herculean effort, the iron flake seemed to tear itself from its webby prison and fall towards freedom.

Elle's voice was growing louder but it was still incomprehensible. My brain clicked and suddenly I was very aware of the moment as all of my senses kicked in with a whoosh. The pain kicked back in with a vengeance and I growled in annoyance. I remembered what one of my instructors said about shock wounds, if there was no medical assistance nearby then you had to make a tourniquet, and fast. I looked down at my right arm and I could see that it was still bleeding, so I used my left arm to rip off my sleeve of my right arm. I knew that I had to place the fabric above the wound or the blood would continue to pour out of my arm.

I was just about to tie the tourniquet above my wound when I hesitated, if I did this it could save my life but I might also lose my arm. While for most people it would be a no brainier, I was not like most people and I still had other options. I had never used my gift like this but I had to try.

I closed my eyes and tuned into the chaos of my body and everywhere I could see the damage of the searing burning, wound. I ignored the pandemonium of my body and search along the nerve highways of my body to get to the source of the terror.

I could almost see the crackling energy lodged in some muscle in my arm, contracting the muscle uncontrollably. This was actually not too bad. It meant that the discharge was not too far from the surface of my skin. I quickly set to work.

I gritted my teeth, and I felt my gift travel along my arm, almost like a curious monkey. It reached the wild electricity and I tightened my grip on it and it dove into the muscles around it. The muscle was suddenly under my control, consciously. I was the muscle and my viewpoint of the world was shifted. I could feel a jagged hole inside of me, the discharged electricity of the gun wreaking havoc my arm and I could feel the fibres that made me up being torn. I gasped at the sensations. I began to use the various fibres of my muscles like ropes to wrap around the hole, and with concerted effort I began to pull at it.

The pain was rippling through me, but I ignored it. A sudden thought illuminated my brain; since pain was a nerve cell's way of telling the brain about certain damages to the structure it's attached to then maybe I can dial it down! I sent a small portion of my gift to the nerves surrounding me, the severity of the pain went down like a dimmer switch.

I returned all of my attention to the task at hand; I began to wrap my muscle fibres around the shrapnel from the capsule used by the shockray to penetrate the body and pulled again. With a sudden scream I felt the shards of metal fly out of my muscle and out the way it came in.

I snapped back into my brain and I was panting. My skin was pale and clammy and with shaking fingers I picked up the bloody capsule that had just fallen from my arm. I felt my mouth widen, I had never in my wildest dreams thought I could do that. Even as I looked at it in wonder, I felt my gift begin to speed up my healing process, directing my body's resources towards my wound. I could feel my torn flesh being knitted together and within moments the energy blast wound was completely sealed over. I stared at it in wonder. Then I felt a slump in my energy and I was suddenly ravenous. I guessed that my energy reserves were depleted after doing that.

It was worth it.

Merissa! Where are you? Elle's panicked thoughts sliced through my brief sense of relief and I opened my eyes to take in my own surroundings. I sensed Elle and realised that this was the first time that she had ever left the Underbelly, and she did it without a thought.

I was touched by the selflessness of her.

I heard footsteps approaching me. he must have heard my scream. I grunted, I may have healed myself and lost some strength, but I was still stronger than any ordinary human, and still strong enough to take on a vampire. I took a deep breath and got ready to tackle him.

I crept around to the corner of the wall that he was about to come around. I felt my heartbeat begin to speed up in preparation, my breathing deepened and quickened. I felt a trickle of sweat slide down from my forehead to my jaw.

He rounded the corner.

I gave him no time to react. I mercilessly grabbed his wrist, the hand that held his shocker. He grunted in surprise and fell back. Before he fell I grabbed his shocker. He scrambled up and cursed when he saw that he no longer had the shocker but froze when he saw that I had it. He backed away a step.

"Don't move." My voice did not sound like my own, it was the coldest I had ever heard it, and I knew that Chaz could hear death speak through me.

Chaz's dark eyes paled and I saw him hesitate. "Let's be reasonable, Merissa."

I cocked my eyebrow. "Why should I? You shot me without giving me time to explain myself."

Chaz rolled his shoulders in exasperation. "What was I supposed to do?! You were talking to Surface Agents!"

I gave him a pointed stare. "I was and because of that you shot me?"

Chaz looked at me oddly. "Did you fall on your head after I shot you?"

He looked at me closer and frowned. "I shot you in the arm, where's the injury?" He sniffed like a hound and his eyes narrowed in confusion. "There's no fresh blood coming from your wound either, what happened?" I ignored him and he looked at me bemusedly for a moment before continuing. "You know that we are going to war soon so that would be sensitive information that could be given to the Surface."

I laughed. "You shot me for that?! Oh that is rich. You do realise that you would be slaughtered if you went against the Surface? Even if on the ever so slight chance that you manage to hold this city, you do realise that the other Empire cities would retaliate and suffocate you in bodies?"

Chaz remained silent and that could only mean one of two things: either he was stupid enough to believe they could do it, or that the Underbelly had a secret weapon that they were so confident in that they reckoned that they could take on a city and its siblings and win. Either way I had to stick around to stop the bloodbath.

Chaz looked at me quizzically. "So what are you going to do with me?"

I dropped the shock blaster, not caring if it went off. "You're going to pick up that shock blaster and put it back on your belt. Then we are going back to my father."

Chaz looked even more confused. "You're going back to the Underbelly?"

I nodded resolutely. "Yes. I am going back to talk some sense into my old man because if no one does, everyone in the Underbelly will die. I've lost one family member already and I don't intend to lose the rest of them."

Grounded

Without giving Chaz a backwards glance, I walked towards the gate of the Underbelly. I heard him scrambling after me and I saw him coming up in my peripheral vision. He was silent for a moment before he spoke. "What do you expect your father to do when you say what you say?"

I threw my hands up in exasperation. "Honestly, I'm not sure, and I'm just hoping that if I tell him how hopelessly outclassed he is that he will listen to reason."

Chaz snorted. "You do realise who you'll be talking to?"

I growled in response.

Elle joined us and nuzzled her snout against my cheek and it tickled when her scales rubbed against my skin. She fixed Chaz with a glare, hissed with her own impressive fangs on display and Chaz looked both defiant and chagrined.

We were silent as we walked through the doors into the reception with the fake prostitution rooms. The young guy was still there, he acknowledged Chaz but ignored me, obviously my gift was still working on him. The curious thing was that he also seemed to be ignoring Elle also. Elle shrugged. *I'm not sure, I think since we're bonded any minds that you influence are also influenced by me but I'm not certain.*

Chaz gave him a confused look. "Why are you ignoring her Miles?"

I coughed before Miles could speak. "He can't see me Chaz, I made him forget me."

Chaz turned to me incredulous. "You made him forget you?! How is that even possible?"

Miles looked at him in total bewilderment. "What are you talking about man? Who are you talking to?" A sudden realisation came over him. "Ah, is the stress of the job getting to you dude, or are you due a drink? When's the last time you took a holiday or had a glass of juice?"

Juice is the common term night people use to talk about blood in front of humans.

He continued babbling on in the background but Chaz was ignoring him, skewering me with his hostile dark lavender eyes. "How on earth am I supposed to trust you if you wield this kind of power?"

I opened my mouth to reply but Miles finally caught on that something strange was happening to him. "Whoa man, you mean one of those mutants did this to me? Since when could they go invisible?!"

Chaz looked at him darkly. "She's not invisible, she went out for a little walk but didn't want you to stop her so she did something to you."

Miles' face lost what colour was on his face and his face looked deathly pale and his voice was hardly above a whisper. "Whoa, am I like dying man?"

Chaz raised an eyebrow at me and I threw my hands up again. "For crying out loud, it's only a temporary block! It should be gone by the time he wakes up in the morning! But since you're both so worried I'll get rid of it now. Jeesh."

I walked around the desk that Miles was sitting behind. Miles was following Chaz's eyes trailing me and his eyes widened when he saw Chaz looking at me beside him. "Whoa dude. Is she, like, beside me now?"

Chaz nodded and Miles began to back away but I gripped his arm firmly and then he began to really freak out. "Dude! I can't move my arm! Why the fuck can't I move my arm?!" I jerked him over to me and he began to scream.

I heard a bang and I saw that a door had burst open, and the small weasel man who was here when I came through the first time with Jeffery and commented on my hair. He looked at Chaz and began roaring. "What is the meaning of this?! Girl, why are you bothering Miles?" Miles tried to turn around but I pressed my fingers to his forehead and drained back all of the residues of my gift.

Miles looked at me, the girl who had just materialised in front of him. "Oh, you're that chick who came here the other day to meet the Bossman." He frowned as Elle also popped into existence on my shoulder. "Whoa! And you've gotten a dragon too? Wicked!"

I smiled and turned to walk back towards the lift. The lift opened with its customary groan but dutifully stayed open until Chaz and I were inside. The last thing I saw before the doors closed was Miles looking at me with a hint of fear in his eyes and the weasel man looking at me with narrowed, suspicious eyes.

We were silent as the lift continued its laborious journey back to the Underbelly, but I could sense the agitation coming from Chaz. I was tempted to tackle the thoughts in his mind now, but I had a feeling that he was a man that liked to have his thoughts ordered before he hashed them out. So I gave him time.

Even Elle was subdued and I could tell that she was not looking forward to confronting Frans. Almost as nervous as I was about dealing with my Dad.

The lift stopped and opened. Dad was waiting there. Frans, sitting down beside him, had her electric blue eyes fixed on us. I suddenly felt like a little girl who had just been caught sneaking out. He sent me a level gaze. "Come." That single word spoke legions. Oh crap. Elle echoed my sentiments.

Chaz made to follow us but Dad looked at him sharply, and he backed off. I straightened my spine and followed my father at a leisurely pace. I had to remind myself that I was not a little girl, and the he no longer had power over me. He ignored my defiance and let me set the pace.

He led me to his office without a single word. I knew that I was in serious trouble. He went to his desk and faced his fire with his back to me and Frans coiled beside the desk and stared unblinkingly at both of us.

He was silent for a moment before he spoke. "Was I wrong to trust my own flesh and blood Merissa? Has the Surface twisted you so much that you do not recognise your own family and where your loyalties should lie?"

I felt my own anger stir at his words. "What are you on about old man? Maybe if you actually let go of your obsessive hatred of the Surface then you would see that you're going to get everyone here killed if you go to war with the Surface! Including my little brothers and sisters!"

He rounded on me with fury blazing in his eyes. "What would you know of obsessive hatred? You were so intent on killing me that you were going to do it in the middle of my own home. Did you think you would make it out alive if you did? Instead of letting you try that I decided to try to change your mind and show you the truth and, by extension, save your life and give you the closure you seek. You repay me by meeting up with the very agents that were part of the group that hounded your mother and I across the globe!"

I started and then snorted. "Don't be delusional old man, they part of the CPF. They are a bloody civilian force! They wouldn't have the firepower to go after you." Then I faltered, I did see them in Chaz's memory…

My father threw his desk to the side and it slammed against the wall, leaving a sizable dent in the wall, Elle tensed and Frans matched her. I flinched momentarily, but reprimanded myself. I was stronger than him, but Frans was stronger than Elle. With that sobering thought I bit my tongue.

He was roaring now with spittle flying from his lips. "You have no idea do you?! They were sent to get you but through some freak of coincidence you weren't there when they were looking for you. They tortured your mother to find you but she wouldn't crack and so they killed her! Hoping that when you heard that you would come looking for them with revenge in mind."

I was stunned silent. I remembered that night vividly. I had returned from a camping trip with my college friends and I saw the congealed blood all over the sitting room. I had thought that my father had finally lost control in a fight with my mother and killed her so I went looking for help, to get revenge. I ended up outside the CPF offices after a couple of years of searching. They told me about my father, who was a security risk to every good law abiding citizen of the Dynomamian Empire and that my mother was one of the many victims my father had claimed.

My father was obviously reading my emotions. "Yes, you stupid child, you played right into their hands. They were hitting two birds with one stone. They got to train up an assassin with the best chance of killing me, but who would be highly unlikely to survive the ordeal."

I felt the shock fade a little as I muddled through my questions. "But why would they want to kill you if you if you're not a security risk? Why would they want me dead? Is it just because I'm your daughter?"

Dad shook his head. "I am a security risk. Not to the ordinary people of the Dynomamian Empire, but to their rulers, specifically Emperor Sidario. That's why they want me, and those like me, dead. We're too hard to control. We were made to help control the Empire but instead, they made a people who can stand up to them. It's why they hunted all of those children's parents. And many others besides."

I frowned. "I thought that there were only eight of you?"

Dad grunted. "In the first batch yes, but they continued the experiments and made about three hundred, total. But when I ran away, I think they began to execute them indiscriminately because they realised that we were not blindly loyal and could think for ourselves."

He pursed his lips thoughtfully, "Truth be told the most efficient way to deal with you now would be to kill you. You know too much and you're a traitor."

I put my hand up at that and said calmly despite my furiously beating heart. "I love the way that everyone assumes that I am a traitor. I'm not. I had intended to kill you and leave. Everything changed once I saw my little brothers and sisters, and I bonded to Elle. I wasn't sent here as a spy, just as an assassin. That means that they are not expecting to uncover any information, but if you're smart, you could use me to feed them false information."

My father laughed at that. "You may not have been trained as a spy but you seem to have the mind of one." He paced back and forth for a few minutes as I steadied my breathing and my racing heart. I could feel Elle's anxiety and she melded her mind with mine and I saw how far she was willing to go for me. She was willing to turn her back on everything that she had ever known if it would mean that I could live. I was humbled by that. Elle replied fiercely. *Of course, we're a team.*

Suddenly Dad snapped towards me his eyes alight with anticipation. "Ok I'll take you up on your offer. But before I make it official I have to know what you told those agents, and leave nothing out."

I thought it over for a moment. "I told them that you were still alive and too well protected but that I had earned your trust already." Dad snorted again at that and I continued, pointedly ignoring that. "They asked if there were any other unnaturals with you and I said that there weren't. They then told me to stay here and take you out when the opportunity came, and to get as much information about the Underbelly as possible. And help them invade it."

Dad eyes widened slightly at that. "Do you know when they plan on doing so?"

I shrugged. "Since they probably intend on killing me, I doubt they'll tell me. They'll just kill me in the invasion if I survive killing you."

Dad was silent for a moment. "I see. This game is going to have to sped up it seems. I had hoped to have a couple of months to prepare, but I think we're going to be lucky to have a couple of weeks. Now go get some rest. You have a hard couple of weeks ahead of you, we're going to punish you by making you the best soldier the world has ever seen."

I rolled my eyes. "Alright. I'll get going but one last thing;even if you manage to somehow overwhelm Limondium, you do realise that the other Empire cities are going to invade and possibly the Hangerion warships might also blockade us, not to mention the Wolfton air force would raze us to the ground?"

Dad had a mischievous look in his eyes. "I guess it's a good thing the other Underbellies will be rising with us. We're going to give them hell!"

I saw what he did there. What did he do? I don't get it.

It means, Elle, that because the Surface has always associated the Underbelly and the Underworld with death and hell; we are going to make it a reality for the Empire in our fight for freedom.

I yelped when Dad came over and grabbed me in a big bear hug and Frans nudged me gently with her dark snout. I felt a little safer in my Dad's arms.

The Ball

There was a festive atmosphere hanging over the Underbelly as it was Yelena's thirteenth birthday. In honour of her birthday, Dad was throwing her a public party. It was also my first official introduction to the Underbelly.

Since my agreement with Dad, I had been training for weeks with both Chaz and the team of scientist I had met in the tree lab. Elle had grown quickly in the last week or so, and was now the size of a large dog. A fact that she constantly bemoaned, *I've been a comfortable size for the last fifteen years, why am I suddenly growing? I feel fat.*

I had, of course, made the appropriate reassurances but being my bond-mate she could tell that I did not think that it was a bad thing she was finally growing. In fact, I was rather relieved. I had doubts that she would ever grow, and that she would never leave my shoulder alone as she hitched ride after ride. Over the last day or so she had come to accept her changing physique.

I was in my room, getting ready for the ball. This was a welcome break from the intense workouts and experiments. Dr Oslo and Dr Terry had run experiment after experiment on me, and I could tell that something was bothering them. I could sense the bewilderment leaking off of them every time they looked at the results of the most recent experiments we conducted together.

Oh well, I guess we're both freaks. Elle commented as she observed my thoughts, referring to the puzzled looks that Dr Oslo and Dr Terry had shown when they saw the newly emerging colours that appeared on Elle's scales.

Dr Yuyo and Dr Andrew were constantly asking me to participate in their pilot studies with their suits, armor designed to enhance Spliced Soldier's gifts. So far, the suits of armor were not as successful as they had hoped they would be. The last suit had almost burned me as it short circuited, and Elle nearly bit the leg off of one of the butlers who was aiding the scientists to show her displeasure.

Yelena was supposed to have a group of stylists help her get ready, but she had insisted that I be the one to help her get ready. I had smiled when she had put her demands to Dad, she had not one flash of fear as she put her requests forward.

It was such a different childhood from the one that I had been given. After my moment of bitterness, I realised that I was happy that my little sister was so confident.

So when Dad had looked at me with a crooked smile and asked if I would be so inclined as to help Yelena get ready for her big night, of course, I couldn't refuse.

So that was where I found myself; standing behind Yelena as she sat in front of the small mirror in my room. She was chatting away excitedly about the night that she said that people have been planning for the last month for her. She was so excited that her enthusiasm seeped into to me, and I couldn't help but feel excited myself. Even Elle, who did not seem to particularly delighted about mingling with strangers, was infected with Yelena's excitement.

She was perched on my stool, like an excited starling, and she was asking a constant stream of questions. "What do you think people will think of us when we walk in? What dress are you going to wear? How are we going to do our hair? I'm so excited!"

I smiled in delight at her childishly joyous expression. "Hold still Yelena! If you keep jumping around like a songbird, your make-up will be ruined!"

Yelena went deathly still before a huge exclamation shrieked out of her. "That's what I want! I want you to do me up like a starling! Oh can you do that for me Merissa? I would love that so much!"

I laughed and Elle ruffled with laughter, and I replied. "I can hardly deny the birthday girl, can I now? Ok now hold still, this will require all of my attention if we're going to pull this off…"

I slipped into a trance and the rest of the physical world melted away until there was nothing in front of me but the inks, paints and powders with their brushes. I knew what I had in mind when she asked that I turn her into a starling.

I set to work and layered delicate powders onto her face to make it shine like the moon was personally lighting it. As soon as I was satisfied with the subtle silver glow on her face I set to work on her eyes, I stroked them with a dark pencil to make them black, bold and beautiful.

Next was her eye shadow, it had to be violet and as I looked at the choice set before me I picked out some likely candidates. Once I was satisfied with the best choice I applied it to her eyelid, taking care to be gentle.

When I was done Yelena opened her eyes and blushed, her rosy cheeks looking gorgeous with her pale skin. "Oh wow Merissa. It looks beautiful! It's so pretty!"

I stroked her hair. "No, silly. You are beautiful. This is just showing you how others see you." I finished with a smile and Yelena's blush deepened.

"Close your eyes again" I commanded, Yelena complied though with a hint of surprise, to truly make her like a starling she had to have their signature green speckles. So I picked up a sparkling mascara that had the green she wanted and applied it ever so gently.

I stood back to admire my handiwork and I had to admit that it was definitely one of my finer experiments with make-up. She was looking at me shyly with her bold beautiful face, "Well, what do you think?" I smiled and instead of answering her, I turned her around to look at the mirror. She gasped in pleasure, "Oh my god! It looks amazing!"

She turned back to me and went to give me a huge hug but I held her at bay laughing. "Careful Yelena! You don't want to ruin your face just before the big party!" She laughed, too, and went back to admiring her face. As she was examining herself, I quickly reapplied my own makeup. Nothing too fancy; just my cherry red lipstick being my most extravagant part, and I evened out my skin with foundation.

I pursed my lips as I looked at Yelena, or more specifically her hair. On an impulse I walked over and released her hair from its customary plaits. I flicked a brush through her hair as it unravelled with great flowing waves, settling gracefully into ringlets that framed her face and flowed down her back like a blonde river.

I brought my face down to hers as we both peered into the mirror. "There. Now you're ready." Yelena just nodded, spellbound. You are truly beautiful Yelena. Yelena's green dragon Jandre was watching us from beside Elle, his alert moss green taking in everything.

I hooked my arm through Yelena's, and we both rose from our seats. I could feel Yelena wavering slightly in her heels, but I could also sense her natural balance kicking in and she steadied herself.

We walked down the academy steps together arm in arm, fashionably late and escorted by our dragons. I marvelled at how much the Underbelly had changed for the occasion. The cobblestones that we were walking on had a red carpet laid out for us to follow to the party, protecting our shoes and ankles. The cold air of the Underbelly was kept at bay with the aid of the black suns that were blazing on full power tonight.

As Yelena and I travelled with our dragons along the red carpet, we were joined by more late comers, most were unfamiliar but there were a few familiar faces.

Chaz joined us and he looked great in his black and white suit. He looked at Yelena and his lavender eyes widened. "Wow! You look so grown up Yelena! Your eyes look so pretty!"

Yelena's smile was bright enough to power the Underbelly. "Thanks Chaz, Merissa did it for me! She made me look like a starling!"

Chaz's eyes flickered to me for a moment before replying. "You're so lucky to have a big sister like Merissa."

Yelena's grin grew wider. "I know! So, why don't you ask her out already?"

I nearly fell with shock and Chaz spluttered for a moment but he was saved from having to answer as we arrived at the party, a large empty marquee.

See, even your little sister sees it. Elle was amused and I could feel the mirth running off of Yelena and Jandre. I studiously strove to ignore them but they could see the scarlet splotches on my cheeks.

We had just walked into the empty marquee when everyone had appeared out of thin air and yelled "SURPRISE!" Yelena squealed in shock but then was laughing in delight and we were suddenly swarmed by everyone, with Dad at the front of the crowd, his face alight with sheer joy.

I slipped off to the side and sat down as the people began to wish Yelena happy birthday. I expelled a lungful of air in relief when I saw that no one had noticed Elle and I slipping away. Well, almost no one.

As I was sitting down on a stone bench, being kept warm by a black sun radiating down on me, I was joined by a figure. I to find Dr Yuyo sitting beside me, clutching a beaker firmly between his hands.

He was silent for a moment before talking in his unusually musical voice, a voice that seemed to be both filled with sorrow and joy simultaneously. "Well met, Merissa. I hope that you are well on this fine evening."

I raised my eyebrow and replied politely. "I am Dr Yuyo."

The vampire smiled. "Please dear, call me Yuyo. We don't need to wrap ourselves up in unnecessary complications, the world will do that well enough for us!"

Yuyo's facial expression became more animated, the most life I had ever seen in it as he became increasingly excited and he took a deep gulp from his beaker and then exclaimed. "My dear! I am so utterly glad that you are here with us! You have filled us with hope that I have not seen on this dreary planet for centuries."

I started. This had taken a sudden unexpected turn and I treaded cautiously. "Hope? In centuries? I'm afraid I must point out my ignorance and ask you to clarify what you mean."

The vampire chuckled. "I had forgotten that humans on this planet are not as experienced with vampires as they are on Origin or other settled planets."

The more the drunken vampire spoke, the more confused I became and he laughed raucously. "Oh my dear! Pray tell, are you ignorant of your own history?"

I felt like this was a test of some sort, and Elle was melding with my mind again., *This is most intriguing. I was always aware that Dr Yuyo was among the oldest vampires in the world but I have not given it much thought truthfully. Perhaps it would be prudent to find out what we can.*

I answered Yuyo carefully. "History is a very complicated and delicate study; it would be unwise to say that one is an expert in it."

Yuyo laughed again and slapped my back. "Spoken like a true Politian Merissa! You are your father's daughter alright. All right I have a tale to spin and it is a long one so get comfy."

Yuyo then crossed his legs and drained the last of his juice and spoke with a deep sonorous voice that was perfect for storytelling. "Humans did not originate from this planet. You come from a planet very far away from here, a paradise called Origin. The actual name is different in every planet but the meaning is clear, it is the beginning of humanity. It is a planet of islands with warm breezes, flowing emerald tropical forests and brilliant blue oceans and the sands, oh the sands Merissa! The beaches are pristine, white beaches that lusciously caress your feet."

He had fallen silent as he reminisced the past and then shook his head and said, "Once the technology became available, the more adventurous of you began to spread amongst the stars and settled down in new homes.

"However these adventurers were not alone, we accompanied them. We share the same home and we have lived harmoniously for millennia together. Though vampires are stronger and faster than humans, we are dependent on you, we need your blood to remain healthy. Though there were points in our history where vampires tried to subjugate humans, you were too numerous to control. Empires always fall, even vampiric ones.

"So we travelled amongst the stars and founded great civilisations, and created peace and prosperity. I was not one of these original travellers but my father was."

I had to interrupt then. "I'm sorry but how old are you?"

Yuyo shrugged. "I've lost count. Travelling between solar systems takes time. But, if I had to say, I would say in around twenty thousand years old."

Oh. Wow.

Elle shared my shock, and I felt huge implications fringing in on my mind. "Ok, so you've been around a while. How do we stop the Empire?"

Yuyo shrugged again. "The same way that every other Empire falls, when the people have had enough, it will fall, not before then."

"Anyways… on with my story. I was enjoying myself as I satisfied my wanderlust; about four hundred years ago I arrived here with about forty other vampires and a travelling ship full of human explorers. We had heard that a ship had crashed on this planet about a thousand years ago and we were curious to see what survivors may have built in the meantime. We were not let down.

"We arrived to see a thriving human population spread across the three continents. They had unfortunately lost much of their technology and we spent a hundred years bringing them up to our level. Then this harmonious planet was plunged into a savage war, led by the first Emperor Ferro Jecha. In the space of a handful of years the Dynomamian dominated the globe. Most of the leaders across the globe had been executed and all technology that could be used to call for help destroyed. Vampires were hunted to near extinction."

He was silent for a moment. "I had lost my wife in that first purge. I was in mourning for a very long time." He tapped the lid of the empty beaker. "I would have probably ended my life had I not seen the formation of the Underbellies. I saw their potential."

He snorted. "Humans used to be capable of so much, it wasn't just your technology that made you so powerful, but also your ability to harness the energy of the Universe. You were Gods with your magic. But this planet has long since forgotten how to use its magic."

I felt cold all over, like I was remembering an old forgotten secret. I didn't want Yuyo to stop. "With the experimentation of the Spliced Soldiers, it seems to have awakened something in some of you. But the magic is different, it's not as powerful or primal but it's a start."

Yuyo fixed me with an intense gaze with his lavender eyes. "You, in particular, are important. Your magic seems to be less restricted than the others and that must mean something."

Yuyo suddenly cocked his head to one side and seemed to hear something and briskly stood up. "I must go now, there is someone else who wishes to speak with you and I'll not delay him any longer." And with that he slipped back into the merry crowd.

Chaz sidled up beside me and sat down. He was scowling slightly. "What was my old man saying to you?"

There was a slight slur on his words and I could smell the alcohol on him. I laughed, surprised. "Dr Yuyo is your father? That would explain the grouchiness anyway!"

Chaz pretended to scowl for a moment and then grinned his small little smile. "I hope he hasn't been filling your head with his past, he gets very imaginative when he's had a few drinks."

I laughed again. "No of course not! He was just asking me a few things about the suit I was trying for him the other day."

I don't know why but I did not want anyone else apart from Elle to know what Dr Yuyo had just told me. It felt too important and private.

Chaz was silent for a moment before speaking in a low voice. "Yelena looks very beautiful tonight, thank you for doing that for her."

I cast him an askew glance. "No problem."

Before he could say anything else, Dad noticed me and jerked his head, indicating for me to join him. I nodded, and got up and walked towards him. I looked back to see if Chaz was following, but he was nowhere to be seen. I looked around for Elle. *It's ok. I'll rest here for a bit. Those flying exercises that Frans makes me do are torture, and frankly, I need the rest. Just shout out to me if you need me.* I mentally shrugged and prepared myself to greet all of the people that Dad wanted me to be introduced to.

This should be fun. I knew that Dad was going to use me as a political weapon to both intimidate and wow people. The prodigal Surface girl who not only could do more things than the rest of my gifted relatives, but also bonded with the only multi-coloured dragon.

I joined Dad, who was resplendent in his dark suit and red shirt. It contrasted well with his ivory skin, and complimented his dark hair and eyes. He was talking to a young couple who were clearly in awe of him. With a quick look at Dad I could see the tell-tale signs of him working his gift.

A few moments later, the young couple were sent on their way. I raised my eyebrow and my father shrugged his shoulders in mock innocence, "I'm innocent until proven guilty, you know. Now come." He placed his arms around my shoulder and began to steer me towards a small group of people that were standing awkwardly beside the crystal fountains that were spewing wine, judging from the smell.

Several of the young men in the group saw us approach, and even I could sense the apprehension that was burning like wildfire amongst the group. Dad continued to walk towards them, with his winning smile, and they quickly began to dart glances at each other. I could see them taking in their breath collectively.

Dad was still beaming, ignoring their unease, and slapped one of the men on his back. "Rory, how are you? I hope your new baby is not keeping you up too long!"

The young red haired man stuttered for a moment before clearing his throat. "Yes sir, thank you for asking."

Dad began talking to the rest of the group. He was on a first name basis with most of them, but it was clear that everyone was on edge while speaking with him. But, as he continued in his small talk, I noticed small changes. The people began to relax, and some even began to take some of the glasses that were in a ring on the edge of the fountain of wine and began drinking. Soon the group were regaling their tales of the missions they get up to on the Surface. It was then that I was told that this group of people were actually soldiers, a specialised branch called Runners.

One of the young women, Violet, was talking with such enthusiasm that her arms were thrashing about as she told us about that time she was sent to the Surface to organise a prison break, "Oh, You'd never believe it! It was bloody terrifying let me tell you! It was myself and Jamie here that had to break into the prison to bust out a couple of our guys."

She took a swing of her wine and began gesticulating wildly again. "We were backed in a corner and we even had those bloody Spliced Soldiers after us." She nodded to my Dad. "No offense intended, sir." Dad just laughed and Violet continued. "We were back in a corner and dopey Jamie falls and hits something in the wall and lo and behold, there's a secret cellar, filled to the brim with glorious wine!"

She laughed heartily and a few of the young men began slagging Jamie, who was blushing with the attention, but Violet was not finished. "So we got down there ASAP and just in the bloody nick of time." She took another long drink and then gestured to the wine flowing from the fountain. "And now we are drinking the bastards' wine!" Her story's end was met with a massive cheer that followed like a Mexican wave throughout the party.

Dad was still grinning and I could still see the tell- tail signs of him pulling at people's emotional strings. Being a leader must be difficult, constantly boosting those that would otherwise be too meek and keeping the arrogant in check observed Elle and I had to agree with her.

Sometime later, I was walking alongside one of the underground rivers, taking a break from the party. Elle was stretching her wings as she glided through the air casually.

I had thought when I had first come here that the underground springs of the Underbelly would be horrendously smelly. But, before entering the domain of Dad, it is all treated and strawberry essence is even added to the water to give it the characteristic smell of the strawberry Underbelly air.

An otter was swimming sinuously through the clear silver water. The water here is so clean that tiny micro ecosystems with a family of otters and the small schools of fish flitting through the shadows were totally sustainable. The Surface could not even claim that.

All of our parks were diseased and sick. The trees were twisted and their leaves moulted and rotten, the rivers were overrun with algae blooms, killing off all the other wildlife in the rivers. The air was stagnant and malnourished. The birds rarely sing anymore; I only hear them out in the mountains where the cities haven't swarmed.

Our planet is dying.

The thought chilled me to the core but then dawning comprehension stole over me. Our planet is not dying; we are. The planet is just a massive lump of rock; it will endure until the sun has swallowed it up but we are not immortal.

Footsteps startled me out of my reviver and I felt a presence settle beside me.

Chaz leaned in towards me, his breathing was slow and measured. I felt Elle pause up in the air but remained where she was. My breath was shallow and rapid. I was surprised at his directness, but then I could smell his breath and I saw the stain of red wine on his teeth. I couldn't help but chuckling and it arose him from his stupor, "What are you laughing at Rissa? It's rude to laugh at people you know."

That was hardly going to make me stop.

We stood side by side near the railings for a while as the party continued in the background. I was still lost in my thoughts when Chaz spoke again. "You know that I'm glad I found you before we invade the Surface."

I raised my eyebrow but Chaz still had his eyes closed so he didn't see. "And why is that?"

Chaz kept his eyes closed but I could see a smile creeping across his face. "Fishing for compliments again?"

Before I could retort he interrupted me. "I'm glad because I could see what you could do and I can see what you can do now. You'd be one of those Spliced Soldier Captains that we would be praying not to run into."

I looked at him in surprise. "Spliced Soldier Captains?"

Chaz opened his eyes and regarded me seriously. "Yes, Spliced Soldier Captains. They are the Splice Soldiers that are both incredibly intelligent and hugely gifted. Basically supermen without the morals."

I shuddered. "And you think I can take them on?"

Chaz's smile sprung out of nowhere. "That's what we're training you for."

Lovely, they are not only training me to rule the Underbelly, but also to take on an army of supermen.

Lovely.

He hiccupped again. "I'm also glad I found you before I went on my mission."

I felt my heartbeat race a little. "What mission are you going on?"

He giggled like a little girl. "Top secret Rissa. Top secret."

Epiphany

It had been several days since I spoke to Chaz, and I imagined that he was on his secret mission. I tried to put it out of my mind but something kept me on edge.

I was sparring with Zack, with both my mind and my body. Zack feinted to the side, I was stronger than Zack but he was faster. So he had no problem dodging my attacks and slipping in and out of my defences, but my mind was another matter entirely.

As he dashed in and out of my reach, like a dancer, my mind was like an impenetrable steel wall. He couldn't gain access and I could see the sweaty sheen on his face as he tried to avoid my fists and slither into my mind.

After a few moments I could hear this glorious golden sound, almost like liquid silver swirling through the air. I felt my body relax and become more sluggish. With a roar of victory Zack slammed into my mind and scattered my defences.

Suddenly everything was all black and I felt like I was floating in the vast expanse of space, there was no concept of sensation. Suddenly I was catapulted into a world of rich sensations and I was back in the academy and Zack was standing over me with a smug expression. "You lose sis."

I was about to retort with something snappy but my mind suddenly bloomed with a dark image in my head. When Zack or another illusionist fills your head with an image, it's like you are there. But this image was different, it was almost like I was there as an observer.

It was a dark room, but it was sterile. Men dressed in white were pacing around the room, occasionally checking pristine steel instruments dotted around the small room. Powerful lights suddenly flared on and flooded the room with bleaching light. There was a loud bang and the door slammed open and three men stumbled into the room.

The reason for their lack of grace was apparent when it became clear that the man in the centre was struggling against the other two men. I watched with morbid curiosity. It was fascinating to see someone struggling so violently against the will of others, and the audacity of another person to impose their wishes on another.

The prisoner was shoved into the chair and before he could jump back up, the straps on the arms of the chair sprung to life and constricted around him and embraced him like a snake.

The men in white began to converge on him like a group of cold angels. The fear was starting to leak from the man and the cloth that covered his face then was lifted and Chaz's panic was answered with a scream.

Mine.

Merissa! I could feel the naked terror in Elle's voice and I sensed her frantically flapping her wings as she sped towards me from the training sessions that she took part in up in the air with Frans.

Strong arms grappled with me and I lashed out with my gifts and I heard curses. I opened my eyes and I saw that I was back in the academy, Zack and Ray were rubbing red welts smattered across them ruefully and several vampires in red were running to us.

I felt like an animal in a trap. Snatching breath. Terrified. Surging adrenaline. Erratic electricity was crackling through me.

I lost the track of time and by the time I had come back to my senses I had a small crowd collected around me and I heard humming and I saw that Elle was looking at me with concern in her eyes. I saw scared white faces peering at me and several trainers in red were looking at me in worry. One of them, Geraldine, offered a strong hand to help me up. I grasped it gratefully and pulled myself up.

I took in a shaky breath and focused on all of the sensory information coming in from my tongue, I desperately tried to take it all in. The sweat of the people around me, the moist ground beneath me and the constant lingering strawberries on the air. Anything to blot out the image growing in my mind like a poisonous weed.

My heart was racing as the image began to solidify in my mind. Suddenly it reached a point that I couldn't hold it back anymore and the image became a video in my mind and I was catapulted back to that horrible room.

Chaz was already bleeding from shallow slices that decorated his arm like a perverted painting. The men in white were no longer in pure white as the blood soaked through their sleeves as they worked on him.

Chaz was gritting his teeth in concentration as he attempted to resist their torture. A man stepped out of the shadowy corner and casually walked over to Chaz, giving him temporary respite from the blinding light as he blotted out the light.

He bent over and peered into Chaz's eyes. "Well, well, well. What do we have here? We actually caught a vampire. I had thought that the rest of you had long passed to the shadows." Chaz froze and the man straightened up and turned around and I saw his face for the first time. It was a deeply lined face, and appeared cracked, like parched soil. His skin was grey and lacked any other colour save for his eyes, which were the most horrific red colour. A dead, red colour. The colour of congealed blood.

His voice was soft and it reminded me of a snake. "Oh yes. I know all about Alistair's freakish army, dragons, mutants and leeches. No matter. They won't be able to do much against true Dynomian justice." Chaz tried to speak but nothing came out. The forbidding man laughed cruelly. "Save your breath. No one can save you. Not yourself, not Alastair."

He turned suddenly and looked right into my eyes. "No, not even her Chaz."

I opened my eyes and I found myself in a hospital bed. There were several tubes inserted into my arm and I promptly removed them and several machines began beeping. Dr Oslo and Dr Terry flew into the room, their white coats flapping like a startled bird's wings.

Dr Terry went straight to my lightly bleeding arm clucked like a mother hen, while Dr Oslo began tinkering with the machines. Dr Terry bandaged my arms and pressed the back of her hand to my forehead and sighed. "I really never understood why patients insist on removing needles as soon as they are awake, it's silly really!"

Dr Oslo was humming, a sound that reminded me of the dragon's humming. I felt oddly comforted by it, and with a satisfied exclamation the machines went silent and a deep menacing voice cut through the new born silence. "Now can I see to my daughter?" This was punctured by a growl of a dragon.

Unfazed Dr Terry continued to look at a few more things, making sure that my eyelids were a peaky red and that the bruises underneath my eyelids were not too dark. "One moment, Alastair and Elle. All of the Spliced Soldiers have an extremely robust immune system and I've never seen any of you just faint like that. I need to make sure that there's nothing wrong. Ideally we could run a gel scan to get a perfect picture of what is going on but I guess that might be overboard."

Dad lost his patience and burst into the room, followed by Elle. I realised that the two scientists must have been talking to him outside the infirmary before they rushed in when they heard the machines go off. I also saw that Elle had gotten two new rings of white around her eyes.

Dad looked dangerous, but there was also an uncharacteristic flood of vulnerability reeking off of him. Catching my gaze, he spoke gruffly. "What happened Merissa?"

I swallowed past a dry lump in my throat and I spoke, my voice wavering. "I saw Chaz. He's being tortured."

My voice hitched and a strong sob broke through and Dad looked stricken, having never seen me cry. He came over and murmured comfort into my ear. "It's ok Merissa, I'll get my best people on it right away."

There was a pointed silence from the two scientists and gazing over my father's massive shoulders, I saw the two scientists involved in a heated silent argument. Then Dr Oslo exploded angrily at his wife. "We can't just sit on our hands about this Terry! They should know about it."

I had expected to hear some commentary from Elle by now but she was still silent and I sent a questioning probe towards her, she was looking at me intently and I frowned, why wasn't she answering? Then it hit me, our link had been severed!

Blind panic washed through me but I took a deep breath and centred myself and I felt my mind relax and expand and I heard her. *Merissa! I thought something awful had happened.*

I raised my eyebrows and Elle relented, *I thought it was permanent. Thank god you figured it out, I was worried that I was going to be mute again.*

I was confused by that, and Elle explained. *Dragons can't communicate without a bond-mate, so I need you as much as you need me to point out obvious things to you.* She grinned her dragon smile and I rubbed her snout fondly.

Dad was regarding us worriedly, but had calmed down when we did. He went stiff and disengaged from me and looked at both scientists. They looked meek under his glare. "What should we know Terry?"

Dr Terry who was calm while under my father's bluster as she examined me earlier now quailed under his mounting fury.

Dr Oslo jumped in to save his wife. "This is all just speculation, but I think it might be prudent to tell you our theories." Dr Terry looked mutinous but stayed silent on the matter, and so Dr Oslo continued. "As you know, Merissa, we took a few genetic samples from you several months ago and have been comparing it to the other Spliced Soldiers here." I frowned, for some reason I did not like where this was going.

Dr Oslo continued on. "Now, the strange thing about Merissa's DNA is that it's very…unstable."

I felt a growing sense of unease, but my Father's curiosity was aroused and he leaned forward with interest. "What do you mean by unstable Dr Oslo?"

Dr Oslo licked his lips nervously and looked at his wife for support. With a sigh, Dr Terry continued the explanation. "It's actually quite simple in concept. In order for anything to evolve there must be some ability for the DNA to mutate randomly. We see that in Merissa, except that it's much more frequent. The other strange thing is that it's only certain parts of her genome that are unstable, specifically the parts that make her superhuman really."

I threw my hands up in exasperation. "What does all this science mumbo jumbo even mean?" I interjected.

The two scientists looked at each other uneasily and Dr Oslo shrugged. "We're not entirely sure and that was one of the reasons Terry did not want to tell you yet. There's no point in worrying you if there's nothing to worry about. However, with your recent vision w-"

I held my hand up. "Whoa. Hold up. I never said it was a vision."

The two scientists looked at each other again and I barked out. "I really wished you would both stop sending each other silent messages and just tell me already what on earth is going on."

This time it was Dr Terry who spoke. "Well, like Oslo said, we're not sure what your genome is, but one thing that we're pretty certain of is the durability of the Spliced Soldiers. We know you that you're one of the toughest of them, and you don't just faint."

I shuffled uncomfortably. "I was shocked, people sometimes faint when they are shocked."

Dr Terry was shaking her head and she spoke as soon as I was finished, "No, you don't understand. All of your emotional and physical durability is much higher than other people's. That's why we were so concerned initially. Now, we're satisfied that you're ok, however, like my husband said, it does lead us to think that there's something going on."

"FOR THE LOVE AND HONOR OF GOD CAN YOU PLEASE JUST GIVE US A STRAIGHT ANSWER?!" Dad's patience had run out.

Dr Oslo took a deep breath. "Basically, Merissa can act as a chameleon, and her DNA seems to adapt to her environment. We suspect its why Elle constantly adding colours to her scales."

I blinked and Elle perked up at that, turning her head to see as much of her body as she could. "So you think that I can do what exactly?"

The silence stretched on for an age before Dr Oslo finally answered, each word dragged out reluctantly. "We think that there is no limit to your gift."

Lovely, now you're going to get a huge head, commented Elle dryly.

Breaking the Rules- Again

I was in my bed again. I'd been sent back to my room a few hours ago by Dr Oslo and Dr Terry, once they were satisfied that I was not in danger of fainting again. Elle was on constant watch duty and she only left to go to relief herself.

I focused as much as I could on the spider cracks that danced across the ceiling, but no matter how much I tried to focus on each infinitival detail, all I could see were the look of terror that was in Chaz's bloodshot lavender eyes just before my vision faded.

A huge surge of pressure flooded through my chest and I bolted upright as though a lightning bolt struck me.

I have to do this.

He would do the same.

It's decided.

I guess that it's time. I was surprised at Elle's easy acceptance but her reply cut me short. *I will not be able to protect you up there as much as I would like, I doubt it would be wise to attract attention to us by having a rainbow coloured dragon flying around but I will meld my mind with yours.*

"Would we not be too far apart to stay connected?"

I felt wry amusement from Elle. *I've learned a thing or two in the last couple of weeks and I am confident that I can do it. I won't be able to physically protect you but I can lend the strength of my mind.*

I felt like that there was something that she was hiding from me, but no matter how much I tried to chase the reason, I could not reach it. *You're wasting time, Merissa. Chaz does not have that much time.*

I felt my heart clench a little too tight. I got up from the bed in one fluid motion and opened the door and ran smack right into Zack and Ray.

I growled at them and Ray held up his hands in a placating gesture. "Hey take it easy, big sis, we're just checking up on you. Dad said it would be ok to do it now." I could see the concern radiating from Ray and the subtler concern flowing from Zack. I felt my eyes tear up. It had been a long time since someone checked up on me when I was sick.

Before the flood-works could go into full swing, I could see Ray look at me alarmed. "What are you thinking of doing?" With his limited empathy ability, he was able to sense something of my plans.

I hesitated for a second, but before I could speak Zack cut across me. "Isn't it obvious Ray? She's going to rescue Chaz. She's in love with him."

I looked at Zack shocked, expecting to see contempt, but only saw sadness and even a little empathy. Ray looked progressively more and more alarmed as the conversation continued on. "Wait what?" He turned to me. "You're in love with that grumpy old git?"

I fell silent. I couldn't bear dare to say anything out loud, especially after what I've seen. Ray whistled quietly though his teeth. "Well I guess this changes everything."

It was my turn to be confused.

Ray and Zack grinned in unison and Zack spoke. "Well, we're going up to the Surface with you."

Ray shrugged. "We don't let family fall by the wayside in this family." He paused for an afterthought. "Even if he is a grumpy old git."

I laughed, and the two began to leave with me towards the Academy exit. I swished my hair, looked back at them and gave them a full blast of my charm. "He might be a grumpy old git but he's my grumpy old git. Do you hear me? Especially you, Zack."

Zack' face grew red at that and I turned back to the doors of the academy and braced myself. And I heard Elle's exasperated sigh. It took for him to be captured to realise that you love him. Humans!

Secrecy is Subjective

We slipped through the streets of the Underbelly like a trio of ghostly apparitions. The Underbelly was beginning to wind down, and there were many tired and satisfied faces as they came home from the evening's feast.

As we approached the massive blast doors, I prepared myself for whatever I would have to do to get through the huge doors again. But then Ray took a sharp turn to the left, and led us straight into the chocolatier that was nestled in beside the gigantic doors.

I frowned as I stepped in through the door of the mouth-watering smell of chocolate permeated the building. There was something that was very familiar about this building… *It was the sweet shop you stood beside when you broke to the Surface the first time,* Ella reminded me.

Ray and Zack sauntered up to the counter where a wizened old stooped woman was standing guard as she peered at the two powerful young men walking towards her. She showed no alarm however, her mouth actually beamed open in a wide smile, showing her rotten teeth.

Zack swept right up to her and embraced her in a rare form of open affection over the glass counter, displaying their wonderful chocolate treasures. Ray looked back at me with his eyes sparkling. "Merissa this is Old Maud."

Old Maud peered at me with milky eyes, but I had a feeling that like everyone else in the Underbelly, she could see more than she let on. "Hello Merissa, aren't you a pretty girl?"

I smiled awkwardly. I never really knew what to do with elderly people that insisted in treating you like a child, and Old Maud continued. "Are you one of these fine boys' girlfriend?"

Ew, that woman is a little creepy. I felt a little bad for agreeing with Ella but there was something that was off about the woman, something about her made me uneasy and Ella agreed with me, *Keep an eye on her. There's more to her than meets the eye I think.*

Ray laughed. "No, Maud. This is our oldest sister Merissa!"

At that Old Maud snapped her eyes back to me and her gaze suddenly sharpened and the milky whiteness of her eyes vanished, and her crystal blue eyes gazed at me with such intensity that I stepped back. Elle hissed in my mind.

Ray frowned as he read the emotional atmosphere and opened his mouth to speak, but Old Maud spoke over him to me. "Sorry if I startled you dear, you just reminded me of someone I met a long time ago." I frowned, and she answered my unasked question with a new strength in her voice. "She reminds me of you, she would have been your age when I last saw her. When the time comes, you will need my help, when the shadows of your mind become more real than reality, come find me. Find me and I will help to guide you to igniting the flames within."

Who and what is she talking about Merissa? I had no idea.

Her eyes clouded over and I felt her strength vanish. She looked at me confused, and her weak wavering voice warbled as she spoke. "Sorry. I seem to have forgotten my train of thought. Sorry, dear!"

I felt warm tingling, and I could feel my gift wake up and explore the aura of the strange woman but with her strength and clarity gone, its curiosity was gone.

"Who looks like me?" My question seemed innocent enough, but Zack and Ray were shaking their heads at me from behind Old Maud and the old woman was looking and at me, bemused.

The lights from her eyes then dimmed and she closed her eyes and I could hear her slightly snoring. I blinked. I looked at the two guys. "What just happened? Did she just actually fall asleep?"

Ray shrugged his shoulders. "Old Maud has always been strange. Dad even thinks that she might be gifted but too mentally unstable to be of any use to the Underbelly."

I looked at the peacefully slumbering old frail woman, with her agitation gone, her lined face relaxed and she looked years younger. I wonder, if my father would be so quick to dismiss me if I were not so useful to him?

Ray flipped over the counter and knelt down and began pressing buttons. "Oi Merissa. We've got to go and save your grumpy git remember?" That instantly sobered me up and snapped me back to reality.

Time to save Chaz.

I followed Ray and Zack over the counter, I saw the two guys crouching over a trapdoor that was swung ajar. With a grim smile Zack slipped into the dark gaping maw and Ray quickly followed suit.

I took a deep breath to steady myself. With a controlled but explosive exhalation of air I steadied myself and followed suit.

Breaching the Skin

The tunnel was utterly pitch black and I knew instantly that my eyes would be useless. I remembered a training exercise that we did a few weeks back, we fought blindfolded and this was not dissimilar to that.

I closed my blind eyes and listened with my sharp, ears and an automatic image sprung up in my mind of the rough shape and form of everything around me. As my skin began to feel the whispers of the air, I could tell which way was the way out.

In the darkness I could sense two other warm body masses rustling as they got used to the new environment. After a few moments Zack spoke. "We should start moving, can we all get a good grasp of what's around us?" Ray and I grunted in confirmation.

It's a pity that your smell is not as sharp as mine, I feel odd not being able to smell more. After a moment Elle conceded, *Though walking through the sewers I would say that having a weaker sense of smell would be more advantageous.*

In my life before the Underbelly I would have asked why did we not bring torches but ever since I began training I learned that the darkness can be our greatest ally, and with our superior senses we can travel faster without alerting our enemies to our whereabouts. *Good to see that you're learning, I was beginning to think that you were hopeless.* Having a dragon commenting on your every thought was no easy cross to bear.

I'm a delight, I'll have you know.

As one, we began to swiftly run through the tunnels, and soon we had left behind the strawberry scented tunnels and we were trying not to gag on the rotten stench of the rubbish that floated in the foul river flowing by us.

Suddenly, Zack stopped. Ray and I almost collided into him. I glared at Zack but I remembered too late that he could not see my face and he spoke with finality. "We are here."

All feelings of petty annoyance vanished, and they were replaced with writhing snakes that burrowed deep into my bowels. Ray and Zack turned to me and though I could not see their faces, I could read their emotions, and I could detect apprehension laced with anticipation. Then a flash of light momentarily blinded me and I hissed in pain with my brothers.

I looked up when the glare faded and I saw that there was a crack in the ceiling above and light was filtering through haphazardly. We must be near.

"Let's go," I said. It was the first firm order of the night and I knew that there would be more to come. I felt a sense of unease come from Elle and when I sent a questioning probe her way she mentally shrugged, *it's just odd to see you taking charge. For as well as I know you, I never saw the potential your father saw in you as a leader, and for the first time I do now.* I felt both pride and nerves at her observation.

I looked at Zack and through the light that was filtering through the cracks in the ceiling above, I could see that he nodded and shimmied up the ladder and reached the manhole up at the end. With an almighty shove Zack heaved the thick steel manhole aside. Street light flooded through, illuminating our surroundings. I grimaced when I saw how dire the tunnel was; there was indeed a river running beside us, but I think crawling next to us would be more accurate. It was so choked up with sludge and rubbish that the river was more oozing than flowing.

The walls were slick with slime and condensation, and the various flashes of warmth that I had felt on my run here, were confirmed when I saw flashes of scarlet eyes peering back at me.

Rats.

Ew.

Ray suddenly stiffened, and I thought that he had just seen the rats like I did. But then, he leaned forward with the intent of a hunter and he sprang down the tunnel and vanished into the darkness.

There was a scuffle, and I could hear shouts and a chirping and hissing of a dragon. Ray came back into the light and he had two small figures in tow and I felt my heart stop when I saw who he was tugging along.

Zack was up out of the manhole and he hissed down. "What is going on? We're going to get caught by patrols if we're not careful!"

I called softly up to him. "We had two people and a dragon follow us, Yelena, Max and Tyson." There was a moment of silence then it was shattered by vehement swearing.

There was a sharp clang and the light vanished as Zack covered the manhole and joined us. I did not need to be an empath to see that Zack was more than a little annoyed.

I was in no sweet mood either, and I could feel my throat begin to growl as my control slipped. "What is the meaning of this?"

Max hung his head in shame and Tyson was uncharacteristically silent but Yelena held her dainty head high and looked at me right into my eyes. "I saw him too Merissa."

That must be how you saw him Merissa. What do you mean? *Hush, let her explain.*

For some reason my skin began to crawl. "What do you mean?"

She looked at me with eyes that seemed to harden all of a sudden and her voice was low and full of purpose. "I saw Chaz on the Surface and I can still see him." I held my hand up to my mouth in horror.

Yelena's smile was a little sardonic as she looked at her older brother. "Because she knows that her little sister is able to see things that she would rather not let me see."

Ray and Zack still looked bemused and I knew that I would have to explain it. "It means that Yelena is able to see things as they happen. It's how I can do it."

Zack and Ray looked at me in horror and fascination, and Ray was first to ask a question. "Wait. What do you mean by that's how you can do it?"

I shrugged. "The scientists back home seem to think that I'm some sort of chameleon that is able to adapt to everyone's ability. When Yelena had her vision, I absorbed it."

Zack and Ray took a step back and Zack spoke in a croaky voice that trembled with emotion. "You're some kind of leech?!"

I sighed impatiently. "No, I'm not some kind of ability vampire that sucks your gift, you moron. I'm just like a sponge, that's all. To the best of my knowledge no harm is done."

Ray shook himself. "Merissa is right, she's been with us months and no one has gotten weaker. If anything, we've all improved!"

Zack nodded slowly. "Sorry about that sis. I've never been fond of leeches…"

I rolled my eyes at his melodramatic tendencies and turned my attention to Yelena and Max with my hands on my hips. "Since you know what's in store Yelena, you should know why you can't come."

Yelena regarded me calmly. "Normally you would be right but as a chameleon you know that you have to work harder to achieve the same proficiency as us naturals. So tell me, can you see Chaz now?"

I looked at her blankly for a moment and then swore explosively. I knew that she was right. I threw my hands up in frustration. "Fine. But you're not coming with us, you can still be in contact with us through holochips or something."

I turned to Max, "There is absolutely no reason for you to be here, you have got to go home at once."

Max had the same calm, serene look on his youthful face that Yelena had in her eyes. "But you need me to help infiltrate the prison complex. Yelena can see where Chaz is, but I can see the way to it. And everyone who stands in our way can act as our eyes."

I growled and I heard a hesitant cough behind me and Zack spoke hesitantly. "Merissa, that's actually pretty sound logic. If we take them, we actually have a decent chance of sneaking in. Yelena can pinpoint Chaz's location, and Max can tell if there's someone around a corner without us even having to look or listen. I can make people see things that we want to, and Ray can convince anyone to do anything."

I glared at him. "You're almost saying that I'm useless." Ray laughed. "Hardly. If what you said is true about you being a chameleon then you can back any of us up, not to mention that with a simple touch you can down anyone. Pretty handy if we're to fight any Spliced Soldiers."

I looked around at my motley group of misfits, and realised that I would not win. "Fine. But if anyone of you gets killed, I'm never talking to you again."

As Max and Yelena walked over towards the ladder Zack stopped them and looked at Max and Tyson. "We need to shield him Max, make him invisible otherwise we'll stick out dangerously."

Tyson looked at Max and for a few moments they were silent and then Max nodded. Zack frowned for a second, and then a haze settled over Tyson. Zack nodded and said. "That should do it, unless you know he's there you can't see him but he can still be felt and heard so be careful ok Ty?" Tyson chirped in confirmation.

Tyson was cocking his head oddly at me, like a puppy that was puzzled about something, and Max frowned. "Merissa, Ty says that you smell like Ellesera and it's fresh." His frown deepened. "He also said that it's fresh but that doesn't make sense, because he said that he didn't smell her until he smelled you but she's nowhere to be seen."

I was about to answer but Elle hissed D*on't tell them that I melded with you. Please.*

I was taken aback by her insistence, but I respected her privacy so I shrugged. "I'm not sure to be honest. Maybe her smell is just lingering on me?"

Max grinned but Tyson was looking at me unwaveringly and I was sure that I did not fool him. I hope that you know what you're doing Elle, *I'll explain when we get back.*

Memories

I recognised the neighbourhood Zack brought us up to. I looked around sharply and the others looked at me worriedly. "We gotta move. Now."

Ray shivered and convulsed. "This place feels awful, where are we?"

Zack shrugged. "It's one of the places Dad told me about to go to if we wanted to go to the Surface without getting attention."

I felt my hairs on the back of my neck raise, and I looked at the others and Max nodded. "We're being watched but their minds are strange, almost reminds me of bees or something, hive-like."

Elle was uneasy, *why do you not like this place Merissa? Can we get moving? I don't like it.*

I swore again. "We need to go." I started to walk towards the end of the alley, but shadowy figures began to drift in from the streets beyond.

I had always hated bumping into figures from my past.

"Well, well isn't this fun?" The lead figure was the last person I needed to be dealing with right now, and as she stepped forward I groaned inwardly. "I really need to go now; can we do this some other time? Are you free in twenty years?"

Merissa who's that? I ignored Elle.

The woman stepped forward and lowered her grey hood, exposing a bald head that was laced with tattoos, that have long since lost their distinct shapes. "There was a time you would have been much warmer to me. Do you remember?"

I began to knead my forehead with impatience. "You know that was never real, why can't you just move on?"

Merissa, what are you hiding from me?

My siblings looked back and forth as they watched the exchange and the tattooed woman looked at them with a sour expression and asked, "Do they even know who I am Georgina?"

I sure as hell would lady, sniped Elle.

I rolled my eyes at her in exasperation. "Guys, this is Lady Halo. She was a prisoner of mine when I was working with security."

Lady Halo looked at me with insulted eyes and added. "You forgot the most important thing, and that is that we're lovers."

I had forgotten how annoying she was.

LOVERS?! Explain. Now. I sighed.

I took in a deep breath. "That is not true. She is one of the main leaders of the Bumble Bee Society, the BBS for short. I had to infiltrate their ranks and she was my target, and I brought her down."

I frowned as a thought struck me. "Shouldn't you still be in jail?"

Lady Halo was grinning fiercely. "I looked everywhere for you my love, but when I couldn't find you, I figured that the Surface scum had made you do their dirty work. You have just confirmed my suspicions, my love."

A mad glint entered her eyes. "So much has changed since you were here last. The time of men is over."

You were in love with this thing? She's mad. I do not approve.

I growled, irritated. I was just doing my job.

With that, she raised her arm suddenly and she had a shock blaster pointed it at Zack, who looked unconcerned. Suddenly, with a flash of movement, Lady Halo was lying flat on her back on the rubbish strewn floor and Zack had her shock blaster swirling casually in his grasp.

Several of the other robed women produced firearms, but there were other flashes as my siblings dashed back and forth, ridding them of their weapons.

The robed women, who had given off a constant aura of confidence, were now stinking of fear. Lady Halo righted herself and glared at me. "Since when did you ally yourself with these Surface Spliced freaks?"

I gazed at her, feeling a cold detachment. "The Surface is not the only source of power. You might be fighting the Surface for women everywhere, but as soon as you win, you'd as soon put men beneath your feet. What we fight for is the freedom of all, not any one people."

That is very important, remember that. I will.

We brushed past her and her group of robed women, and Elle commented. *Shame, she seemed like an interesting character, I would like to get to know her better. Even if she is a little mad.*

Maybe so, I agreed. She's part of my past and it is not a time to focus on the past when there are more pressing matters to look to in both the present and the future. If we survive this mess, I promise to bring you in body to their queen and you can spit and hiss at each other.

It's a deal, she proclaimed silently.

Old Friends, New Alliances

We left behind the BBS territory, and it was soon clear that the Lady Halo was not kidding when she said that much had changed. In the last few months, previously safe areas had become warzones. There were burnt out gravicars everywhere, derailed from their magnetic roads and the g-tubes were uprooted from the underground system and smashed and strewn about. I could feel Elle's confusion and I quickly explained. They are glass tubes that people take to certain locations, they were public transport.

Surface security had slipped in the city of Limodium.

As we reached my old apartment, I saw that there was military checkpoint ahead just before my old neighbourhood. I swore at our bad luck. The others were looking at me grimly and I could see the strain starting to affect Yelena and Max. *You might have to use your gift extensively today*. It was going to be a long day.

I bent down and looked right into both of their eyes. "We're nearly at my old apartment. My friend still lives there, but she's a gold soul so you'll be safe there."

Yelena and Max shook their heads fiercely and Yelena spoke for both of them. "No way, we're going all of the way. Anything to stop them hurting Chaz." Max nodded his agreement.

I think that she is still watching him Merissa. Her eyes are still unfocused; Elle's voice was filled with concern.

I looked at Yelena in horror, was she still able to see them torturing Chaz? I peered deep into her eyes and suddenly I felt my mind snap from my body as it propelled itself in the direction of the city centre.

The buildings flashed by, indistinct blurs until I had stopped suddenly in a red room. I realised with gut wrenching terror that the red was actually blood. Some of it was the bright colour red of fresh blood, and other shades were the dark and congealed colours of stale blood, and there were even some splotches that had dried black with age.

Before I could throw up, I tried to focus on the various details in the room. There were three men in the room, one was standing back observing while the second man was attending to the man that was bound to the steel chair.

The third man was bare chested and it was clear from his great heaving breaths that he was in enormous pain. I couldn't tear myself away from the blood that was running down his scarred chest in rivulets.

The man who was casually observing suddenly sprang to attention. "Ah! I see that we have guests! Well let's not be rude." He turned to face me and I saw that he was the same man that had seen me the first time I had seen Chaz, and I felt the same shiver when I saw his dark red eyes.

His previously dead red eyes were now alight with passion, and I could see that the menace was still in them. Instead of looking like a helpless but malevolent grandfather, he suddenly looked very capable of committing the atrocities that his bloody eyes craved. His grey, lined face deepened as he smiled.

"This must be the Merissa and Ellesera I have been hearing so much about. And who's this? Oh Yelena is your name?"

I froze with shock as a multitude of thoughts ran through my mind, one was that Yelena was watching this horrific spectacle. Another was that this man could not only sense me, but he could read my mind at the same time and so must be Spliced. And the last was, *RUN! We need to get out of here Merissa! He's powerful!*

I wasn't sure how I did it, but I managed to wrap myself and Yelena in some sort of mental shroud, and I began to drag us away from this terrible man.

But before I had fully vanished the elderly man spoke, his voice slithering like snakes. "Leaving so soon? Oh well I guess I'll be seeing you soon anyways. General Fatweather will be bringing you and your siblings to me and a word of advice, don't resist."

With a scream I pulled tremendously and I felt a plug pop inside of my mind and with a swirl of colours the room rapidly disappeared but not before I heard Chaz scream. "MERISSA!"

I sucked in a great lungful of air and I found myself back in my old bed, in my old apartment. I sat up and for one surreal moment, I thought that the last few months were a dream, but then I saw Tyson flutter his colourless wings and chirp harshly. Door opened and Max came in with a relieved grin on his face. "Oh. Thank the Creator, you're up. Yelena was up hours ago but then when she saw that you were still out, well she's been crying ever since." *You do sleep deeply,* Elle! *Yes, I'm still here. I didn't get shut out like last time.*

Just then the door exploded open and a blur of blonde hair hurtled itself at me, and with a hard thud, I felt my lungs unwittingly expel the air I had greedily taken in. I was coughing too hard to see who it was that was crying uncontrollably on my chest.

After a few moments, I caught my breath and my vision settled. I saw that it was Yelena dry heaving into my chest. I swept back her proud blonde hair. "It's ok, no need to cry."

But Yelena was inconsolable, and a few minutes later there was a slow knock on my door and it swung open and a blast from the past stepped right back into my life.

A tall Amazonian woman stood and glared at me with her hands on her hips as her dark face scrunched up with a frown. "Well, Merissa. Care to explain all this?"

I couldn't help but grin. "It's good to see you too Rena."

My old roommate stood still as she looked at me, but then shrugged and grinned. "By the Creator, Merissa! I swear I might have even missed your sulky face!"

With that I knew that all that well. I was home.

Action

Elle was filling me in about what happened after I had fainted. Apparently, she was still able to absorb things from my mind though I was unconscious, which is a skill that I planned to keep in mind. After I had started to convulse and spasm, it had attracted the guards' attentions and when one came over to investigate Ray had blasted him with his charm and he was instant putty in his hands. Using his gift on multiple people, Ray was able to get us into the apartment complex without the required ID.

I whistled through my teeth. It was hard enough to charm one person, but multiple people was a feat worth celebrating. I returned my attention to the people in the room and Rena was rubbing her arms ruefully. "I had a wee bit of a shock when Ray and Zack turned up with you in their arms, and those two looking so terrified".

Max and Yelena looked a little miffed at that, but they remained silent on the huge cushions that were strewn on the living room floor. Ray was sitting on the chair I used at the desk when I was working on reports for the CPF, with it back to front. "So, what's the next move then, Merissa?"

Zack was leaning against the wall, his face growing steadily more scowling. "Why do you keep fainting Merissa?" He threw his hands up in frustration. "We can't afford to make plans if every time you have a vision you decide to take a nap!"

Flashes of what I had seen that Chaz was being put through kept flooding into my mind and pulling me back and forth, until I lost my sense of self. But being the target of Zack's frustration snapped me to reality and I felt my own temper rise in my defence. "I can assure you, Zachery, that I am not taking a nap. Obviously, this gift is more taxing than others, and it will take me a while to adjust. You don't need to worry about me being the weakest link."

Take it easy Merissa, Elle soothed. *He means no insult.*

Deep breaths. In and out, in and out. I felt some of the irrational anger seep out of my system and Zack did not seem so irritating.

Zack bristled at me using his full name, but before he could retort, Rena stepped in and looked at me disapprovingly. "Whoa, what's going on? Why all of the needless aggression?"

Ray was smiling wryly. "This is unfortunately how our family sorts out its problems."

Rena blinked for a moment, and I could see the penny drop. She turned to me with an incredulous expression on her face. "Family?! Are you married or something?!"

I like her. She is direct. Elle's approval radiated from within my mind and it distracted me for a moment.

Of course, Rena knew all too well that I was an orphan and an only child, and so the only logical explanation that she could come up with was that I had gotten married in the past few months and these were my brother in laws.

If only life was so simple.

I sighed and I began to tell her of my adventures over the past few months, tracking down my father and finding out that I had many half siblings.

I hesitated. Although I knew that Rena was my best friend, I was still unsure if I should divulge everything. She might not agree with me and call me a traitor.

Are you sure that you should even be thinking of telling this to Rena? She is a likable person and your best friend but we're about to go to war, we can't afford mistakes.

No, I replied silently. We were sisters in all but blood. I've supported her all through her life and she through mine. There is no way that she would turn me in. With that rare sense of certainty, I continued with my tale, I told her of the Underbelly and how they were arming for war against the tyranny of the Surface.

Zack's face was white with fury when I got to that part, but a quick shake of Ray's head silenced him, and he resorted to glaring and sending me glowering faces.

Rena clapped her hands in glee when I told her of Chaz, and I saw the girl who I used to go camping with. "Oh Merissa, this is amazing isn't it?! A Night Person to boot, so dangerous and sexy!"

She clasped her knees and looked at me with rapt attention. "So. Tell me everything about him."

I looked down, and couldn't find the words to answer.

A look of horror crossed her face. "He's the reason that you're here isn't he?" I nodded mutely. A speculative look entered Rena's eyes, "Hmm. So what do you know about his situation? The rest of your story can wait until then."

I smiled gratefully. "I appreciate that." I pointed at Yelena and then back at myself. "Yelena and I have the gift of now sight. We can see events as they happen and so we know that Chaz is being held in the CPF headquarters."

I saw that Yelena's eyes scrunched up in confusion. "How do you know where it is, Merissa? Even I couldn't tell where we were in those visions, and I'm better at them than you."

I sighed, I guessed it was time to tell them. I could see Rena raise an eyebrow in surprise and I nodded and she blew out a deep breath, trying to steady her nerves for the inevitable confrontation.

If Rena knows about this and is nervous for you, what does that say about her? That she is loyal to you alone, afraid of us in the Underbelly, or something else entirely?

I shared Elle's unease as I looked at my family, trying to not look deceitful. "I know where Chaz is because I have been there before."

Zack went really still and I could tell that Ray was tasting my emotional aura. Yelena was shaking her head slowly, she could see where this was going and Max was almost as still as Zack. Even Tyson, was rigid.

Rena had her hands up to her face in exasperation. "Riss, when will you learn not to be so secretive? They are family!"

Before I could defend myself Zack's cold voice cut across the room. "What secret is it, Riss?"

Zack's use of Rena's nickname for me had the same effect as me using his full name earlier and I felt my hackles rise.

I quickly and viciously retorted. "I'm not the only one with secrets Zachery. Remember Christopher? Remember how that could have killed everyone here?"

Zack's face went grey at that and he fell silent and the others were looking at him with curiosity now.

I felt mildly guilty after that, and decided to draw attention away from Zack. "The reason I know the place is because I used to work there."

Shocked gasped travelled around the room and I could see that Zack was almost smiling appreciatively to me for diverting attention away from him, but he was nevertheless shocked also.

You need to learn to manage your temper better if you're to run the Underbelly, tutted Elle.

Ray was the first to recover. "By working there I assume it wasn't secretarial work you were doing?"

I nodded. "That's right. I was part of the elite unit that was in charge of taking care of the biggest criminals in the city. Our nickname was the Hornet Squad."

I smiled wryly. "That's how I got to know Lady Halo. I was supposed to take her down, and I did."

Rena jumped in then. "Wait there, girl. Lady Halo? Did you bump into that crazy bitch again?"

I nodded sourly and Rena harrumphed. I quickly explained to the others. "Rena and Lady Halo never eye-to-eye."

Rena sniffed. "That savage gives the rest of the lesbians of the city a bad name. Thanks to her, there are now huge restrictions on lesbians everywhere all over the city, and some are applied to women citywide."

She turned and looked out the dark window. "They're only adding fuel to the fire when they put more rules on women. This is making women everywhere turn to the BBS for protection, and their numbers are growing every day."

I looked at my old friend and I saw that she was visibly older than the last time I had seen her. Lady Halo was right; the city had changed in the last few months.

I wonder what laws they placed on women? I dismissed the question, it was not the right time for probing questions.

After squeezing reassurance into Rena through her arm, I continued on with my story. "So after a couple of years, I became more and more specialised. It didn't hurt that at this stage my gifts were beginning to manifest themselves, and I had a huge edge over the people I was trying to put behind bars. Thanks to my skills, I rose through the ranks quickly, and before long I was out in the Hornet's division."

Rena frowned. "You never old me what division you were part of. I can't believe you were a part of that horrible squad!"

Ray looked uneasy and Zack asked with his voice hard. "What was the Hornet squad?"

I shrugged. "Hornets are known for slaughtering whole colonies of bees, and Emperor Sidario thought it had a nice ring to it."

Everyone froze, including Rena. Zack spoke through clenched teeth. "You know Emperor Sidario?"

You've had an interesting past Merissa. I shook my head. "Hardly, he does not associate himself with common staff but yes, my commander to reported him and relayed his orders. When the BBS got troublesome we were sent in to eliminate them. I wasn't particularly proud of it but I saw the necessity… "

I was lost in my thoughts for a moment. All of my efforts had been aimed at revenging my mother. Each punch was a punch for her, every drop of blood, sweat and tear was for her memories. We had always joked that one day I would be a great general one day in the army like her, even if we did not know then how close I would actually come to that reality.

I heard coughing and I was snapped back out of my musings, and I saw that Ray and the others were looking at me expectantly. I quickly hurried on to cover my embarrassment. "Yes, well, I continued on like that for a few years but then I finally got the assignment that I was looking for."

This is it, they could kill me after this.

I'll protect you as much as I can, Elle reassured me.

I took a deep breath. "You see guys, when I arrived back from my camping trip with Rena and a few others, I found my mother in a bloody mess in the sitting room."

Flashes of the terrible night flashed in my inner eye and I tried to ignore them; the congealed darkened blood that spun around my mother's still body like macabre wings, the awful stillness in her eyes and her horrifyingly pale skin.

I drove on. "So I felt a little part of me die that night and then I saw the damning evidence." The air caught in my throat. "It was a message written on the wall, in blood." The others' eyes were round as plates, even Rena, who had never heard the finer details, was looking at me with rapt attention. "The message said "Merissa, your mother should have never crossed me."

Then the memory hit me with full force.

I was standing back in my cramped sitting room and the smell of coppery blood drenched the air. My mother was strewn across the armchair that she always curled up in when she was lost in one of her puzzles. Her starlight blonde hair was stained red and ripped in brutal clumps and cast around the room. Her body was contorted, twisted unnaturally and I could see her broken bones beneath her skin.

I had vomited then.

The others were looking at me with alarmed expressions, and even Zack looked a bit queasy. Rena stepped forward. "It's ok Riss. It's a long time ago now." She wrapped me in one of her deep hugs and I felt my tears slide down my face. I felt Elle's muted horror in my mind and she sent me waves of comfort.

I sniffed. "We don't have much more time, but I can tell the rest quickly enough; basically, I had thought it was Dad who had done it. So when I was given the assignment to assassinate him, I took it."

Shocked silence greeted me and I felt the atmosphere cool rapidly in the room. I rolled my tear filled eyes, that made more tears fall. "Cut me some slack, guys. Obviously, Dad and I worked out our differences. I realise now that it was the Surface authorities that had authorised the murder of my mother and I will not rest until I know why, and until I know who had ordered it. And I will make them pay."

Ray was looking at me with a mixture of hope and worry. Eventually, his natural optimism won out. "Well, I have trusted Dad as far as this, and if he has nothing to worry then neither do I." Yelena and Max were both nodding their agreement.

Zack looked more reserved for a moment, and then shrugged his shoulders. "You've had far more than one opportunity to ruin us, and me personally, and never took it. If that doesn't show that you're trustworthy, I don't know what does."

Ray grinned brightly and I was startled. Before I knew what was going on Ray roared, "GROUP HUG!" Everyone converged on me grabbed me into a massive hug.

Family, gotta love them.

Family comes first Merissa, cherish them.

About to Hit the Fan

We were all sitting around the old coffee table that Rena bought at some yard sale and I never had the heart to tell her that it was horrendous. Rena had gone into full mother hen mode, and made sure that everyone had a cup of steaming beverage in their hands.

While Rena was taking orders for the drinks, Max had asked shyly for some sugared water. Though confused, Rena had done as asked, and when she saw the sugared water being lapped up without anyone touching it, she had grown a little alarmed. So I had to explain to her that Max had a companion that helped him see. While I trusted Rena with my life, I knew that telling her that a dragon was in our living room was going a little far, and she would freak out. She had nodded slowly and continued to serve the drinks.

I gulped my tea gratefully; the heat was adding much needed strength after the last few hours. I looked around at my group. "Right then. Are we clear on what we need to do?" There were nods all around and I nodded myself, "Let's do it."

It's a risky plan, Merissa. I knew that but it was all that we had.

We stood up to leave, and when the last of my new family had left, I turned to Rena. "Thank you so much for your hospitality."

She smiled in return. "Don't be silly; this is as much your house as it is mine. As long as you keep paying the rent!"

I laughed at that, but then and I sobered up and said with my voice lowered. "In all seriousness, take care of yourself."

A hesitant spark entered Rena's eyes. It was uncharacteristic for her to be shy about anything she wants, so it piqued my interest. "What is it?"

She bit her lip. "I want to go with you."

I shook my head but she hurried on before I could talk sense into her.

"Not to the CPF headquarters, to the Underbelly. That's where I want to go. It seems like that people like me could be useful there."

I smiled. It was typical of Rena to think like that. I felt my frown slide over my smile as I peered at her. "Why would you want to go there? It's dangerous."

Rena was holding her left arm with her right hand and she refused to meet my eyes. "Things have gotten…difficult."

My empathy spiked, and I saw her in a wash of colours, her normally bright vibrant colours seemed more leeched and I instinctively did not like it. I growled, "What's wrong? Has someone hurt you?"

She shook her head quickly, her eyes darting back and forth. I felt a well of frustration wash through me. "Then tell me why things are difficult!"

She sighed. "In the last few weeks, maybe months now, things have been getting weird up here. People are edgy, people are going missing and there's more soldiers on the streets."

My eyes were narrowed. "That's hardly enough of a reason to want to leave your whole life, what about your patients?"

Rena scowled. "I've been more or less told by the other doctors that I'm not fit for surgery. They are following orders, that female doctors are no longer allowed to perform surgery. There's no real reason for me to stay here." She stopped and brought her fierce gaze up to meet mine. "I will not be made useless by some conservative fools. If the Underbelly will have me, I will more than gladly offer my services."

I paused for a moment and then I shrugged. "I don't see why not; you'll have to be ready soon though. After tonight, I won't be able to pretend to be a law abiding citizen."

Rena nodded grimly. "Where will I meet you?"

I thought about it. "I don't know how long we'll be, we might be done within the hour or we might be all day. We might be on foot, or we might be in a stolen vehicle. It's hard to tell... Tell you what, meet us at the bridge by the Wolfton ambassador's house, ok?" She nodded.

I gave her a final hug, and left behind my old apartment for the last time.

No you'll see Rena again, remember? So you're not really leaving anything behind. That made me feel a little better.

I quickly caught up with the others, who were waiting for me just before the checkpoint. I nodded at Zack and the two of us linked minds and pooled our energies together and began to weave an illusion. It was a simple one, just instead of a group of young people we were elderly group on our way to a bridge competition.

We walked towards the military checkpoint, one of the younger men was smiling at us and I felt a little nervous under his scrutiny. There was a man leaning against the gate casually. "Where are we off to folks?"

It was Ray's turn. "If it doesn't bother you, my friends and I are off to our annual bridge competition, over on Castle Street."

The man waved his hands. "Open her up boys."

One of the other men, pulled his hand through his silver hair. "I don't know captain; they shouldn't be leaving their homes for trivial matters."

The captain twirled around and smacked the silver haired man across the cheek, "If I ask for your opinion, Slewen, I'll let you know. Otherwise, keep your gob shut!"

Ray winced, and I itched my lips to hide my smile. I guess he over did his persuasion with the captain. The captain turned back to face us, "Apologies for that, ladies and gents, but some people these days have very little respect for their elders and superiors."

Ray grinned wanly and we filed past them. As soon as we were out of sight of the checkpoint, Zack and I let the illusion slip. I turned to look at Ray, "You could've gone a little easier on the charisma back there, Ray!" Ray rolled his eyes and endured our teasing good naturedly until Max gave us his warning.

"Uh… guys? Another checkpoint up ahead. These guys are a little warier than the other guys."

I looked around at my group. "Into positions guys."

We had passed by through several checkpoints when I heard a scuffle off of the street that we were walking on, down a dark, dank alleyway.

Rolls of terror were streaming from the alleyway. Without a moment's thought I strode into the alleyway and stopped.

In front of me was a small group of men, maybe seven or eight of them. At their feet lay a man who'd been badly beaten. The man groaned and clutched at his sides, he rolled around and I saw his pale skin and he opened his lavender eyes and looked at me pleadingly.

A man from the group, with short cropped ginger hair, turned and grinned when he saw me. "Well, well, lads. Looks like we've got ourselves an audience. And she's brought her babies with her."

I could hear my crew come up behind me as cold rage grew inside me. "What is the meaning of this?"

The ginger man grinned lecherously, "Don't you know lass? The Emperor has put a massive bounty on each vampire head that is brought to him."

Suddenly, I saw the genius of the currency system that was used in the Underbelly. Monsters like this can't be born in that system. I growled, and the ginger man stumbled back as the rest of his group laughed at him.

One of them with buck teeth sneered. "What's the matter with you Hugo? Did the pretty little girl catch your tongue?"

The ginger man named Hugo snarled, "Why don't you take her then Ronson? If you're so tough?" Ronson laughed and ran towards me with his fists raised. Bad move.

I almost felt sorry for him.

He swung first, but I easily sidestepped him. With the lightest brush of my finger along the back of his neck, he screamed and crumpled down to the ground. The rest of my group exploded into action and in a mere two seconds, the rest of the small group of men were also unconscious on the ground.

I walked over to the injured vampire and gently placed my hand on his injuries and with a push of my mind, the worst of them vanished. The young man looked up with an expression of awe. "Who are you people?"

I ignored this deliberately, and said instead. "You need to go to the Underbelly. It's no longer safe for vampires on the Surface. You will have your mind examined by a man called Marcus, but you will have to accept it if you want access."

The young vampire sat up abruptly. "I can't thank you enough, I'll need to get my family first and then we'll go as soon as possible. Who will I say sent me?"

I paused for a moment and said with deliberate slowness. "Tell them that the future Underworlder of the Underbelly sent you." The young vampire looked confused but nodded and quickly ran out of the alleyway.

I looked around at my family and saw newfound respect in their eyes. I nodded. "Right. We have another vampire to save, let's move out."

Going towards the city centre was always like stepping into a different world. The sunken houses and boxy apartments gave away to luxurious and spacious houses that competed for our attention as they displayed their wealth and status. Cheap wood, carbon metal and concrete gave way to glass, titanium and marble.

We stepped into the market square, filled with tall glistening glass corporate towers; the heart of the Surface's power. Men and women in suits ran and ducked through the rush hour traffic. The gravicars were sleeker in this part of town, and the noxious gasses spluttering out of the cheaper models in the outskirts of town were nowhere to be seen.

It's so loud, how did you ever function in this hellhole?

I mentally shrugged. You just got on with it, I suppose.

We stopped in front of the tall imposing doors of the CPF tower. A continuous stream of men and women in smart clothes rushed in and out of the building. I looked at our dark but practical clothes. There was no way we would be able to sneak into here without suspicion unless we were disguised by one of Zack's illusions.

I looked at my family and they gazed back at me with fierce determination. I nodded and Yelena grinned. "Come on, Merissa; let's get your grumpy git."

Into the Lion's Den

We breathed into the cool atrium, and I was struck at the cold beauty of the place. The cream marble floor spread out beneath us like sand. The golden fountain that stood in the centre of the sea of marble was shaped like a tree, intrinsically entwined with silver ivy. The water cascading from the enormous fountain was the only perceptual sound in the startling silence. Though I had been here many times before, I'd never really taken in the building. As I moved closer to Chaz, I felt like a silver cloth was being laid over me. Each movement was dreamlike, each detail of the world strongly contrasting with the surrealism of my reality. I had to focus. Otherwise, I would risk someone catching me unawares.

Deep breaths. In and out, in and out.

Even with my advanced hearing, I could hardly hear the silent crowd swirling around us. I shared an uneasy glance with Max, and I saw his forehead crease in concentration. When he spoke, it was strained with effort. "They're strange, almost like those hive like minds of the BBS, but they are different…" Tyson fluttered agitatedly his translucent wings as he sensed his bond-mate's unease.

Suddenly, his head snapped upright and he stood rigid. "That's where we need to go."

I peered around the large fountain and I saw where he was pointing. It was a door. People were running through the door with no consideration for others, but it was strange. They ran together like a synchronised flock of birds, and no one crashed into each other.

There is something at work here Merissa, be careful.

I stepped forward, but Max grabbed my arm tightly. "Careful, there are people watching the door whose minds are clear of whatever it is that's affecting these people here."

I nodded grimly and I saw Zack and Ray square up. It was time for the next stage of the plan.

We glided up to the door, imitating the flock of people around us. We drew up close to the door, and I saw that there was actually a pair of soldiers lounging against a security booth. Their gaze searching each and every person who came through the door.

I'm not sure what gave us away but they zeroed in on us in seconds. With a flash of movement, one of the security guards grabbed my wrists, and I felt my blood drain from my face.

He was a Spliced Soldier.

He had to be. There was no way a normal human would be able to move that fast. His narrowed blue eyes stole right past my illusion; I wasn't sure how but I felt it being stripped away. I felt Elle in the back of my mind, lending me her strength for the fight to come.

His eyes widened in recognition and I felt my brain do one of its intuitive leaps and I knew that whatever the man was thinking, I did not want him to act on it. I sent an impulse through my hand but it was blocked. I frowned and the man leered at me. "It will take more than that to break me sweetie."

Elle swirled in my mind and I felt our energies become one and I looked right into the man's blue eyes. "So be it."

I unleashed the full strength of my gift and it thundered against the wall of his mind. Instead of ploughing against it relentlessly like a tidal wave of water against a cliff face, I felt Elle slip between little cracks in the wall that were too small for me to grasp and pry them open wide enough for my gift to latch into them. My gift surged forwards and ripped chunks of his wall apart. After a moment his mental defences crumbled and I flooded in. I had complete control of his thoughts, sleep, and he went limp.

His colleague looked at me in alarm and turned to run, but Ray sprang in front of him and I felt a flood of power surge from him. I heard his low melodious voice soothe the terrified man.

After a moment his shoulders slumped, and suddenly Max jumped in glee. "I can access his mind like Tyson now!" He was silent for a moment and then his eyes went as round as polished marbles. "He's some sort of pacifier. He's used by the boss to placate the workers in order to get them to do what he wants. Only Spliced people are resistant to their gift."

He frowned as another thought whispered into his mind from the unconscious man. "The man Merissa downed is a blocker. They are immune to all gifts that the Spliced Soldiers can do. They act as the pacifier's bodyguards." He cackled like a hyena. "No wonder he was crapping his pants; he saw that Merissa broke the blocker's shield and he knew that he was a goner if he didn't make a run for it."

Zack was shaking his head. "Dad will love this now, Merissa can now break unbreakable shields." He cast me a wry grin but I could see shadows flicker in his eyes. Once upon a time he would have been resentful about my new ability, but he was beginning to see the amount of pressure I'd be put under.

About bloody time, I thought.

We've all started to grow up a little I think. Ella was impressed with all of our teamwork.

Yelena clicked her tongue. "Guys, we need to move. Chaz is on his own." The seriousness of the situation then crashed into me.

I felt my stomach constrict like there was a nest of pythons writhing inside.

I nodded and Ray looked at me. "What should we do with him? I can make him hide himself for a few hours if you want."

I shook my head. "No, he could prove useful. If he can placate people, that might come in handy if we meet any unsavoury types. Make him follow us."

I didn't mention that now that I'd been exposed to the placator and blocker, I now had their gifts. At least, I did if Terry and Oslo are right.

Guess that means that when I return to my body I'll have new colours on my body, they had better be nice colours.

Thanks to Bruce, the placator, Max had an inside view of the CPF tower. We made rapid progress through sections that I had little knowledge of. Max was crouched in the corner of a hallway and I tensed my legs, ready to snap. We'd been here almost three minutes solid and Max showed no sign of moving.

Bruce then rounded the corner and Max breathed a sigh of relief. "Ok, we're clear." I rolled my eyes and turned around the corner myself and stopped.

Lining the hallway were the prone figures of a small crowd of people, I pressed my hands up to my mouth and whirled to look at Max, who was grinning. His face withered when he saw the look of total fury on my face. "Why did you do this?"

Max stared, shocked, and Ray stepped forward and grabbed my shoulder. "It's ok Merissa, they're just spaced out. Max just made Bruce overwhelm them with his gift."

I whirled on him and I saw Ray flinch, and Zack snorted sarcastically. "Your shadows are at it again." It barely registered but then I saw the flickering shadows in the periphery of my vision.

Damn it. Merissa discipline yourself, you're growing in power and if you give into your emotions like this then you're going to hurt the people that you love.

I took a deep breath and tried to calm myself. I thought of strawberries and chocolate and I felt the ugly anger grudgingly go back into its cage. Good, deep breaths, good.

I expelled a gutsful of air from my lungs and the last of the rage vanished. "Come on, let's bring Chaz home."

The others looked at each other for a moment and after it was clear I wasn't going to become death personified, they followed me with my wrathful shadows.

You're Never Really Ready

Yelena led the way forward and I swear I actually caught her sniffing like a bloodhound as she marched down the corridor, with the rest of us in tow.

Zack and Ray weren't needed anymore, as it was clear that the upper levels of the CPF was almost deserted. All the security we came to was easily bypassed with a swipe of a card that Bruce had in his possession.

So they waited and rested for the mayhem that will ensue on our way out.

Before long Yelena went rigid and I felt it too. The awful feeling of recognition, we had been down this corridor before. The startling white walls, the cold glass doors, and even the red stains that had not been totally removed were all too uncomfortably familiar.

Yelena looked at me. "I think this is it Merissa, he's behind one of those doors." I looked at Max and he nodded, and after a few silent moments he exhaled and I felt the group relax minutely.

He smiled at me. "Found him. He's behind that door there." He pointed at a door that was near the end of the hall.

We rushed towards it and Ray commanded Bruce to open it. Bruce lifted up his card and swiped it against the security pad. Nothing. The light stayed a persistent red. I felt sweat beginning to bead on the back of my neck and I heard Ray repeat the command. The uneven beep from the security panel was the only answer.

I lost my patience. *Not again Merissa.*

I shoved Bruce aside desperately and he stumbled to the ground. I brought my leg up and crunched it against the door. The door bowed from the impact, and with another mighty kick, the door crumpled and flew inwards.

I strode into the room and I recognised it instantly. The walls were washed down and so there were no scarlet stains soaking the walls, but that couldn't mask the terror that these walls have felt. In the centre of the room, bound to the chair that he was sitting in, was Chaz. He was deathly still.

My heart stopped for a moment but then restarted when I saw him take a shuddering, gasping breath. I rushed to him, all plans flooded from my mind. I gingerly touched him, careful not to cause him any more pain. Despite my caution, his face scrunched up in a wince as deep lines ran down his face. Elle was studying him from a different angle and I saw through her mind that the physical injuries weren't as severe as my panic led me to believe.

I withdrew my hands and I looked at him, helpless. Then I felt a nudge at my elbow and I looked up to see Yelena peering down at both at me and Chaz. "You can heal him, remember?"

I could have smacked myself.

With a greater sense of urgency, mindful of the ticking time, I gently placed my hands on his broken face. He weakly resisted, but I persevered and he quickly ran out of strength. I sought his mind as my gift responded to my dire need. I felt the power sweep down my arm, different from when I used it to hurt. A flood of water, as opposed to a torrent of fire.

It reached his face and slowed. It almost seemed to understand that it needed to be soothing and careful. It pooled delicately around the most damaged parts of his face. His eye socket was crushed and I sensed the gift swell around the damaged bone, as it began to rapidly knit together the bone.

Though the majority of the focus of my gift was on his face, I could also see the distant echoes of it sweeping through his body, targeting the huge bruises on his various organs, helping his innate ability to heal rapidly.

The whole experience was surreal, I breathed a sigh of relief as I felt injury after injury began to repair itself. Before long, Chaz began to breathe a little easier and I sat back, feeling like I had just climbed a mountain while carrying three people on my back.

Well done. That was very well done, you're becoming a force to be reckoned with Merissa.

"Well that was a thrilling show you put you on Merissa. Chaz was right, you are special indeed."

I stiffened and I turned around to see a figure was standing in the shadows.

I already knew who it was, but I still spoke. "Who's that? Come out of there."

"With pleasure."

The elderly man stepped out of the shadows, his cracked skin and dark red eyes were even more macabre in real life. The light bounced off of his bald head, a detail that I did not notice before. He moved with the grace of someone who had been an athlete all his life. His skin seemed to whisper as the draught from the air conditioning washed over it, it was so cracked. The others stiffened and I felt a spring of relief as they also sensed that there was more to this man than meets the eye. Yelena in particular looked pale but she glared at the old man with a determined expression.

The elderly man beamed at all of us as though he were a grandfather seeing his grandchildren for the first time in a long time. He smiled at Zack. "Zachery, you are one of the most accomplished illusionists I have seen in a long time, maintaining that illusion for hours was pretty impressive, not to mention hiding Tyson there for as long as you have."

He turned his attention to Ray. "Let's not forget your twin Raymond. Only he could make a placator his slave and open all of the security we have in the CPF."

Max's eyes widened. "Guys! He's a mind reader!"

The elderly man nodded sagely. "You are indeed right, Maximus. I am most intrigued by your particular gift, I have never seen anything like it, and I am looking forward to seeing the possibilities that it can open up for us." Tyson hissed and the bald man clapped his hands delightedly. "It's been much too long since I have seen one of the Fae."

Elle was suddenly very interested in what Fae were. And I asked for her. "Fae? What's a Fae?"

At that, the bald man turned his gaze towards me. "And let's not forget the jewel in the crown, Merissa. A healer, a blocker, and a seer. You, my dear, I am most interested in working with."

I felt a flash of anger and Elle shouted in alarm but it was too late, a shadow flickered from my left hand and the bald man's gaze sharpened and he pursed his lips, in displeasure.

Yelena stepped out in front of the predatory gaze of the old man and glared at him with inner strength that I was proud of. "You leave us alone, you creepy old man! You're an awful person, how could you do that to innocent people?" She was pointing at Chaz, who was beginning to struggle to his feet.

The old man snorted. "That man is not innocent. He is a vampire, and so needs to be culled. He was also caught attempting to assassinate a dear old friend of mine."

Yelena looked aghast, and Chaz snorted himself softly. "He may have been your friend Frost, but Fatweather is a man that needs to be put down like a dog."

The elderly man, Frost, shook his head sadly. "It is this kind of barbarity that stops the Surface and the Underbelly from working together."

I'd had enough.

I cleared my throat. "Right. That's great and all, but we're leaving now."

Frost spread his hands out wide. "Why are you in such a hurry to leave Merissa? You haven't even heard my offer yet."

I raised my eyebrow in derision. "Unless it's the keys to the rest of the Surface, I'm really not interested."

Frost's cold red eyes gleamed like new born ice. "Oh but I could, Merissa. You, in particular, I am interested in seeing in my experiments; a healer whose thoughts I can't hear and an illusionist that can conjure shadows. Could I ask for a better subject?"

It was right then that I knew we had to get out. I agree.

I shot a look at Zack, saw his nod, and then I saw his illusion throw itself up and envelope itself around Frost. He looked slightly dazed, but I knew that it would not hold him for long and that was confirmed when Chaz growled. "We need to move. He becomes immune pretty quickly."

I tried not to think about what Chaz must have tried to do in his desperation to escape.

Just then I heard a piercing wail shatter the illusion of calm in the room, and Max swore vehemently. I turned to stare at the young boy but he was shaking his head aggressively. "That blocker we left behind has woken up and raised the alarm." He frowned and went pale. "There's a man that I did not sense before coming our way. I've never seen a mind like his before. It's so twisted and evil, and it's coming fast."

Max trailed off, an expression of utter hopelessness enveloping his youthful face. It aged him horribly and I could see what he would look as an old man in decades to come, his lined face, and his watery weary eyes. Ray shouted in alarm. "Max!" He rushed over and tried to shake him but Tyson was spitting venom as he thrashed back and forth as his own mind was ravaged.

Chaz swore. "That's Fatweather, for sure. We need to get out of here. I don't think that even we could all take him. He has the power of apathy."

Lovely. Max snapped to attention and I could see that he had shaken off the influence of Fatweatherand was back to his old youthful self.

I whistled to the group and everyone stood to attention, even Chaz, and I began issuing orders. "Right then. Max you are to be our eyes while we get out of here. I don't want any annoying ambushes along the way. Yelena try and get a fix on Rena, she'll be waiting for us on a bridge. Ray and Zack, you both know what to do." Nods all around.

Chaz propped himself up and grinned at me. "What should I do captain?" I resisted the urge to roll my eyes. "Just try not to get yourself killed, that would make this a waste of a mission."

Chaz's grin dropped and I thought I had offended him and I was about to apologise, but then I saw that he was looking pensively at Frost.

"We should kill him." I was expecting it, but it was still a shock to hear him say it out loud.

I shook my head. "No this was a retrieve and rescue mission, not an assassination mission. We also don't know what gifts this man has to protect him while he's like this."

Chaz's expression darkened. "I'd never met Frost before this, but I had heard of him. He was supposed to be heavily involved in hunting down the original Spliced Soldiers. He might have even had something to do with your mother's murder."

I looked at Frost, I could see that the illusion was beginning to wear off. It would be so simple to avenge my mother but I stayed my hand. I could not be certain that this was the man responsible for my mother's murder and I could not in good conscience kill somebody on a rumour.

He's powerful, we should kill him while we have got the chance. I was surprised at the venom in Elle's voice and she growled, There's something that's abominable about him.

I shook my head again, at both Elle and Chaz. "We leave now, nothing stops that. Fatweather is too dangerous."

Chaz saw the decision in my eyes and nodded slowly in agreement. I gazed around at the others, and with a collective deep breath we left the elderly man Frost gazing vacantly out the window.

Just before we left behind Frost I saw him looking back at me and he winked. With horror, I realised that he was never under an illusion.

Run! Elle was shouting.

I fled.

Water Across the Surface

We slipped through the building like shadows, my heart was beating louder and louder as I heard our hunters closed in. Getting out of the CPF headquarters was surprisingly easy, we had just smashed a window and jumped out of the twentieth floor and landed on the roof of one of the lower buildings. Chaz needed a few minutes to recover, but we were soon on our way.

It was not long, however until the surrounding areas were swarming with soldiers. Currently, we were hiding in an abattoir. The grinding squeaks of the steel hooks were beginning to grate on my nerves, and on more than one occasion I bolted up, thinking that I had heard voices in the bloody slaughterhouse.

Ray returned from his scouting mission. He slumped down beside the steel container used to drain blood away from the corpses. He expelled a weary breath. "As far as I can see, they have become more dispersed. It looks like that they have begun turning over every rock to find us."

Chaz was gazing out to the city, lost in the sparkling of the dark city but he snapped his attention to us as Ray continued. "They will use us as a reason to use more force on the citizens and will say that it's to protect them from us. This will probably be the push the Surface will use to unite the citizens against us."

He coughed and I automatically approached him, using my gift to target the source of his coughing, and it eased off. He smiled gratefully. "Thank you, but we need to get back to the Underbelly as soon as possible. We are on borrowed time right now."

I pursed my lips. "You're right. I think that you need to take the others and go back home."

Chaz frowned. "And what exactly will you be doing?"

I shrugged. "I have a promise to keep, I'll meet you back there."

Before he could question me further, I stood up abruptly and he could read the determination in my face and nodded unhappily.

I think he's starting to respect you, Merissa.

The others were looking at me with apprehension, and I smiled to reassure them. "Don't worry, I'll see you all soon."

Zack and Ray nodded slowly and Max followed suit but Yelena held me in an unwavering gaze. "I expect you back home promptly Merissa."

I almost laughed, the shy girl who had never had her hair done or her face done up in make-up was nowhere to be seen. I smiled again. "I promise."

Before I left, I looked at Chaz and the sun caught on his face and it highlighted him in a way that the black suns could never do justice. With a pang I realised that the proud people of the vampires were never meant to be banished to the shadows. I then frowned and I gestured for Chaz to follow me and he did, wary.

Elle was also nervous. *Be careful Merissa, vampires' have strong hunting urges.*

I knew what I was doing.

Chaz looked at me with quizzical lavender eyes and I impulsively brushed his black hair out of his eyes and he went still. Hardly breathing. I asked in an almost non-existent whisper. "When was the last time you fed?"

I did not know how often vampires needed to feed but judging from what his father Dr Yuyo was saying, it was a pretty important part of their diet. I assumed that after being put through such an ordeal, Chaz would need blood.

Chaz's lavender eyes widened and he backed away. "No, Merissa. I couldn't ask you to do that, I'll be ok."

I stepped right into his personal space. "I'm not offering it to you as a favour. I'm ordering you to take a mouthful so that you don't faint along the way back home."

Chaz's face looked torn, the most expression I had ever seen on a vampire's face.

He shuddered and stepped forward and murmured. "I'm sorry Merissa, please don't remember me like this."

His arms slid gently around my torso and he pulled me towards him, bringing his head down towards my shoulder. I took a sharp breath, and then felt a sharp pinch as he bit quickly into my neck, followed by a surge of pleasure as the endorphins from his saliva entered my bloodstream.

After a moment, he pushed me away and wiped at his mouth, refusing to meet my gaze. Already, I felt my gift repairing the wound on my neck. I looked at Chaz for the longest moment, and he finally met my eyes. I wasn't sure what, but something powerful was happening. I felt something shift in not just my heart, but my soul as well. This was meant to be part of the greater plan.

With that I ran towards the window and leapt through it swiftly. The wind was cool for this time of year, bracing but welcoming. I ran with purpose across the slate tiles beneath my feet, leaping with confidence from rooftop to rooftop. There was deep yearning in Elle when she saw the vast sky above. I could feel her desire to stretch her wings and fly beneath the stars and between the cotton clouds. As I hurtled from roof to roof, I made a private promise to myself while Elle was distracted, she would one day get the chance to fly in the open sky.

I soon reached my destination. I shimmied down the wall with the grace of a snake and landed with a lithe jump into the alleyway. As the sun began to set the alleyway became darker and cooler, and I knew that I did not have much time, she might not even be there after the uproar of the city.

I stepped out into the busy street and lost myself in the throngs of people. The energy of this crowd was one of nerves and I could hear snatches of conversations as I slipped in between them. A couple of co-workers were talking as they passed me with steaming coffee in their hands as they eagerly gossiped on their way home from work. "Did you hear about the break in at CPF?" The balding man was saying to his younger co-worker. "It's had the army out in the whole city, whoever's done it has made the Emperor very nervous!"

The younger co-worker was shaking her head. "Be reasonable, Harold. There has to be a better reason for..."

They slipped beyond my hearing range, but a young boy was tugging at the skirts of his mother. "Mommy, why are there big men with big plasmarays running around? Are they not afraid they will hurt someone?"

The mother looked terrified, as though one of the soldiers would beat the child for saying something so traitorous and hurriedly hushed her son.

I pushed past the crowds of people and finally reached the bridge. I quickly cast my gaze down the crowded bridge and then I could see her and I breathed a sigh of relief.

I ran towards Rena and it took me a little longer than it should have to recognise that there was something amiss. But her face was pinched in panic that intensified when she saw me getting closer. It was then that I saw the man that was standing beside her and I blanched when I saw the intention in his mind. He was going to use her to get me to co-operate. *Bastard.* It was the first time Elle had ever sworn and I had almost smiled despite myself.

He called out in a casual drawl. "Merissa, stay where you are please. We don't want to make any more people to get hurt than absolutely necessary."

I snarled, startling Rena. People around us had begun to notice the blatant hostility radiating between us and gave us a wide berth.

Good.

With cold calculated rage I felt my gift slip free of its restraint and it launched itself at the man across the distance that separated us from each other. The man stumbled back and yelped from the onslaught and then succumbed to the pain. Rena ran towards me and I grabbed her, the two of us fleeing through the crowd. I saw figures detach themselves from the crowd and give chase. Judging from their speed, they were Spliced.

With a curse, I slung Rena across my back. She yelped, but she held on tightly, I then began to sprint as quickly as I could through the busy streets. The faces flashed by in blurs, and I knew that I was not far from where I needed to be.

The grand houses gave way to more modest dwellings until these finally gave way to hovels. I stopped to catch my breath. The crowds had grown larger and it was harder to avoid people and I knew that I was going to need my full strength to fight off the Spliced Soldiers.

Rena slid off of my back and looked slightly winded herself. "Geez, Merissa, I never knew you could do that!"

I shrugged by way of answer. "I had a lot of training, you know that."

Rena laughed. "There's training, and then there's superhuman feats. That was a superhuman feat. What has the Underbelly been feeding you?"

I shook my head. "There's no time to answer. We're still being followed, and we need to lose them."

Rena fell silent then, but gazed around the neighbourhood, her expression darkened and she looked at me accusingly. "Why are we here Merissa?"

I sighed. "It's the only way."

Before Rena could retort angrily, the first of the soldiers melted out of the crowd and approached us. Then, a warning sonic-boom and a crack and a slash of concrete sliced through the air.

"Men are not in power here." The voice seemed to have no source, but I knew from past experience that there were probably several sharpshooters in the buildings around us.

I cursed, the BBS have gotten sonic weapons. I had hoped that they had been restricted to bullets. Sonics are unlimited in ammunition, perfect for long drawn out fights. Not to mention they were just as lethal as plasmafire.

The soldier was slowly backing away, but then roaring plasmafire exploded out of the crowd and the unarmed civilians began screaming and running for cover. I dragged Rena towards the alleyway we had come up earlier that day.

Several windows in the hovels were vibrating as the BBS began firing on the Spliced Soldiers. The air shimmered as the lethal invisible rays of energy shouted through the air. There was more than one ear splitting screech as the plasmafire crashed into the sonic blasts.

Then, one of the derelict buildings took a shell from one of the assault troops and exploded violently. I looked around and located an assault tank hovering down the street. The suspension systems it used kept it an inch above the ground, and the gleaming metal was reflecting the purple rounds radiating from its laserfire cannon.

A huge concussion of sound buffeted me and Rena, and I felt myself fall down as the assault tank fired relentlessly on the BBS.

I knew that it was time to go. Agreed.

I dragged Rena away from the infernal carnage and towards the manhole. Rena froze when she saw where I was going. "We're going in there?!"

There was a note of hysteria in her voice, and I knew I needed to steady her nerves. "Down there is the Underbelly. Up here is death and destruction. Take your pick." Rena paused to deliberate for a split second, but then nodded her decision.

In we went.

As I slid the manhole back over, the sounds of screaming battle began to fade. I could not help wonder how long it would take for the Surface to bring its war to us.

Snakes and Lions

After checking to make sure that we were all ok, and to mind read Rena to confirm her intentions, Dad had told the rest of us to get some rest and to be ready for intense training in the morning that involved running laps all around the Underbelly and scaling huge walls.

We trained. It was brutal, getting up ridiculously early and pushing ourselves until dusk. I did things over the next few weeks and months that I did not think were humanly possible; running up a 5-story vertical wall, holding my breath for almost an hour whilst swimming, and even running through a tunnel of fire without being burned.

We heard tales of brutality coming from the Surface world all of the time. The trickle of people seeking sanctuary in the Underbelly increased, so much so that in order to make sure that the security of the Underbelly was not compromised, Marcus had to set up his interviews on the Surface to ensure that none were spies attempting to infiltrate the Underbelly. I'd had to accompany him on several occasions to offer my own mind reading skills, and I was always shocked and angered by the state of the people seeking shelter.

By far the most haggard of all of the groups were the vampires and the small groups of women fleeing the harsh laws of the Empire. They were slowly being robbed of their dignity and their rights. One woman owned her own successful business that acted as a bridge between employees and employers. But as she offered her hand to me for my mental inspection, I saw that the scabbed and worn hand was a world away from the dignified hand it was several months ago, when she had control over her life. The agents came and told her that it was now illegal for women to own their own businesses, and took the business into the Empire's control. I could see from the woman's memories that the business had already been run into the ground. All those years wasted.

Elle was never happy whenever I went to the Surface and had wanted to join me but Dad and Frans had forbidden it. They said that dragons had to remain a secret for as long as possible. Though, at the time she had been arguing that Frost already knew about Tyson. But her logic fell on deaf ears, and so she resorted to mind melding, a technique that she still refuses for me to see or to explain. On the day I returned from the Surface, she had been waiting for me with Dad and Frans, feigning innocence.

There weren't just the physical trials, there were mental ones, too. Trials designed to train each of our gifts. In the end, Chaz couldn't decide what I specialised in, as I could do a little of everything, and so had me train in all of the disciplines.

I was not as proficient as the others in their specialities but I was quickly catching up.

"Concentrate!" Zack was tutoring me in illusions, one of my weaker disciplines since because it required non-physical contact to be effective. If I were touching Zack it would have been easy enough for me to conjure up the desert I was supposed to make him see, but the air acting as a barrier for my gift. I found it immensely difficult to bridge the distance between us, without burning need to guide me.

After several hours of sweaty effort, I managed to make some contact. I could see the desert forming in his mind like an uncertain mirage. "Good Merissa, now see if-" I gasped as I lost my concentration. Zack scowled and began to growl something, but I saw red. My hours of frustrations boiled down to this singular moment, and I felt my gift reach out, strong and sure. Zack stopped and looked glazed. "Well done, Merissa! If I didn't know better, I'd be very scared right now."

His condescending tone began to grate on me, and I felt my annoyance flare into something darker. I could feel Zack begin to appear uneasy. As well as he should, because he was surrounded by lions in his mind. I made them advance, fur rippling and their snouts pulled back in a fearsome savage scowl with their yellowed teeth glinting paly in the sun of the Damoovil plains.

"Merissa, stop it now. You've made your point. Please stop!" Zack's fear was growing stronger. As the panic rose in him, his own mental defences began to crumble and the lions crept ever closer. With a terrifying yowl, the lead lioness jumped and swiped at Zack. Zack screamed and fell back, and his mind went blank with fear. I could see his whole essence in front of me. I felt a morbid curiosity at seeing this strong man being reduced to this, then I saw what he saw of me; cold, malicious and malevolent. Cruelty personified.

Merissa! Elle was distracted from the flying exercise that she was doing with Frans and Jandre. Stop it, *you'll hurt him!*

I snapped back out of his mind and I looked at him, curled and shaking on the floor. With alarm, I saw that he had a bleeding arm, and three large gashes. They were bleeding, badly. I rushed to him with a towel I had grabbed from the small pile on the table. I knelt down by him and began to apply pressure. I could feel panic rising in me as I thought of what to do, the darkness in my mind warping my thoughts.

My eyes darted back and forth and I could feel the sheer panic beginning to overwhelm me, all the while Zack was growing paler by the moment. Suddenly the door to our training room burst open and my father strode through with a couple of people, including Chaz.

He made his way right over to Zack without looking at me. He pried Zack from my bloody fingertips and nodded to one of the young girls who hurried over and placed her hand on his ravaged arm.

She closed her bright green eyes for a moment in concentration and after a few seconds I could see that Zack's flesh was swiftly and cleanly knitting together, and I could have slapped myself! I had utterly and completely forgotten about my healing lessons. I was so panicked about Zack, and felt so guilty, that I had thought only of the problem and not the solution.

Merissa, this lack of control had got to stop. You're getting dangerous.

The burning feeling of rage burnt itself out and left only the feeling of cold shame.

Some hours later, after all of the drama began to calm down, I was lying on my bed in my room, staring at the ceiling when I heard a knock.

"Come in," I replied morosely.

The door opened and my father stood in the doorway. I hadn't seen much of him these past few weeks with both of us being busy, me with my training and him with his invasion plans. He stood there awkwardly for a moment before entering.

He settled down at the bottom of my bed. He looked tired, almost as tired as I felt. "How are you doing Merissa?"

I shrugged by way of an answer and he sighed. "Zack is more or less recovered."

I was still silent and he tried again. "Have you been talking to those two agents again?"

I sighed myself this time, "No, and it makes me think that Frost put two and two together and realised that I was the agent sent to assassinate you."

Dad ruffled my hair, ruining it. "That's ok. You did splendidly. You had them going for a long time."

It always amazed me how much he loved seeing people being manipulated. We've often theorised that our gifts manifest themselves according to our personality. However, my recent advances with my own particular gift has had my father stumped, he had eventually shrugged and just concluded that I was an anomaly.

He sighed again. "I need to talk to you about what happened with Zachery."

I felt my stomach tighten with unease and I looked away from him. He continued on, his voice a little harder. "You need to explain to me what happened, exactly."

So I did, I left nothing out, not even my ugly rage. My father was looking at me sadly, but also with a tinge of pride. "Watching you grow up was a privilege. I'm sorry that life has worked out this way between us, but I hope that the last couple of months have at least made a step in the right direction. Your gifts are going to be the stuff of legends. If what you said is true, what you did was more than just a mere illusion; you made Zachery's brain think that he was being attacked by those lionesses and his body ripped itself apart, as that was the reality it had perceived."

He began to beam. "You are going to save so many lives with your talents!"

My unspoken thought was how many lives was I going to have to take to save all of those lives, would I be able to do it? It's horrible to think that this is what the world has come to. That we need to act violently to get justice.

I honestly didn't know what to say. It felt wrong to take pride in the fact that I can convince a body to rip itself apart. At the same time, I couldn't deny that when I felt that power, that it had a certain intoxicating edge to it. It awakened a dark hunger in me to consume and pulverise. The instinct to dominate.

To distract myself I asked the first question that popped into my mind. "Why were you not mad that Zack, Ray, Yelena, Max and I went to the Surface without your permission?"

Dad grinned. "Oh, but I did authorise it!"

I was confused and Dad explained himself. "I told you that I was going to get the best people for the job and so I did."

That would mean that he expected you to go try to rescue Chaz with or without his permission. He knows you better than you think Merissa.

My father looked at me for a moment and nodded to himself. "You're starting to make yourself known to the wider community of the Underbelly, and I believe it is time for them to meet you. They had a chance to observe you at the Ball, but their imagination will run wild, they are quite paranoid. They might start saying things like a look from your red eyes can blow people up! And I won't have people saying that you have red eyes when you clearly have beautiful brown eyes."

I rolled my eyes, he had no problem with them saying that I can blow people up, of course.

Without further ado, my father stood up. I knew what he was thinking; there was no time like the present and sure enough when I made no move to leave my comfortable bed, he began tapping his foot with impatience. Bloody criminals and their timetables.

We left the Academy and made quick progress to his office. When we arrived, he gestured for me to sit down and then clicked a button on his watch. Suddenly, I was swarmed by a multitude of servants in swirling grey. They plucked, pulled and pushed at all the different parts of my face. They spotted, sprinkled and smoothed creams and pastes into my face, and I tried not to wince as they did their work.

Another team was at my hair, twisting and braiding it into a French braid. While they were at work my father was giving me a lecture. "Tonight, I am going to bring you to my council as an honorary guest. I want you to observe, only to observe. The people you're going to meet are criminals. They might be respectable criminals but that doesn't mean that they wouldn't hesitate to use you as political leverage against me."

I opened my mouth to respond but father beat me to it. "Not a word Merissa. Seriously."

I mockingly drew my fingers across my lips and threw away the imaginary key, but the act was marred by my wince as a servant pulled particularly tight at my hair. My father's laughter did little to help.

After I had sulked appropriately enough at the mistreatment that my father made me endure, we made our way to council. It was mostly silent with only the watery emotions coming off of my father to keep us company.

Even though he was acting like he was in charge of the world I could tell that he was nervous. That, of course, naturally made me nervous.

We ended up outside a rather unimpressive building in the residential district. It was similar to the other houses that surrounded it in this neighbourhood.

I raised an eyebrow at my father. "Is this it?"

My father grinned. "Oh yes. The other council members don't have our gifts to protect themselves, and so are a little on the paranoid side."

He strode up to the door with a swagger and knocked on the door. A peephole materialised suddenly on the door, and a gruff voice demanded. "Password?"

Father looked in and said with a straight face. "Unicorns."

The gruff voice paused. "Sorry sir, but that is not the password. Goodnight."

Dad peered in. "Let me in, you buffoon. I don't have time for this."

The gruff voice was quiet for a moment. "Sorry sir but the master of the Underbelly himself said that no one, but no one, can enter the council chambers without the password."

At this, Dad lost his patience. "Remind me to not hire you again, now stand aside you moron!" Dad kicked the door and it burst inwards.

Dad looked at me with his snakelike smile, similar to the one that he had flashed to me when I had met him in his office all those months ago. "After you my dear."

I rolled my eyes and straightened my own spine and walked with a confidence which put my father's swagger to shame, into the lion's den.

Drama Queen

I pushed past the small man that was guarding the door. I glanced behind, and my father gestured forwards, and so I continued on the long dank corridor. The smell of damp permeated the air and I wrinkled my sensitive nose in disgust.

I came to a stop at the end of the corridor at a plain wooden door, and I heard my father following me. I hesitated for a moment more before the wooden door swung itself open by itself. I stepped through into a large plain room. There was a hollowed circular table set in the centre of the room, ringed by chairs.

Most of the chairs were occupied by various men and women, the other rulers of the Underbelly. There were also men ringing the room in dark uniforms with red masks pulled over them. Guards, I presumed. There were quiet conversations being spoken across the room just before I entered. Upon my entrance, many of the men and women sitting in the chairs turned their attention to me, their eyes alight with interest.

However, their eyes were quickly averted once my father had entered. I saw now why he wanted me to go in first. He wanted me to be aware just how people would view me without his influence. I had no doubts whatsoever that they would use me for their political gains, after seeing their reactions.

We made our way to two seats that were empty beside each other. I ended up sitting beside an elflike woman with her high cheekbones and raven coloured straight hair. She looked at my father imperiously. "What is the meaning of this Alistair? Why are you bringing your children to this meeting?"

My father smiled at her good naturedly, but I could detect a little hostility emanating from him. "My goodness, Felecia. I expect my children to take my place in the ruling of the Underbelly one day. How will they know how to do it if they don't know how to deal with dry old hags like yourself?"

Felicia gave a derisive snort in reply, but before she could rebuttal a young silver haired man spoke. "As untactful as that was Mr Forts, Madame Felicia is correct. How are we to know if she is to be trusted? Why not even a few weeks ago she was seen consorting with the enemy!"

I felt myself bristle inside, but I remained calm. Well, somewhat. Dad was rapidly losing his patience. "I will not have an insolent pup like you speak out of turn!"

The young man looked at my father with blazing eyes, but before he could retort angrily an elderly man spoke with a fatherly scowl resting on his forehead spoke.

"Alistair must you try to bring out the worst in us when meeting your daughter for the first time? I can only imagine what she must be thinking!"

Dad grinned. "Merissa, please allow me to introduce Simon. He was my mentor when I first took up the role of Underworlder." The elderly man bowed his head in acknowledgment. "You are too kind, Alastair. But the question, though rather tactless, about your daughter is a legitimate one."

I felt all of the eyes that were looking at me subtly previously, were now gazing openly at me as Simon directed attention towards me. I squared my shoulders and drew myself up to my full height. "My name is Merissa and I am Alistair Forts' eldest daughter. I am here to meet the other Underworlders of the Underbelly." I paused then decided to follow my instincts and continued.. "And to be brutally honest, I'm not impressed. You're more like frightened and squabbling children than you are the mighty women and men who I was raised to fear on the Surface." They are not going to like that.

A thick, bull-set man rose abruptly and began to stride towards me with rage puncturing each step. "Listen here you little bitch," he reached over to stab at my chest with one stubby finger, but I, of course, never let anyone touch me without my permission.

I grabbed his finger and pulled it backwards until it cracked with a sickening pop. His wide face went white with pain, and he went down on one knee. Two men, as big as he, rushed from the shadows of the wall to apprehend me, but they too went down in a flurry of limbs and loud cursing.

One reached for my exposed ankle, but as soon as he made skin contact my gift ripped across him. He began to convulse and thrashed away from me. No one made a move towards me after that.

I looked over the crowd of the elites of the Underbelly and felt cold rage roll over me. "Listen, and listen well. You are all preparing for the war against the Surface, but your chances are laughably abysmal."

I had their attention now, the electricity in the room was almost visible as the tension cracked up a few notches. "You don't stand a chance in the conventional sense, but that doesn't mean we can't win with unconventional tactics. You will be slaughtered if you can't put aside your petty bickering. You will be annihilated if you don't stand strong. And you will be obliterated if you don't inspire others to believe that they can win with you. If you don't do all of those things, I will. It will be my name that will be remembered across history for toppling the tyrannical Empire, and not yours."

Simon, who was gently reprimanding my father a few minutes spoke up then. "How do you suggest that we do this then young lady?"

I tried to ignore how much the young lady remark bothered me and focused on the question. "Simple. We use people like me and my father. We use the vampires, the dragons and the black suns. We have an arsenal of weaponry that the Surface has never seen the likes of. We also have two more things that they don't have."

Simon leaned forward, his weathered hands propping his head on the table, and his watery eyes were full of interest. "Interesting proposal, but what is it that we have, that they don't have?"

I grinned and said something that they were not expecting. "Passion and creativity."

The uproar that followed took a while to settle down, some people were calling me crazy saying that my gifts have given me a god complex. It was the lady called Felicia, and the young man whose name turned out to be Henry, who proved to be the biggest advocates of that theory, while my father and the Simon were trying to discuss the merits of my plan.

Eventually my father lost his patience. "ENOUGH!" His voice reverberated throughout the secret council chamber. It was not just his loud authoritative voice that was lending him his powerful presence. I could sense his gift becoming agitated as he expressed irritation with the other Underworlder's, making him more threatening. It filled to the brim with passion, silencing the uproar.

"We will vote on this now, now those in favour-"

A loud bang interrupted my father and an unwelcome familiar figure stood in the doorway of the council chambers. Jeffery looked at my father with the look of someone bearing horrendous news. "The Underbelly is besieged. They've found us."

His voice was dead and monotone. Then his scarred face contorted and he glared at me. His voice filled with hatred and loathing. "And she is the one who led them here."

Oh shit.

Calm Before the Storm

Jeffery's furiously trembling fingers were still pointing accusingly at me, and more and more eyes began to harden as the accusations began to sink in. Henry's high voice racked up the tension. "Is this true?"

I shook my head resolutely, but Felecia snorted derisively. "Of course she is going to play innocent! This is the perfect ploy. Gain access to the Underworlders of the Underbelly, and assassinate us so that we cannot direct our troops. Guards, take her!"

My father stood with a roar, and any guards that were about to follow Felecia's orders hesitated. My father looked at Felecia with wrathful eyes. "You will not issue any orders, Felecia, while you are a guest here. I have known that this was going to happen for a while now."

This was greeted with further uproar, but the calm commanding voice of Simon sliced through the cacophony of voices. "If you've known this for a while Alistair, why have you not told us before this? Do you not trust us?"

Even without my gifts I could hear the implied threat, and my empathic gifts allowed me to see the undercurrent frustration of Simon, being kept in the dark.

My father spread his hands in a placating gesture. "I do not think that anyone here would willingly help the enemy, Simon, but you must remember that the enemy does have spies down here. Despite my and my children's best efforts, some of them have eluded us, and some of those spies may be mind readers. I had to make sure that any sensitive data was protected."

The aggressive atmosphere of the room was slowly receding as Underworlders of the Underbelly grumbled their understanding. But a small plump ginger woman suddenly exclaimed; "What do you mean that the enemy might have mind readers?! I thought the whole basis of us following you and your children was that you would give us the edge with your gifts!"

She had a point.

My father looked momentarily stumped but I stepped in before his lapse became apparent. "Simple. There are more of us and many of us have been born with the gifts we have."

"Our gifts are organic to us, even now I have surpassed my father in regards of the strength of my gifts and he was among the strongest of his programme. when all this started decades ago. They might have Spliced Soldiers, but we live and breathe our gifts. We'd destroy them in one on one combat."

The ginger woman nodded once, seemingly reassured. But looking at the others, it was clear that there was still some major convincing to do. However, this was not the time. We have a siege to break.

I'll meet you at the academy.

I looked at my father and he nodded, guessing which way my thoughts had headed. "Go and get the rest of the family. They will be needed to level the playing field. I will make sure that the rest of the army is ready and in position." I nodded and left him to deal with the politics of the Underbelly.

I stepped back outside and breathed in the relatively fresh air, with the tint of strawberries emanating in the breeze. The streets were much busier now, people were thronging but there was no outright panic; these were a warrior people indeed. Even the children were calm and composed.

I began to slip between the gaps in the crowds towards the Academy, back towards my family and my home. Pretty soon, however, the crowds were milling tighter together than the great sardine schools that swim in the Harso River in Hangeranion.

I had no time for this. I bunched my legs and sprang up onto the roof of one of the nearby buildings. I landed on the shale tiles with a sure thud. I then began to sprint in earnest for the Academy. I'll be damned if my family is harmed.

We will not let that happen.

I looked up to see dozens of dragons gliding through the air, they ranged in size from a medium sized dog to a large antigravcar.

It was an awe inspiring sight.

I arrived at the grand stone steps leading up to the great doors of the Academy. I was panting a little, although I think it was more from my sense of urgency than lack of endurance. I hoped it was, otherwise Chaz was going to make me run until I bled.

I pushed the great steel doors aside with little difficulty. Inside, I could see one of the younger guys lounging on the comfortable couches with a book up to his nose. Owen. That was his name. My orders came barking out of me. "We've got an emergency! Get everyone together and bring them to the field. Wait for me."

He looked nonplussed, but nodded. Just then a klaxon alarm began to blare and it stabbed at both my and Owen's sensitive eardrums, and we both winced. We both raced for the lift and began our descent.

As soon as we reached the bottom, we split up and began banging on doors. As luck would have it, it was Zack's room that I knocked on first. His weary face was hostile once he registered that it was me. His arm was still in a sling and I could still smell his blood. The slashes from the lions from his illusion still hadn't clotted over, resistant so they were to our healing.

"What are you doing here?" His voice was passive aggressive and normally I wouldn't blame him, but this is no time to play nice and my voice came out brisk and rapid. "We need to go. In case you haven't noticed, there's an invasion happening and we're needed." His woolly eyes sharpened and the alarm suddenly registered. "Oh."

It was all that he said but he nodded determinedly, and strode back into his room. In less than ten seconds, he was ready and standing fully dressed.

His free hand was on his hip. "Well let's go then! I'm ready and we need to go and save everyone's asses. You better watch your own though because that is not one that I will be watching."

I grinned, nothing like a war to make someone wake up.

By the time that I had gotten through to Zack, Owen had roused most of the others. Either that, or the shrill screaming of the alarm got them up and out.

I quickly rounded them up in the centre of the athletic field. "Are we all here?" A quick headcount confirmed this.

Chaz stepped out from the crowd and his fellow vampires, dressed in black and looking far more lethal for it, followed suit.

A figure was sprinting to us from the labs of the Academy, and it was followed by a long gravicar that hummed as it hovered above the ground. I saw that the figure was Dr Yuyo and I instinctually looked for Chaz. I saw his lavender eyes tighten, but he said nothing. Dr Yuyo stopped in front of me, panting slightly from the rapid sprint. He collected his breath and then said. "Merissa we did it, Dr Oslo and I finally developed a suit that is totally functional."

I felt initial unease, but then I thought about it. Dr Yuyo was never the one that said that the previous suits might be functional, it was always Dr Oslo, a scientist with considerably less experience. If a twenty-thousand-year vampire is confident it works, then it was worth a try.

I nodded and Dr Yuyo grinned, exposing his full fangs. "Perfect." He turned and clicked a button on his watch and the roof of the long gravicar pulled back seamlessly and several prongs of metal extended out of the gravicar. Hung along the prongs were suits. They were made of a shiny clingy fabric, which was uniform in detail.

The only added detail on the otherwise unimpressive suit was the jewel that was embedded on the forehead of the hood. It was colourless, that but it had a strange quality of shattering the light before it reached the jewel.

I touched a suit and with a cry of alarm, I saw that it moved by itself. It swung itself onto me, morphing into a liquid mass and wriggling into my clothes. It pooled around my body. In seconds it had formed a second skin around my body.

I swung my head back and forth and I marvelled at how the suit had formed over my scalp, but not covered my hair, keeping it free. Then I felt the jewel at the front of the hood begin to heat up and I was about to panic, but then Dr Yuyo stilled my hands. Chaz was there in a flash, his fangs bared. "Leave her go, Father."

I looked between them and Dr Yuyo sighed. "The suit is recognising Merissa as its own. In a matter of moments, it will only be her that will be able to use it. Look."

Chaz did and his lavender eyes widened. I looked down at myself and saw that the previously black suit was now swirling with intricate colours. Reds, greens, blues and even darker black subtly danced with the about a dozen other colours. I was now as colourful as Elle. I heard gasps as others put on their suits and their own colours appeared on their suits.

I felt my gift become amplified by the suit, and with a roar I let lose my gift and a river of shadows erupted from my hands. I abruptly stopped it and everyone looked at me in silence and then began to clap slowly. Before long, they were cheering loudly. I may be a freak but I was their freak.

Just then, a loud wind buffeted us, momentarily drowning out the klaxon. I looked up to see our dragons swooping down to join us. There were whoops as the crowd went to greet their bond-mates, and then everyone fell silent. A dawning awareness that this could be our last day together, began to creep over us. I tenderly touched Elle's dark blue snout, flecked now with green, and deep emotions passed between us, words were not needed.

Chaz stepped beside me and placed his hand inside of mine. I heard Elle, *I told you so.* I stepped away from Elle and looked at Chaz. He was studied me earnestly for a moment, then he leaned forward. His warm breath drifted over lips and then I felt the lightest brush of his lips against my own. It was a small gesture, but it lit me up more than my gift ever did. He stepped away. "I had to do that at least once."

He looked at me for a moment before turning to the rest of the group. "Those of you that are under eighteen follow Anita and she will take you to safety. The rest of you follow me. You all have permission to use each and every of your gifts to kill these Surface bastards."

His short speech was greeted with enthusiastic cheers as the group split, and the younger children were herded by Anita to the safe house.

A small figure pulled away from the group, throwing herself at me. I knelt down to stroke Yelena's blonde hair. I could feel her sobbing against my chest so I hugged her tightly. "Yelena, what is it?"

Yelena's voice came out hitched and broken. "I don't want you...hic... to go! I don't want...hic... you to die!"

I could hardly tell her that these were thoughts that were plaguing my own mind. I hugged her tightly to calm her. "Don't worry, Yelena. I'm not going anywhere. I'm just going to help Dad put these unwelcome guests out of our city, that's all ok? I'll be back before you know it." I hugged her one last time before Anita called Yelena and she reluctantly let go and re-joined the others.

I stood and Chaz approached me. "So what do you think is the best course of action right now?"

I looked at him and grinned. "We give them hell."

Chaz grinned in response. " I couldn't have put it better myself."

We mounted our dragons, and with a massive push, we were propelled into the air. Time to go save my Dad's sorry ass.

Time to find out if our enemies are as strong they believe they are.

This will be interesting to say the least.

Besieged

My heart thudded in my chest and it was becoming harder to breathe. Despite the chaos in my body, I could feel my mind begin to sharpen, feeling more deadly. The twenty or so of us that were over eighteen flew over the rooftops, and we glided effortlessly over the gaps between the buildings. Our vampiric trainers ran across the rooftops below us, keeping pace with the dragons.

This part of the city was almost completely deserted. All of the civilians have already evacuated, and only military personnel were left around here. They gave us a wide berth, as they knew better than to come between the trainers in black, and their charges.

I heard vibrations running up from all around me, and it gave me the chills for some unfathomable reason. I pushed aside the feeling of dread and tried instead to focus on the group following me. I began to strategize in my head, wishing we'd had more time to prepare.

Illusionists and other non-contact psychics would be used as long range weapons, confusing the enemy from afar but swooping in on dragons to cause disarray. The others would need to be in closer contact to support the soldiers and to maximise their gifts. I'll have to be with them. With the exception of my shadows, most of my offensive gifts are short range and will need bodily contact.

The best healers will need to be in the wings, ready to sweep in like angels to heal soldiers. However, they will need to be able to defend themselves too and not be squeamish...

I could see a giant spotlight blazing down by the market place and I knew that father was waiting down for us there. I stopped and everyone stopped along with me, casting me confused looks. I regarded everyone seriously, taking them in, this family that I never knew that I had. Now, they were all mine to protect.

I took a deep breath. "Ok everyone. This is what we're going to do." I laid out my thoughts and plans and when I finished, everyone nodded and moved to their positions, nervous but determined. I knew I needed to calm and steady their nerves. "We've been through so much, trained long and hard for this. We are more than ready for this."

"Remember brothers and sisters, you are not just fighting for yourselves, you're fighting for those who can't. The oppressed, the weak and the broken people. They deserve justice just like you. They've had mothers, fathers, brothers and sisters murdered, assaulted and jailed like us. We fight not just for ourselves but for everyone!" A roar greeted me as human, vampire and dragon roared their approval.

After a few moments I nodded to Chaz as he went with the group that were part of long range team. He looked at me with a little hint of fear in his eyes but he said nothing.

Give him some encouragement Merissa, he's worried for you. I smiled in encouragement, and he replied with a small little smile of his own, before joining the others who were spreading across the rooftops. I turned, heading to the giant blazing torch, on Elle's back.

There were only three others who came with me, Emily, Tommy and Aaron. Emily had a similar gift to my primary gift, a brush of her fingers and she could make you feel whatever she wanted. Tommy was again something similar but with one major difference, he could numb your senses at a touch an apath. Aaron was a bit of an anomaly; he was a pyrokinetic. He could ignite anything with a touch.

When we dismounted our dragons, we were joined by our trainers in black. Together, we approached my father who was barking orders like a general. Frans was coiled like a snake as her forklike tongue flickered in and out as she scented the air. I remembered that he'd been in the army. He saw me and beckoned me over, but scowled when he saw who was with me. "Where is everyone else?"

His voice was a growl, but I had long since lost the fear I used to feel in his presence. I replied without hesitation. "They are all long range attackers. They can do far more damage from afar, and remain safer like that."

He scowled for a moment but I was saved another lecture when Simon interrupted. "Alastair, they are attempting to bomb their way in, do you have any orders?" Well that would explain the tremors I was feeling as I flew across the city.

My father snorted in contempt. "Nothing short of a fission bomb is going to get through those blast doors. We can comfortably ride this out and have everyone evacuated to the various Underbellies."

I frowned myself, "How exactly is that being done? Would the Surface troops just not come in that way?" My father was shaking his head before I was finished, "Not all, they are all escaping in the thousands of escape pods into the sewers and can travel to the other Underbellies."

Something hit my head, and it stung. I frowned and looked at the small rock that was now at my feet, it looked strange, almost jagged... I felt something pulling at me. My insides froze and I drew my gaze up and I saw them.

They were descending like spiders on silk, they must have breached the outer defences of the wall that surrounded the Underbelly and then tunnelled through the rock to penetrate all the way through to the Underbelly. And also like spiders they were pouncing on their prey.

"UP!" The single word screamed from my throat and suddenly there was plasmafire everywhere. Many of the men went limp, but there were so many of them, we were going to be swarmed. My father went stock still and the descending men began to scream and thrash. I knew that my father was making them feel primal fear.

The soldiers began to fire from above but one of my Dad's body guards flicked a switch on a small flat disk and then a shield bubbled out of it and absorbed any plasmafire coming from above.

Some men unclipped their lines and dropped several hundred metres and slammed into the ground but landed lithely on their feet. They didn't even flinch. I felt a coldness spread through my body; Spliced Soldiers.

The men that surrounded us began to unleash a hail of plasmafire at group of twenty or so men but they dodged them with ease. "Stop!" I barked the order at the men and I pointed at the men who were still descending to us. "Stop them and we'll deal with these." I nodded to my gifted group and they squared their shoulders.

We'll cover the rest of the city. It was then I saw that there were soldiers dropping down from the roof in other parts of the city, I mentally sent my agreement and Elle roared and the rest of the dragons and her flew to the air and grappled with the soldiers in the air.

The Spliced Soldiers were waiting for us with their viroblades extended, and we obliged. I wrapped shadows around my right hand and formed a shadow blade. We pounced on them like feral cats but they matched our speed and ferocity. My opponents moved in hard and fast, and I was like flowing water as I danced and weaved between their stabs and thrusts. Every time my shadow blade crashed against the viroblade, it sucked a little more life away from the metal death colonies on the blades. The longer the dual went on the less dangerous their blades became. Soon it was time to go all out.

I grappled with three men. They were stronger, but I was faster. Each time they tried to grab me, I slipped away before they could catch me.

One darted behind me and swung his open fist and it nearly connected, but I managed to swerve out of the way. The other two took advantage of my unbalanced feet, stabbing and slashing at my face.

One swept through my defences and struck my abdomen with the hilt of his viroblade, I grunted and fell back, but the man who was behind me grasped me before I could evade him and locked his limbs. I gasped as he applied brutal pressure and my shadow blades evaporated as my concentration slipped. I knew I had moments before my arms would snap so I did the only thing I could.

I released my gift.

My gift screamed and roared and slammed into him. He yelled in horror and began spasming in pain. The others backed away sharply, but I gave no quarter and rushed after them. I grabbed each of them by the shoulder and send floods of pain crackling through their body. They both screamed as their eyes rolled in their heads.

Die. The thought came unbidden into my mind and each of the men went instantly silent. I could feel my mouth drop open in horror.

Had I just killed with a thought? What the fuck am I?

My other comrades had quickly dispatched their adversaries also. The smell of charred flesh wafted towards me as Aaron set the last of his opponents alight. He turned to smile, running high from the adrenaline from fighting, at me and I offered a wan one in response. I still felt slightly sick.

The man who I had knocked out a few minutes ago was beginning to stir. I looked at him for a moment and steeled myself for what had to be done. I walked over to him and knelt by him and placed my hand on his throat. I could feel his heartbeat, pulsing in my hand. I felt my gift respond to my wishes and flow into him, it waited questioningly for my orders. Kill.

The heartbeat stopped.

A sudden explosion ripped at my sensitive ears and I saw that an explosion had shredded the blast doors apart.

Impossible!

My father looked at me with true terror in his eyes. "RUN!"

I grabbed the others' hands and saw my father and his men standing between us and the flood of soldiers that flowed through the breach, while the raining soldiers from above continued their descent.

If I ever had any doubts that this man loved me dearly, they vanished when I saw him and Frans stand resolutely between me and certain death.

I sprinted towards one of the lower buildings, the chocolatier where I had snuck out of the Underbelly so long ago. I used it as a platform to get to the higher buildings that the others were standing on. They had stood still, many of them too terrified to move. When he saw me, Chaz snapped to attention and began roaring at people to move. And they all did, apart from Zack.

Zack was staring out towards the advancing army and I saw shadows leaking from his eyes and with a scream I saw his suit flash gold and the shadows ripped from him like a tidal wave. With a maniacal laugh, he sent the boiling and seething wave of shadows towards the Surface army.

With horrendous crunches I could hear bones snapping, and flesh being vaporised. I looked at my brother in horror, the shadows were still coming from his eyes but also his outstretched hands.

If I don't stop this, he will die.

The thought came to me and I was utterly sure that it was true, and I was not going to let my brother die. I slapped him and he turned to me in godly fury and he blasted shadows at me but I was expecting it and I had a shield of my own shadows protecting me. Zack growled and was about to physically charge me when I saw a golden dragon fly down.

Feron began to hum his dragonsong and Zack faltered. Seeing my chance, I hugged him and I slipped into his mind, sleep. Zack's shadows vanished and he fell unconscious and I looked back over the battlefield and I saw the hundreds of crumpled bodies, all victims of Zack's insanity.

"Forgive me little brother."

I picked up Zack and hurried over to Feron. I hauled Zack up to his saddle and strapped him in. Feron and I then re-joined the others waiting for us. With tears streaming down my face, we fled the battlefield as fast as we could. We jumped to the rooftops and began flitting across, it was not long before we were joined by the dragons, who swooped down and we quickly mounted them. The screaming and the cracking of the plasmafire and the occasional scream of laserfire were still resounding across the Underbelly.

We pushed harder and the dragons zipped through the air. I was certain that they would send Spliced Soldiers after us and so we could not slow down. We reached the escape pods. There were still dozens left, each spherical in shape and a dull grey colour and could probably fit about ten people in each.

The others began to file in. I stopped Chaz before he got in. "Where are the younger ones? Are they still at the safe house?"

Chaz nodded. "We're going there on the way." I felt a momentary moment of relief. Then the silence fell.

NO!

I felt my mind reach out and warp itself, trying to reach Dad. My mind stretched and pulled and suddenly broke free of its restraints and I felt my mind sweep across the entire Underbelly with the speed of a thought.

I crashed into his mind and with a sharp inhalation of the air, I was looking out of his eyes. No, I wasn't looking out. They were my eyes. Somehow, I was my father.

I snarled. These cowardly curs had annihilated my men from above as they were taken by surprise by the exploding doors. Thank the Creator that Merissa and the others are out of the Underbelly by now. It was a little worrying that Zack was becoming so unstable. The others will have to look after him now, especially Merissa.

Thinking of Merissa, I felt a rare surge of pride but it was tinged by sadness. I was going to die. I knew that there were too many blockers around here for me to break through. But thinking of Merissa, Ray, Zack and Yelena made me feel like it didn't matter.

As long as they live I am happy.

Another mind joined in. It was Frans. *You did well Alli. At least we die together.*

I felt a horrified fascination, I was surrounded by the presence of Dad. Once upon a time I would have been repulsed, maybe even terrified but now that I could see the total devotion he had for us, and the people of the Underbelly, I cannot help but feel humbled and awed to have this man as my father.

Something is happening. The men are unsure but expectant. I don't like it. Something strange happened, instead of discrete thoughts flowing from his mind to mine, images that his brain was processing was flowing through instead.

The soldiers were still wary, they shuffled and even if I couldn't sense much beyond the immediate area around me, I could sense their nervous apprehension.

The soldiers snapped to attention and I felt a surge of bizarre déjà vu, a time when I would snap my heels together whenever my captain would enter my tent. It was a long time ago but I knew what it meant, whoever was coming was important.

Just then an elderly bald man stepped through the torn and shredded gates of the Underbelly. His age was an illusion, however, as he moved with the grace and confidence of someone much younger and more powerful than his body would suggest.

Frost.

As I sensed my Dad's loathing for the elderly man ambling towards him, I was taken aback by the ferocity of his rage. It was pure, unadulterated and murderous. And personal. What did Frost do?

I felt my heart begin to race as my anger grew, but I knew that I could not act on it. If I gave in to it, I would lose valuable time for the rest of my family to escape.

Frost's teeth gleamed as he smiled.. "It's so sweet of you to think of your family in your final moments." He sighed theatrically, "It's a pity you never thought like that about me."

I saw red and I lost track of my thoughts for a minute, but when I calmed down I was pinned to the ground with a hard boot pressed against the side of my face.

I inhaled the dust of the Underbelly and I smelt the fragrance of the sweet strawberries. I felt my lips move up in an involuntary smile. I heard a sigh and I was hoisted up and my arms bound behind my back.

Frost bit his lip with perfect white teeth. "What am I going to do with you, son? Ever since you were a little boy you've been disobedient. You've even instigated a rebellion against me! You know that we'll attract attention from above if we're not careful!"

I saw red again but I did not lose control again but I felt a sharp retort slip out of me of its own accord. "You're no father of mine." Frost's eyes flashed with his own cold rage and he raised his hand and slapped my face with resounding force.

I laughed, there was no humour in it, but I knew it drove Frost crazy and I was not above pettiness. Frost was seething in cold rage and he leaned in close and I could feel the fury washing off of him in waves. Just then he smiled.

The transformation was so utterly startling that I flinched. Frost laughed. "Oh, my boy, you have no idea that we have an audience do you?" What was he talking about?

Just then it came to me, Merissa.

Frost's eyes gleamed. "Oh yes, my son. My granddaughter is watching us as we speak. The poor woman has no idea of the things she can do, you tried to protect her mother and her by leaving them alone but all you did was leave them helpless. You know how much I despise loose ends."

The awful realisation came crashing down, my own father killed the love of my life.

Frost was continuing to talk. "This has gone on long enough, say goodbye to Merissa, Alastair. We need to tie up more loose ends."

Just then he placed his cool weathered hands on the sides of my face and I felt something shift inside of my mind and then with a gut-wrenching scream I could hear Merissa.

I began to growl-

There was an awful silence for a moment and then the scream of plasmafire and the roar of a dragon wrecked the illusion of calm.

Suddenly there were several pairs of arms wrapped around me and I felt my gift lash out and all but one left me. I screamed and thrashed like the man I had shocked. Yet no matter how much struggling I did I could not get free.

As swiftly as the manic episode came over me, it dissipated and I was myself. I turned to the chest of the person who had managed to hold onto me and began sobbing into a large chest. I felt his chest rise and fall as he stroked my hair. "It's ok Rissa. It will be all ok."

Elle was humming her dragonsong again, no doubt to calm me down.

Chaz continued to console me, and as he did so I was aware that we were walking. He led me to the last of the spheres and waited for me to get in. But I resisted. If I went in the last sphere, I was admitting to it and I couldn't face it.

Chaz looked at me with sad dark eyes. "Don't let it be in vain Rissa." I felt more tears falling down my face and I nodded and I stepped in.

I had admitted it. By walking in I just said that my father was dead.

I am an orphan.

With The Flow

I was not aware of what was going on around me, I let myself sink into a numbed confusion; it was easier than trying to function. Thoughts kept jumping in and out of me, almost as if my life was giving me vertigo. My mind was spinning and twisting, hurling out of control like a roller-coaster ride that has just been derailed.

I could feel the memories of my past coming to me, my mother combing my hair and me feeling very safe in her embrace, my father was no longer the big bad man of my nightmares in my mind when I thought of him. He was the man who took me in when I had nowhere to go, he was the man who gave up everything so that I could have a chance to live a normal life with my mother. Even when that was taken away from me, he gave me the training and tools to fight back.

A sob hitched out of my throat; he died so that we could get away. I felt something begin to shift inside of me, my father died so that we could live. Dad knows now that we can never live a normal life, he wouldn't have sacrificed himself just for us to get away. He would have only sacrificed himself if he knew that we stood a chance in taking on the Surface.

And we will.

That we will. Elle was rubbing me with her snout gently and sending me consoling vibes.

I opened my eyes for the first time in forever and I felt like I had just breached the surface of a lake I was drowning in, and was gulping the air graciously and gratefully. I could see Chaz and Elle sitting and curled up in front of me. Chaz looked at me with sad eyes, and there was also a hint of that fear that I saw before the battle of the Underbelly except this time it was directed at me. And I felt ashamed for that.

I smiled and felt the skin on my face crinkle as the stains of the tears broke and splintered apart and I forced a question up my torn throat. "What's going on?"

Chaz was watching me carefully, almost like he was expecting me to flee at a moment's notice. He seemed satisfied and he relied carefully. "We're nearly at the safe house, the rest of them are waiting for us there."

He paused for a moment and I grunted in annoyance. "Just spit it out, I really don't want to be beating around the bush right now."

Chaz nodded slowly. "Ok then. A new Underworld boss is going to be chosen."

I cocked my head to the side, feeling a little slow. "Underworld? Don't you mean Underbelly?"

Chaz shook his head. "When your father rose to power, people were terrified of his gifts. In order to appease the people, he made up a new position that he would occupy, the ruler of the Underworld as opposed to the Underbelly. It made people feel like they had more of a say if normal people ran the Underbelly, when in reality your father was the ruler of the Underbelly."

He shrugged his shoulders. "It was more of a reactive to the political climate of the time but now it might actually be an issue, only a gifted person can be the ruler of the Underworld but since that person is the actual ruler of the Underbelly, the various Underworld councils will be vehemently opposed to anyone ungifted taking that post."

I finally got it. If the ruler of the Underworld had to be gifted, then realistically it had to be one of the Academy students. That was why the council was against it, most of us were too young and those of us that were old enough, they didn't trust enough to control.

Bloody politics. *But it must be tackled Merissa, for your father if nothing else.*

I felt my gift begin to writhe in agitation and Chaz must have sensed something because he was now looking at me in apprehension. "Whoa, let's remember who the real enemy is Rissa." His stupid nickname irked me enough that it snapped me out of my dark mood.

"Don't call me that! You know I don't like it." My voice was half distracted as my brain raced ahead into the future, plans began to snap together and potential obstacles were studied and potential solutions presented themselves.

Chaz coughed. "Did you hear me?"

I gave him my full attention. "No sorry I was thinking, what did you say?" Chaz schootched closer to me and lurched forward when the escape pod swerved sharply, and spilled over my lap. He laughed and with that sound, the last of my murderous mood evaporated. "Listen Chaz," My serious tone snapped his attention to me. My voice was clear and strong, everything that I really did not feel right now. "My father believed with all of his fibre that the Surface, especially the Empire, oppresses people and that they need to be removed in order for people to experience true liberty."

I turned away for a moment to catch my breath, my sobs robbing me of my breath, and I turned back to him to race over the finish line. "I honestly did not believe him, I thought that he was delusional. I thought that the Empire was corrupt and evil, but not oppressive. I thought, naively, that if I was away from them that they would leave me alone. But they are not content with destroying their home, they want to spread their evil."

I paused to catch my breath, as I neared the end of my speech. "I knew it in the moment they blew up the blast doors."

Chaz was following me with rapt attention but at that he frowned quizzically. "What do you mean? I don't get it."

I regarded him sadly. "I explicitly remember my father saying that nothing short of a fission bomb would be able to blow apart the door, then I thought about it. The doors were blown outwards."

Horrified comprehension dawned on Chaz's face. "You mean...?"

I nodded woodenly. "They were blown open from the inside and since there were no soldiers from their side even down from the roof yet, other than the few my group and I were fighting, that means that someone must have planted the bomb there before the battle."

"It means that we have traitors in our midst and I will not rest until they are dead."

Promises

That was three weeks ago, it has been three weeks since the main Underbelly city had fallen and my father had been killed. It has been three weeks since I told my brothers and sisters that we were all orphans, and I had tried to comfort them through their grief. It has been three weeks since I made that promise to Chaz that I would do whatever it took to be free of the Empire's tyranny.

Today was my Dad's funeral.

We had no body of course, but we could still say our goodbyes. I sat with my family and the various people who Dad had ruled alongside for the last thirty years or so, and waited for the funeral to start. I could feel myself replaying over what had happened when I got to the safe house that all of my younger siblings had retreated to.

All of the empaths burst into tears instantly, Yelena had thrown herself and howled with grievous grief. Her tears had torn me out of my own lethargic sadness and drove me into active mode. The next several hours were filled with a flurry of activities that had me focusing on the younger members of my family, especially Yelena and the younger twins, Michael and Erin.

Zack was comatose and has, since conjuring the wave of broiling wave of shadows, spent the last three weeks being tended to by Dr Oslo and Dr Terry, guarded by Feron. Between Zack and the little ones, I was pushed to my emotional limits with caring for the younger Academy students.

I was not the only one, Chaz and the other older ones were helping me, comforting the younger ones. We spent the night around the campfire while talking, roasting strawberries and crying when the smell of the strawberries would remind us of our father's eccentric taste in air freshener.

Today of course the pain was not as raw for them, they were sad, sure. But they would live. Like Dad would have wanted.

"But what about you?" I jerked to attention and I heard Chaz chuckle lightly, a far too rare sound these days. "Sorry, you were murmuring under your breath and when you said that the younger ones will be ok, I asked, what about you?"

I could lie but what would be the point? I looked Chaz right in his lavender eyes and said with brutal honesty. "I really and truly don't know. If you had asked me several months ago what I would feel at my Dad's funeral, I would have said nothing. I buried any feelings I had for him a long time ago, but..."

Chaz finished for me. "When you realised that he was not the monster you thought he was, you began to love him as a daughter."

I nodded, tears falling and ruining my makeup. I didn't trust my voice so I just kept nodding. He walked over to me and gently pushed my hair away from my face, pressing his warm lips against my third eye, and I felt a little better.

A deep sonorous bell sounded and I knew that it was time. We stood up, and Simon, in a dark suit, stood at the front of the congregation. The people of the Underbelly lived under the Surface for as long as anyone has remembered and have never trusted anyone above them. This in turn meant that there were no serious religions practiced in the Underbelly, and so funerals were a community event and would be led by the people.

But every people needs a voice, and Simon would lead us in the procession. "Alastair Forts was an extraordinary man. He will be missed." We echoed him, "He was a man of vision and integrity. He will be mourned." We repeated him. "Even though he may be gone. We will remember him, now and forever. May he rest in peace."

Sometime later, I was leaving the dinner that was thrown in honour of my father. Truth be told, I was escaping, rather than just leaving. Constantly dealing with people who were wishing their condolences and feeling their insincerity as they clasped my hand was exhausting. I didn't have to read their mind to know that they were only there to make a political move, to gauge me.

They made me sick.

That was why I was outside with Elle, as much as I can be outside underground, watching the fluorescent bugs dance and flicker in the air. It was not long before I was joined by someone and judging by how awkwardly they were moving, they would have to be old. A quick glance out of the corner of my eye confirmed this. Simon settled down beside me on the seat and was silent.

We sat like that for a while and soon I grew curious, despite myself. "What is it that you want Simon?"

Simon smiled slightly for a moment. "Many of the politicians in that room back there never knew the extent of your father's gift. I believe that they constantly underestimated him as a result." He paused for a moment. "I believe that you would be wise to do the same."

I cocked my head to the side. "Why would I do that?"

Simon looked at me reproachfully. "Come now child, don't play coy. You know as well as I do that your father was grooming you for the last few months to take over. Granted, it happened far more quickly than he had anticipated, but he would have thought of that and obviously still thought that it was worth pursuing."

Is he friend or foe? Elle's question had me on edge.

I felt my thoughts churn and he continued. "I know that it's hard, it's never easy to lose a parent, regardless of the circumstances. But your father was part of something much bigger than himself. He died to give that something a chance to live."

I held up my hand but he continued and hurried on. "You're a very capable young woman. In fact, you remind me of him when he was your age." He said the last part with a smile, but it soon turned rueful, "He was a masterful manipulator and became a very powerful political figure very quickly. I had thought that he was just another young man lusting after power."

He paused to catch his breath. "I was so very wrong, one night he told me of his vision; one where a person can live, love and die without persecution. It was then I knew that he would start the war we needed to take on the Surface and win back our freedom."

He coughed and gestured about him. "This is no place for people to live. We crave sunshine, rain, and the wind. We need the open sky. But the elite of the Surface have branded us criminals because we dare to defy. We-"

I interrupted. "I'll do it." Simon stopped mid-sentence, and I repeated myself. "I'll do it, I'll finish what my father started, I'll free the Underbelly from the influence of the Surface."

Simon grinned like a young boy who had just been promised a feast after a fast. "Good."

We're going to change history Merissa.